All Your Life

LILY FOSTER

SHOREFRONT BOOKS

Also by Lily Foster

THE LET ME SERIES

Let Me Be the One

Let Me Love You

Let Me Go

Let Me Heal Your Heart

Let Me Fall

When I Let You Go

THE BLACKBIRD SERIES

When the Night is Over

Your Hand in Mine

Ghost on the Shore

All Your Life

First paperback edition June 2023

ISBN: 9780998916781 (eBook)
ISBN: 9798988606208 (paperback)

Cover: Megan Barker Designs

All Your Life

Prologue: Audrey Hamilton

When did everything change?

She used to snuggle in so close it was hard to tell where I ended and she began. And the way she used to look at me? I was this wonderful creature, the center of her universe. She'd sit perched on my bed, watching me put on makeup and jewelry, taking it all in as if she wanted nothing more than to be me someday.

"You're so pretty, Mommy."

"I love you, Mommy."

She still says that last one, but Mommy has been shortened to Mom, and her delivery is routine, just a task to cross off her list. Brushes her teeth, pokes her head in the doorway, tells each of us goodnight and that she loves us.

When did I become ridiculous in her eyes? Everything I do is embarrassing, everything I say is wrong. It's like navigating a minefield, and the eye rolls coupled with her disappointed sighs have blown me to bits more times than I'd care to admit.

He tells me it's just the teenage years, it will pass, I'm being too sensitive—I've heard it all. He doesn't understand, and how could he? She still smiles when she tells her father she loves him, still asks him to come to the stables with her, still abandons what she's doing and hops off the couch if he asks her to ride into town with him to run errands. A new wardrobe, a spa day, ditching school for a Wednesday matinee on Broadway—she won't bite. No, when *I* suggest any kind of outing she has too much schoolwork, and how can I argue with that?

I'd love to chalk it up to adolescent angst, but I can't.

She sees through me, examines me and finds me lacking. It's the same way I looked at my own mother years ago. My life would be more, I'd do better, climb higher. I looked at my mother and saw a life with no meaning. She didn't earn, didn't create, didn't dream. I would be different. Yet here I am, a few months shy of fifty, and what have I accomplished? I live in a beautiful home, in a neighborhood with high manicured hedges and long driveways, with staff arriving on alternate days to handle the gardening, upkeep and cleaning. I traded in my dreams, my aspirations and my career for the comfortable life I now live.

I tell myself that I love my life, but that sparkle I used to see when I caught my reflection in the mirror isn't there anymore. I have everything I thought I ever wanted: the handsome, successful man, the beautiful child, the perfect family. But it's not enough. Now when I look in the mirror and force myself to take a long, hard look, I feel hollow.

I feel unnecessary.

My marriage is somewhat of an achievement, especially if I'm comparing us to the other couples we know. We share a deep, abiding love, there is mutual respect and the sex is still decent, so I see us as better than most in that regard. I used to view parenthood in that same way: a status I'd achieved and something I was good at, especially since our road to becoming parents was a years-long, uphill battle. But when that child begins to look at you with an expression that manages to be both dismissive and pitying, it's impossible to feel successful.

Does she know?

It's become that thing we don't talk about. I'm convinced every family has one. In my family it was infidelity, in my husband's family it was the decades-long rift between his mother and his aunt that they took to their graves.

We always planned to tell her. When she was six, seven...We reasoned that it would only confuse her. When she was nine, ten, eleven...We were so blissfully happy it was something I wouldn't even consider. When she was twelve, thirteen...I told my husband it would only hurt her. And more recently, when she was changing right before my very eyes, I told myself to hold on tight, with everything I had. She was ours, *our* daughter.

Not hers.

I used to dig that envelope out every once in a while, study the picture the social worker handed over as my husband waited for me by the elevators with our precious newborn strapped into her top-of-the-line car seat. She was only a few years older than Sarah is now. The realization makes me shudder.

Back on that hot August morning I felt victorious, absconding with our treasure. I saw that girl in the drab hospital gown as a threat, as someone who could change her mind and crush me. After everything we'd endured on the road to becoming parents, I didn't think I could survive another loss. I never truly knew the meaning of the word relieved until the waiting period had expired and I was certain she had no recourse, no way of taking her away from us.

It's in my nightstand now. Sarah asking me out of the blue

to tell her about the day she was born made me fish it out, but only after I was sure she was asleep for the night. It's grainy and unfocused, but it takes me right back to that spot in the corridor where I stood with shaking hands.

The Kate Spade sleeveless sheath, a navy cardigan draped over my shoulders, brand-new Chanel loafers and my lucky pearl studs. It's ridiculous that I remember every detail of what I wore, but not surprising given the amount of thought I put into that outfit. I wanted our outward appearance to assure anyone who mattered that we were established, deserving, and would give this child a good home. No, not just a *good* home, the best kind of upbringing imaginable. I wanted everyone: the social workers, nurses, maybe even the birth mother herself, to know beyond a shadow of a doubt that this child would be better off with us.

The social worker told me she didn't even want to look at the baby, let alone hold her. *It took some convincing*, she said. I had to suppress my urge to slap the woman. Why on Earth would she want her to hold my baby, to—God forbid—bond with her? I knew the well-meaning woman was giving the girl an opportunity to change her mind, but that was obviously the last thing I wanted.

Holding my gaze, the social worker handed over the Polaroid she'd snapped. I guess since the girl's face wasn't visible there was no breach of confidentiality, but it wasn't right. I was tempted to voice my disapproval, but thought better of it as I took the picture and carefully slid it into my purse.

I didn't feel an ounce of sympathy for her then, not one. But looking at that snapshot now, I'm back in that moment and feel the loss as if it's me curled up on the bed.

Why do I keep referring to the subject of the picture as *the girl, she, her,* when there's no secret? I know her name. I know her *full* name, her date of birth, where she attended university, her blood type and pertinent medical history. And with the background check we conducted on her, I could go on, believe me.

That day in the hospital, I circled back for one last look at Grace Dawson. Like a Peeping Tom I stood at a distance, sneaking a look while trying to be discreet and nonchalant. She was facing the wall, hiding herself. Hiding tears? Yes, her shoulders were shaking and her arms were wrapped tight around her middle. She was alone. No mother to hold her hand, no boy to shoulder this ache with her, no friends.

I didn't think much of her. Don't get me wrong, I was grateful, but not to her. I was grateful for this blessing, for this happy turn of events, but in no way did I feel personally indebted to this girl, and I certainly didn't take a moment to acknowledge what she was sacrificing. Honestly, I looked down on her, wondered what kind of person could sign those papers. Not only signing away her child, but signing an agreement that was basically a pledge to never interfere in our lives. Who knows if it was even legally binding.

Maybe she was happy to get on with her life and put it all behind her. That's what I told myself back then, and I do hope that was the case. I don't like to think of her as a young woman with regrets, sadness, or a longing for the child she gave away.

The child she gave to me.

My Sarah is seventeen today. I planned a night out for her and several friends in Manhattan, and no expense has been spared. They'll be having dinner at La Grenouille, a spot where they're likely to sight a celebrity or two, and then off to the Garden to see Taylor in concert. My husband doesn't balk at much, but I didn't see any upside in sharing the obscene amount of money we parted with for those seats.

I considered putting a small cooler in the hired car with a few of those spiked seltzers, but my husband put the kibosh on that. Harmless fun, I argued—it's not like I was suggesting a bottle of vodka—but he wasn't having it. He's right, I suppose. I'd about die if one of the other mothers found out and disapproved.

The party bus is arriving in one hour and—right on cue—she's sulking. She doesn't want this, that's what she told me last week after I'd already sent out invitations, booked a Mercedes sprinter van, spent an ungodly sum on those tickets, and hounded my husband's secretary to secure the dinner reservation. This night has taken *months* to plan.

Those girls aren't my friends, she tells me with tears streaming down her cheeks. They are—at least three out of the ten I invited are friends of hers. She needs to widen her circle, open herself up to opportunities. And I'm friends with the girls' mothers, so it's going to go well.

I'm sure of it.

The mothers are staying for drinks after the girls leave. It's a kickoff to our daughters' senior year, so there will be no shortage of topics for conversation. Two of the women are in my tennis league, and the rest belong to our club, so I know them to say hello in the very least. You see, I'm looking to widen my circle too, but that's the difference between me and my daughter: I like the challenge.

Sarah does perk up when Penny arrives. To be honest, Penny is her one and only friend. Sarah could take or leave the others. And if I was being brutally honest, I'd admit that my daughter prefers the company of her horse over actual humans. She'd be pleased as punch if I called off the birthday party and dropped her at the stable to talk to her horse all damn day.

It's like we're from different planets, but it wasn't always that way. I seesaw back and forth from asking myself what I can do to get us back to that good place, and resenting her right back for being so difficult, so...ungrateful.

I want to tell her the story of how she came to us, and one day I will, but how much will I share? Will I tell her how sad her birth mother appeared, shattered and alone, looking so very young in that hospital room? Will I ever tell Sarah that the girl needed to be coaxed to hold her, and not because she was unfeeling, but because she probably felt like she'd actually die from the pain and grief? Will I tell her that when I was expecting, it got to the point that I panicked whenever I had the urge to pee, so fearful of the bloodstains that broke my heart time after time after time? Will she ever understand the depths of our sadness, or how many times I was curled up just like that girl, with her father comforting me in the obstetrician's office after yet another loss? I was *desperate* for her—there is no other way to describe the feeling.

The two of us used to watch her sleep, struck with the wonder of it all. I was never tired and neither was Daniel. Sleepy-eyed, we'd shoot a quick smile between us as we woke for midnight feedings and diaper changes.

Will she ever fully realize the extent of my love for her? Elated, ecstatic, overflowing with joy—motherhood was every single thing I'd hoped for and more.

I breathe out once the driver pulls away. She played the part, smiled on cue and greeted everyone as they arrived, but I didn't miss that one brief look back as she walked out the door. It was a look that said, *I hate you*. No one else noticed.

I'm sure of it.

Blue eyes…It's virtually impossible.

Parker snaps his fingers until I look up. He thinks he's being funny, when in reality the move is borderline aggressive.

"Earth to Sarah," he teases.

My fingernails dig into his skin for a split second before I push him away. "Get your hand out of my face."

I'm usually easy going and oh so agreeable, so the force of my anger surprises him. "What's the matter with you?" He looks behind him to where his two lap dogs are waiting before turning back to me. "Got your period or something?"

"Nope…Got *your* period?"

Still reeling from what I found out this morning, I'm surprised his lame insult even registers. It's just another item on the ever-growing list of things that irritate me about Parker. He has a habit of quoting poets he doesn't understand, plagiarizing term papers off the internet, using ridiculous words like ubiquitous with a straight face, and wearing a blazer to school for no reason other than to make himself look important.

Parker presents himself to the world as a distinguished,

powerful man, with the lineage, connections and money to make his future a guaranteed success. And while he does have all of those things, he hasn't lifted a finger to earn any of it. He's not particularly bright, but it's all but guaranteed he'll be admitted to one of the finest private universities in the country based on his legacy connections alone. He has no worries and lacks ambition, but what does it matter? Like most of the people I've been surrounded by since birth, Parker benefits from the ruthless ambition of his ancestors.

Ancestors.

Shake it off.

Right, I just have to get through the next hour or so before I can hunker down and figure this shit out.

Smiling up at my dumbstruck boyfriend, I muster up a more conciliatory tone. "Are we going to lunch or what?"

He backs up a step and lets me pass. I walk a pace ahead of them, half-listening to their sickening bro-talk all the way to the cafeteria.

"What up, Jessie?"

Coming from my girl Penny it's not a dig, but I can't say the same for the others.

My tendency to come into school with pieces of hay stuck to my jacket earned me that nickname back in middle school. Back then I was so crazy about my horse that I'd beg my mother to swing by the stables on my way to school just so I could brush Shadow and talk to her for a few minutes every morning.

And while I still ride Shadow more days a week than I don't, I'm not obsessed the way I used to be. Show jumping may look pretty, but that world is intense. When my coach started talking to my parents about boarding down in

Wellington for the winter—a necessity if one is to be considered serious in the sport—that's when I bailed.

So now, whenever I bow out from an afternoon at the mall, or pass on day drinking at one of my unsupervised friend's estates so that I can ride, I'm *pulling a Jessie*, a reference to that hillbilly cowgirl from some old movie. Fine with me.

This is northeast horse country, so a lot of people ride, but my besties are overachievers in other ways. Penny sails, my friend Clara is somewhat competitive on the junior tennis circuit, and Tatiana has already had her photography featured in a gallery in New York. It was her mom's gallery, but still.

We are the offspring of the one percent. We attend private schools where the crew, fencing and squash teams compete alongside the football, field hockey and basketball players. And golf? We have our very own nine-hole course on campus, naturally. We get our first credit card when we turn sixteen, and a shiny new car when we turn seventeen. I'm not a hypocrite, and I'm certainly not trying to distance myself when I point out the absurdity of this life. Seriously, how could I? I got a freaking horse for my eighth birthday.

Old money versus new money—where I come from it's the only divide that exists. The members of the establishment would like everyone to believe old money is the only money worth having. The kind of money that's linked to a name.

My family is tolerated, but we're new money. Excuse me while I gasp and then stage whisper when I add, *hedge fund money*. It's comical the way they say it. It's as if they're holding their nose to stave off the smell of rotting fish. New money is dirty money in their eyes.

My father, a titan in the world of finance, is only one step above the guy hawking his pillows on the home shopping channel in this neck of the woods. Yep, he earned a full scholarship to a top school, worked his way up and then went out on his own and made a success of his life. He could probably buy and sell most of the blowhards at the country club we belong to, but he's not one of them.

You'd think from the way these morons talk that each and every one of them has a direct link to someone who sailed over on the Mayflower. Let me assure you, they do not.

Parker's family has been here for five generations and their last name is synonymous with banking. Tatiana's family too, but they were bankers in France—ooh la la and *so* much better than being descendant from, say, a Russian oligarch. Penny's family is known for their philanthropy and years of public service. Her great-grandfather was a senator, her grandfather was a cabinet member under President Reagan, and her father is a judge on the federal court of appeals. They have a second home in Georgetown where he spends most of his time. No joke, I haven't seen him live and in person for years. I used to think that was weird, but I've come to understand that marriages come in all shapes and sizes.

My father laughs it off as nonsense, but my mother takes this status stuff seriously. She strives to be one of them, and I'll concede that she has edged her way in, at least to some degree. She plays tennis and pickle ball at the club with the ladies, she's on the board at my tony private school, and she chairs an annual fundraiser for the fair and ethical treatment of animals. I'd like to point out that she does eat meat and shops weekly to feed a nasty leather handbag addiction, so I'm not sure why she chose to support animal welfare over any one of a thousand other worthy causes. But I do know. It's all about who else is on the committee. It's how the game is played.

The fog clears when I catch onto Penny scolding Tatiana, "Leave her alone."

"Sorry, what?"

"Nothing, space cadet. I was just asking if you were coming tonight."

"Where?" I ask Tatiana, and the three of them bust out laughing. I feel out of it, literally and figuratively. I should have snuck off to the library for lunch.

Clara leans into me, wrapping one arm around my shoulders. "Tatiana is having a party tonight. Her parents are away for the weekend."

"So technically," Tatiana says, "I'm having a weekend sleepover." Looking to the three of us, she adds, "Tell your parents you're staying over at my house."

I'm quick to answer, "My mother won't go for that," even though nothing could be further from the truth. Tatiana's mom is on my mother's hit list. And by that, I mean that Tatiana's mom is a top-tier society gal, a card-carrying member of the inner sanctum, and therefore my mother wants in with her more than she wants her next breath.

"I'll mention it to Audrey." He can't see me rolling my eyes, but the girls do. He's always hovering lately, crowding me. I want to tell Parker to mind his own business and to get his hands off my damn shoulders. He's holding on to me like he owns me, giving me a squeeze when he adds, "If I ask, she'll definitely say yes."

It's sad to admit this, but my mother would indeed say yes if her darling Parker asked. She'd give tacit permission for her little girl to lose her virginity if it meant there might be a marriage proposal from *the* Parker Hastings somewhere down the line.

I turn and look up to him, shaking my head. "Thanks, but no. I'll be there tonight but I'm not asking to sleep over." For emphasis, I add, "I'm going riding with my father early tomorrow morning."

The lie slips off my tongue with ease. They always do.

Standing in the doorway of my parents' bedroom a few hours later, I tell another lie when my father asks what's wrong and I tell him I'm fine.

I am not fine.

I sit on their bed and watch them just like I used to when I was little. I was in awe of my mother and father back then, watching in wonder as they transformed from their everyday look into a glamorous couple. Tonight is no different.

My mother is in her late forties, but still effortlessly slim, with glowing skin and a sense of style to rival Coco Chanel's. I watch as she fastens her understated diamond studs and then smiles at her reflection in the mirror as she brushes the apples of both cheeks with blush. Her eyes sparkle when she smiles.

Blue eyes.

My father, too. Early fifties, but I see the younger wives at the club eyeing him with appreciation when he passes by. I think they even dig the laugh lines and the few grays that contrast with his jet-black hair. My mother calls him a silver fox to tease him, but he doesn't look old and he knows it. And tonight he looks sophisticated in his custom-made suit. It's a black-tie affair but he refuses to wear a tux.

"I'm wearing an obscenely expensive suit. If they want their donation check, they'll keep their traps shut." My mother shakes her head even though she doesn't really care, and he walks up behind her to kiss her cheek. "You look gorgeous, by the way."

He smiles at her in the mirror and she winks back at him. His eyes sparkle with mischief and desire just like hers.

Blue eyes.

We covered the basics of genetics in biology back when I was a sophomore, but now I'm taking Anatomy, Physiology and Biomechanics, a college-level course for students considering a career in medicine. It's my first class of the day and it's intense, but this morning's topic of discussion sent me into a tailspin that I haven't come out of just yet.

It's virtually impossible.

Mr. Rogers teaches the class, but he's nothing like the tennis sneaker, cardigan-wearing softy that Tom Hanks played in that movie. No, my Mr. Rogers is a grouchy, pissed-off loser who didn't make it through med school at Johns Hopkins. Hence, he's had to settle for teaching snotty, precocious high school students who park their sweet rides alongside his spruce green mid-level sedan every morning. He's got the look of a man who believes the world owed him something but didn't deliver.

We were doing a lesson on inherited traits, and he let out with a loud, bored sigh when I asked for clarification. I know about recessive and dominant traits, but he was getting into more advanced stuff: monohybrid versus dihybrid crosses, gametes and alleles. On a normal day I'd do my best to follow along and then read up on anything that wasn't crystal clear after class, but today I was stuck, and Rogers was none too happy when I raised my hand for the third time.

"What *exactly* is it that you don't understand, Miss Hamilton?"

"It's just that blue eyes can come from two brown-eyed parents, so why can't two blue-eyed parents produce a child with brown eyes?"

"I said it's possible but *incredibly* rare. As we discussed *already*, it would require a damaged HERC2 gene." He turned back to his laptop, dismissing me. "It's virtually impossible."

Watching my mother twist her hair into a sleek knot, I swallow back the emotion. I don't look anything like my blonde, blue-eyed swan of a mother. She is lean and graceful, nearly matching my father's six-foot frame when she's wearing heels. My father's hair is dark like mine—I check that off in my favor—but there is nothing else. I measure in at five-foot-three on a good day and I'm curvy. Eyes, lips, skin tone, even mannerisms—I don't laugh, talk or move like either one of them.

I have a foggy memory of the words *chosen* and *special* being used to describe me when I was very little, but when I've asked about it in more recent years, I've been diverted with a hug, a kiss and a topic change.

It's a feeling you have, one that's hard to explain. I'm always studying the people around me, half-listening, never one hundred percent engaged. I am an outsider, even when I'm surrounded by family and friends. If I saw a therapist like a solid fifty percent of my classmates do, he or she would tell me that this limbo I find myself in is perfectly normal for my age. The struggle for a sense of identity is real. I know this. But this disconnect I feel, day in and day out, is different. I try and talk myself out of it, tell myself I'm no different from every psychosocially messed up adolescent I know. *You're not special,* I tell myself, even though I know that I am.

I *am* different, but not in some extraordinary, plucky, offbeat kind of way. No, I feel peculiar and abnormal, like an alien trying to fit in amid earthlings.

Chapter Two

I want out.

My friends are all wasted, Tatiana's house is packed wall to wall, and the smell of acrid smoke is turning my stomach.

Cigars are heavy and sweet to my senses. Weed is earthy and rich. But cigarettes just stink—there's nothing redeeming about that stale, toxic stench.

Parker has taken to smoking since spending his spring break in France, poser that he is. And yep, I see that he's got a loose hold on one as he sips from a tumbler of whiskey. I laugh to myself when I see the filter—at least he's not smoking Gauloises.

I came here against my better judgement, knowing I was in no state to fake it tonight. But my mother already knew about the party, thanks to Parker, and I just didn't want to get into it with her. They looked happy, and me feigning a headache as an excuse to stay home would maybe not have wrecked my parents' night, but definitely put a damper on it. I suck down the last of my drink, knowing that Audrey—my mother has taken to correcting my friends when they call her Mrs. Hamilton—would have been disappointed for sure.

My mother doesn't get me, doesn't understand why I'm not spinning in circles and basically thrilled twenty-four-seven. After all, I date the one of the most popular guys in my school, I have a tight group of friends who hail from the best families in our town, and I have every luxury money can buy. That's how she views my life, as some idyllic mix of *High School Musical* innocence and *Gossip Girl*-level excitement. She doesn't know what it takes for me to simply exist in this place. I am a misfit who somehow gives off the impression of fitting in. I spend most of my time second guessing myself and looking over my shoulder. I am uncomfortable at parties, in the hallways of school, and lately there are times when I feel out of place at my own dinner table.

Parker has taken control of the music, and I can't help but smirk when *Used to Love Her* cranks out from the speakers so loud that I can barely make out what Penny is whispering into my ear. I know it's something about a guy she met down at the shore last summer, but I'm never really one hundred percent tuned in, so I'm not following. I'm focused on the lyrics at the moment because I love this song, and I'm also thinking: *Right back 'atcha, Parker.*

Minus that one part. I can't say that I used to love Parker. I don't now and I never have. I'm guilty of parroting the words back to him, but my heart has never been in it. It's just too awkward to stay silent when a guy pledges his love to you. *Gee, thank you,* or *That's nice,* just doesn't cut it. You kind of have to say it back.

And let me just clarify that he's not the absolute jerk I'm making him out to be. He has some good qualities. He's an accomplished athlete, a devoted son, and he's the life of every party. He's figured out a way to move through this world already, collecting friends like bottlecaps and keeping them close.

Swear to God, I don't know what he sees in me. I'm not the prettiest girl in our group, and Parker Hastings can certainly have his pick of the litter. Maybe it's nothing more than wanting what he can't have. I haven't given it up, physically or emotionally, so maybe he just likes the chase.

And right on cue, he sidles up to me, wrapping one strong arm around my shoulders in a way that's meant to provoke. My intuition tells me there's a part of him that gets off on making me uncomfortable, but I fight the urge to wrestle out of his octopus-like grip. Forget it, I take back what I said before. Parker is a jerk, a misogynistic jerk. He likes to be in control, and I take the bait this time because I have no energy to fight him off. I melt into his frame and look up at him batting my eyelashes when I say, "You'd like to see me six feet under, huh?"

"What?" Parker is all wide-eyed innocence as Penny and I crack up. "Oh, the song?" He laughs along with us. Shaking his head, he adds, "Just an oldie but a goodie."

Penny takes my empty cup. "What are you drinking?"

It was plain club soda but I answer back, "Tito's and soda." No one likes a sober girl at a party so I play the role people want me to play. Penny always has a heavy hand, but she's so buzzed right now that I'm sure the drink she hands back will be vodka rocks with a teeny-weeny splash of soda.

Parker leans down to whisper, "You're not really going home tonight, are you?"

"I have to."

It's a lie and he knows it. He drops his hand from my shoulder and turns to watch Tatiana. My friend is wearing a tube dress that's practically exposing her ass cheeks as she makes out with her boyfriend of the month. "I can't wait forever, Sarah."

My cheeks heat and my jaw is clenched tight when I whisper back, "I'm not ready."

He takes a gulp from his drink. "Will you ever be ready?"

Today has been an absolute clusterfuck. As in, my life as I knew it has been blown to smithereens while I've been smiling my way through stupid small talk and everyday adolescent drama. *Will* Penny hook up with that hot townie guy again this summer at the shore? *Should* Parker's bestie, Logan Clark the damn Third, follow in his father's footsteps, or try to make a professional career out of sailing? *Is* Clara really going to move clear across the country if she gets into USC? *Who the fuck cares???* That's what I've wanted to scream at the top of my lungs all day long. And the pressure Parker is laying on me right now is threatening to send me right over the edge.

There's some part of me that wants him to be sympathetic, to understand. I don't let my guard down or show my real self to him in any meaningful way, so I don't know why I expect anything from him in return. But I want that. I want him to look at me and say *I love you* for real. He uses that lame line as a bargaining chip. I love you so let me get in your pants. I love you so give it up to me. I've come to equate those three beautiful words to nothing more than a lie.

My sadness turns to anger, but I swallow it down like I always do. "There are plenty of girls here ready and willing. Take your pick."

He says nothing, just looks off to the side as he takes a long, dramatic drag off his cigarette. Now that I'm up close I can see it's a Marlboro—the brand of cowboys and tough guys all the world over. Is Parker like me underneath it all? Is he trying on different versions of the person he wants to be? One day he's quoting Whitman in an attempt to come off like an intelligent badass, the next day he's watching video tutorials on how to live a greener existence. And while I do doubt his commitment to sustainable living while residing in an eight-thousand square foot home, I have to give him props for at least thinking along those lines. Is he just as mixed up as I am?

And just like that, any sympathy I have for him evaporates much like the smoke he blows back in my face. I cough, and I swear the jerk is pleased when he waves the smoke away and mutters, "Sorry 'bout that."

"No, you're not."

"You know what sucks, Sarah? I know I *could* have any girl here, but for some reason I want you, my girlfriend. It'd be nice if you wanted me back."

Stated in another way, those words would sound tender, but Parker's tone is biting. He's angry and resentful. He believes I owe him and I'm refusing to pay him what's due.

Fuck this. I want my pajamas and my bed.

Parker calls after me as I make my way to the door. It's an exasperated, "I'm sorry, ok?"

He knows he messed up, and I'm sure there's a part of him that is genuinely sorry, but I don't care. I hear Logan call out, "Let her go," and once I'm out of the rain and back in my car, it dawns on me that Parker followed orders. He didn't plead with me to stay or follow me outside.

It's just as well. I'll never be what he wants or what he needs. The sooner he realizes it, the better.

Chapter Three

It's still quiet at this hour.

It's early May but I can still see my breath in the chill of the morning air. I don't mind the cold.

My mother used to obsess over the chances of me contracting pneumonia when I was younger. *This can't be good for her*, I'd hear her complaining to my father. *It's freezing in that stable.* Arms crossed, I'd plead my case to my father, reasoning that if the horses didn't get sick in the winter then neither would I.

He's always had to play the role of referee. It's not that my mother and I butt heads on a regular basis, it's just that we're not like-minded. We tend to disagree about pretty much everything. My father has spent years as the go-between, handling negotiations with the tact of a seasoned diplomat.

And in the end, I won out. It took a couple of winters of me not contracting bronchitis, the flu, or so much as a bad case of the sniffles for her to let up, but eventually she did. And I firmly believe all that time spent out in the elements has toughened me up—you can't tell me anything different.

I breathe in deep, fill my sturdy lungs with that crisp air, and smile when the scent of fresh hay and leather hits me. It's a smell that's so uniquely horsey. I lean in and nuzzle Shadow's mane, and he turns his face to show me some love right back. It never gets old.

The sound of boots on the ground gets my attention. Braids, bright eyes, and a smile that stretches clear across her face. This one can't be more than nine or ten, and she reminds me of myself at that age. You can tell from the look on her face that there's nowhere else on Earth she'd rather be. A girl and her horse. I had that same single-minded obsession way back when.

Back then I spoke to Shadow in the early morning on the weekends, and then every afternoon as soon as I could cast off my school uniform and tug on my boots. I told Shadow everything, even though most of the time I wasn't speaking a word aloud. I believed we had this perfect symbiotic relationship where no words were necessary. I could ease his worry with a gentle brushing, and Shadow could soothe me with a nuzzle, or cheer me up with a whinny.

"You're here early."

"Early?" I don't look up at Mr. Murphy as I go on brushing my baby. "I used to get here before sunrise."

"Still, it's pretty early for a teenager. My nephew was snoring like a bear when I left, and if I don't call him every hour on the hour he'll be late for his shift at noon."

"He snores?"

"Sleeps soundly is a better way of putting it. Guess you could say I'm jealous. Sound sleep isn't easy to come by at my age."

"You're not so old, Mr. Murphy."

"I'll be sixty next month. And my own kids had already

flown the coop by the time my younger sister had this hellion, so don't mind my complaining. I think I'm just too old to be raising a teenager at this stage in my life. I prefer horses," he rustles my hair like he's done since I first started riding here, "present company excluded."

"He lives with you?"

"For the time being." He changes the subject, telling me the farrier is coming on Monday. "Tell your father I'm having him look at Shadow."

"Are his shoes ok for now?"

"Sure, you can ride him today. I just need your dad to approve the expense."

I nod, knowing it's no big deal. Horses are wildly expensive, but my father has never once balked at the boarding, training or vet bills. Where I'm concerned, no expense is spared.

"It looks like rain, little gypsy girl, so if you plan on riding, you best get a move on."

I smile whenever he calls me by that name now, but it used to irk me to no end. When I was a kid I was obsessed with some book, *Gypsy from Nowhere*. I saw myself as Wendy, the girl who gets sent to live on a faraway ranch and comes to rely on a horse to heal her spirit. Sometimes I'd read it out loud to Shadow, using a different voice for each character in the story. You know, to put on a good performance for my animal audience. I think Mr. Murphy got a kick out of my weird behavior.

He made the mistake of calling my horse Gypsy once, and I went off on him like the spoiled little brat that I was back then. *His* name *is Shadow.* And after laying down the law, I proceeded to school Mr. Murphy while he did his best not to laugh. *Gypsy is brown, not black like Shadow. And* my *horse doesn't have weird, different colored eyes like Gypsy, see?*

"Ok, ok...I get it, kid." Mr. Murphy temporarily conceded the win to me, but the next day when I showed up to ride, he greeted me as Gypsy Girl and the nickname stuck.

One brown eye, one blue. A genetic anomaly. Maybe I am more like Gypsy than Wendy.

Gypsy, the *girl* from nowhere.

And today I ride like her—no form, no rules. I warm Shadow up and then take off into the back trails and hills. I am literally off the beaten path, knowing there's a part of me that wants to get lost out here in what passes for wilderness in New Jersey.

By the time we get back, we're both wrung out. My hair is a tangled mess and Shadow is ambling back to the stable like an out of shape runner who just ran a marathon.

Mr. Murphy is red in the face too, but he looks more pissed-off than tired.

"Everything ok?" I ask as he snaps his phone shut. Yes, he still has a flip phone.

"The kid is going to send me to an early grave. If he gets fired from this job..."

"You said his shift is at noon. It's not even ten-thirty."

"Lunch is *served* at noon. He needs to report to the club at eleven. He's probably awake and not answering his phone just to be a pain in my arse."

"He's working *here*?"

Murphy nods. "If you spot a kid covered in tattoos with his hair tied up in man bun, that's him."

I can't help but laugh. "Tattoos? Tell your nephew to roll his sleeves down in the dining room. Some of the members won't be too keen on the ink."

"If *I* tell him to roll his sleeves down, he'll be sure to wear a tank top."

"What's his name?"

"Liam." Mr. Murphy takes the reins from me. "He's about your age, I think."

"A senior in high school?"

Mr. Murphy sighs as he shakes his head. "Well, he *would* be a senior if his mother didn't let him drop out of school two years ago." Handling Shadow with care, he lifts each foot to inspect the shoes. "Looks good. I was getting a little worried...You were out for a long time."

"I won't ride him again until he's ready."

"Tuesday."

Both of us turn when someone clears their throat, loud and angry. His eyes are laser focused on Mr. Murphy as he holds up his phone asking, "Six messages? What's that about?"

And *my* eyes? Oh, they are currently laser focused on the brooding hottie standing before me.

He's gigantic. Like a rugged frontiersman who could wrestle a bear kind of big. I check for a man bun but see that his sandy blond locks are neatly secured at the nape of his neck. Good. He'll get a few side eyes for the long hair but it's not like he's channeling Jason Momoa.

"Just wanted to make sure you're not late on your first day." Mr. Murphy looks down at his watch. "I'd say you're cutting it close."

"Don't worry, Uncle Danny, everyone will get their cucumber finger sandwiches right on time."

He looks my way when I giggle, but his hard eyes cut through me and suck the air from my lungs. I immediately look down to my boots to avoid his glare.

Mr. Murphy looks up to the ceiling and lets out a breath once his nephew leaves. "Like I said...That kid's going to be the death of me."

I take a deep breath too, relieved once his nephew is gone. "All these years and I didn't know your name was Danny. Same as my dad, but everyone calls him Daniel."

He smiles in a way that tells me he knows I'm doing my best to lighten the mood and he's grateful for it. "Need some help with Shadow today?"

"Nope," I tell him as I go on making long, lazy brush-strokes. "I have nowhere I need to be."

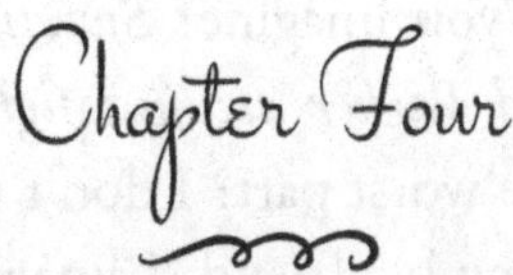

Chapter Four

Busted.

I'm still pissed at Parker, but getting caught in a lie is unsettling.

He's sitting at the kitchen island with an obscenely large bouquet of red roses resting between him and my mother. They're laughing like old pals when I come walking into the kitchen, while my father—yup, he was supposed to be out riding with me—is making himself a cup of coffee.

"I was just about to make Parker some breakfast, Bug. Are you hungry?"

"Nope," I answer, even though I'm damn near starving. "I ate before I left for the club."

My mother shoots me a look because I've just made this little get together awkward, but taking in my father's profile, I see that he's cracking a smile as he's pouring cream into his cup. He's probably wondering what Parker did to his little girl that required an early morning stop at the florist, so my snotty tone and dismissal please him.

"Don't go to any trouble, Mrs. Hamilton. Sarah, you want to take a drive instead and we'll grab an early lunch?"

This exchange would be so much easier if we were alone, but no, we have an audience. I seriously don't want to get into it right now. Could you imagine? *Sweetie, what's the matter? Oh nothing...Me and Parker are just fighting because I won't give up the goods.* The worst part? I don't trust that my mother wouldn't side with my boyfriend. I imagine her advice might go something like: *Well, you* are *almost eighteen...What are you waiting for?*

"Sure...Gimme a minute."

Five minutes later I'm changed into sweats and my hair is in a messy topknot. I want him to see that I'm putting in zero effort. Once we're in the car, he turns to me. "I'm sorry about last night."

"Why?" I shrug when I add, "You're entitled to want what you want."

"I want *you*, Sarah, and putting pressure on you was wrong. *I* was wrong."

"But *why* do you want me?" When he looks away, I ask him again. "I'm being serious, Parker. Sometimes I wonder what it is that you see in me."

His voice is flat when he says, "And sometimes I wonder if you even care about me at all."

His words sting, and I look down into my lap feeling guilty. "I do care. You know that."

He's still looking straight ahead when he reaches over to take one of my hands in his. "I can see us," he says a moment later, giving my hand a gentle squeeze. "I can see a future for us."

"What do you mean?" As the words leave my mouth I'm wondering why I'm even asking the question. Am I fishing for compliments, or some affirmation of my worth? Deep down am I *that* girl? Do I need the "it" guy to tell me that I'm special, wonderful, or, God forbid, pretty?

When I look up I see that he's turned back to face me. "You'll be at Penn, I'll be at Princeton…An hour away. And I'm not looking to chain you to me for the next four years…I know what being at different schools means. But I think about my future and I definitely see you in it."

"You do?" I want to slap myself for sounding so needy, but it's no use.

"I do. And as for what I see in you? Jesus, Sarah, you're smarter than just about everyone I know, you're kind to everyone and you're beautiful. You make me want to be a better person."

I don't know what to say to all that. I've never been able to accept compliments without feeling uncomfortable. When I don't answer, he leans in and kisses me on the cheek. "So can we please just forget about last night? We'll move at your pace, no more pressure. I feel like an absolute ass when I think about what I said to you."

I look down into my lap and nod, and for that I get another chaste kiss. "Good, I'm glad that's settled. Logan is having a thing tonight, but if it's all the same to you, I'd rather skip it and just do something low key like grab take-out and watch a movie. Sound good?"

While I know that I'm being played to a certain degree, there is a part of me that's grateful for the gesture. Because let's face it, for my boyfriend, skipping a party at Logan's house is like the Pope ducking out of Easter Mass at St. Peter's.

"As long as I get to pick the movie."

"Fine," he leans over and nuzzles into that spot beneath my ear where he knows I'm ticklish, "but then I'm taking lead on chow. Do you want to hang out now, or just see me later on? I know you like to get your act together on Saturdays, and that back there was just a ploy to get you out of the house."

"I do need to study, so yeah, I'll see you around seven?"

He gives my hand another gentle squeeze and whispers, "Love you," when I turn to get out of the car.

"Love you, too," I parrot back.

Same as always.

Chapter Five

LIAM

It's all I can do not to rev my engine and tear out of the parking lot at the end of my shift, but as much as I play the part of ungrateful ward, I do love my aunt and uncle, so I refrain from doing anything to jeopardize Uncle Danny's job at this uppity, fucktard-infested club.

How does he do it? Catering to these people for a few measly hours has me on edge—like literally on the verge of breaking shit—but my uncle has been serving the ultra-rich for years with a smile on his face, and an attitude that seems genuinely warm. He talks about them to my Aunt Maeve, telling funny stories about the horse-crazy kids, or the parents who try their hand at riding lessons for a hot minute as a part of some mid-life quest to fill their empty days and add purpose to their lives.

And today was nothing. Just had to deal with the ladies who lunch crowd, all on strict, no-carb diets, and a few father-son tables fresh off the links. I recognized one of the kids from the shore. Some jerk who owns a big-ass sailboat that probably costs upwards of a hundred grand. In truth, I have no idea what it costs, but it's a Beneteau and I know that's the top of the line.

My buddy Mike works at the marina, maintaining boats and filling gas tanks for people who think nothing of dropping over five-hundred bucks in fuel for a one-day pleasure ride. He knows some of those kids, considers them friends. He's even invited them to a few of the parties us locals throw down on the beach.

I don't like to go assuming the worst about people who are different from me—seriously, it's something I'm working on—but I couldn't help but study their faces as they took in the scene last summer. They're all the same, scanning the crowd around the bonfire and smiling, but I see the superiority in their eyes.

I sigh mulling it over, admitting to myself that maybe I read into the class warfare crap too intently. Is it possible that they just want to cut loose sometimes? Trade the polo shirt in for a ratty tee and drink non-craft beer? I try to convince myself that I need to give people the benefit of the doubt, but when they can't manage to rustle up a t-shirt that doesn't have that pretentious little whale on the chest pocket, they don't make it easy on guys like me. No, they like to slum it once in a while. That's the conclusion I've drawn.

I hooked up with one of their girls last summer. She was on the arm of one of them when they made their way down the dunes, but sidled up to me after the guy I thought was her man found someone else to entertain him. Can't remember her name, can't even remember the details of her face. I just remember that she was aggressive and none too pleased when I passed on her offer.

I don't like being used or being the butt of a joke.

Shaking my head as I turn onto the main road, I wonder what my life would have been like if I hadn't kicked and screamed my way out of accepting that scholarship.

I remember my mother insisting on that button-down shirt —the one she'd done a piss poor job of cleaning and ironing. It had that ring around the collar that laughs in the face of the strongest stain removers, and being that it belonged to Jeff, it was too small around my armpits and my neck in a way that reminded me of the way he treated me back then. My pants were also an inch too short.

I'd like to say I can look back on that visual and laugh, but it still stings. Pulling on my collar, I remember sweating in the headmaster's office as he rattled off my academic achievements and my stellar score on the state-wide test for gifted and talented students. Homing in on the banter of the kids who passed in the hallway as he gave me the grand tour, I could feel my heart racing and knew I was sweating through the pits of that cheap plaid shirt. Some ignored me, some gave me curious looks, turning their heads for no more than a split second. I wasn't slighted in an obvious way, there were no snickers or people covering their laughter as they took in my cheap clothes. It was nothing like what you see in those stupid teen movies. But I felt like a fish out of water, and wanted out of there, pronto. Made my decision even before the headmaster asked me about my future goals and I stammered out some incoherent nonsense like an imbecile.

The kids who attend those school are practiced in the art of conversation and social graces. Giving a firm handshake and maintaining eye contact are second nature to them. Their education begins at an early age. They learn at the dinner table, on the golf and tennis courts, from the copies of The Economist and The New York Times that arrive at their homes and wait to be devoured. They don't scarf their cereal down, reading the nutritional panel on the box over and over again just to block out the arguing coming from some corner of their shoebox-sized home.

It's not a caste system, but your station in life isn't exactly fluid either. In this world it's us and them—always has and always will be. *Fuck them*, I say in my head. I wouldn't want to be one of those stuck-up, self-important assholes. But then I remember the look on my face, how red I was, sweating as I walked back to my mother's beat-up minivan. I saw my reflection in the window, impatient as my mom took her sweet time leaning over to undo the passenger-side lock. She was looking to be supportive when she asked how it went, I knew that, but I lashed out at her anyway. *What a beautiful school*, she offered up as a gesture of peace. And I practically spat at her in return, telling her she was dumb for making me go on that stupid interview because acceptance or not, I was never going there.

Ashamed and inferior, that's how I felt. My cheap, ill-fitting clothes, my teeth, which I suddenly noticed were crooked in comparison—I even remember thinking that those kids smelled better than I did. And today, just having to smile and ask, "And how would you like your steak cooked?" Damn, I have to grip the steering wheel and breathe deep as it all comes rushing back.

I don't have the luxury of walking away. People who need money—people like me—have to swallow it down, paste on a smile and suppress our emotions. It's just the way it is.

Chapter Six

SARAH

My mother is waiting at the door when I come home from school today. Two weeks have passed since that day in science class, but I still haven't worked up the nerve to ask her or my father what I so desperately want to know.

I went digging instead. I asked my mother for my birth certificate, and she handed it over without blinking an eye. I've seen it before, and I don't recall seeing anything unusual about it, but now I want to scour every detail on that paper. It doesn't get me anywhere. My parents are listed under mother and father, there's no indication of a name change, birthday is what I've always been told. Nothing to see there. But a little internet sleuthing uncovers some interesting information. For one, New Jersey is a sealed records state, but a law was passed fairly recently allowing adoptees access to their original birth certificate. *Original* birth certificate? A little more digging informs me that there would be no discernible difference

43

between the original and the one issued to adoptive parents after the process is finalized. My birth certificate could be an amended version.

That's fascinating, but still, I'm back to square one.

She calls out to me, asking if I want to get a manicure with her in town, but accepts my *no thanks, got a lot work to do* without nagging. My mother doesn't expect anything but my default response. And it's generally not bullshit. I *am* bogged down with homework and studying, but she also knows I'd rather do just about anything than primp alongside her and the other mom-daughter super duos. She used to try and sweeten the pot with a stop for ice cream afterwards, but when I started ordering double scoops and put on more than a few pounds during my freshman year, she put an end to it. And without my chocolate peanut butter cup incentive, heavy on the sprinkles, I was out.

Once I hear the crunch of gravel underneath tires, I know I'm in the clear. It will be at least an hour before she gets home, if not two, so I take my time. I go through every drawer, feeling like a total creeper when I come across items I am *not* meant to see.

Go Mom, I think to myself, giggling when I come across her vibrator, but my face reddens and I shut my father's nightstand drawer quick when I unearth a bottle of lube. I should be grateful my parents have a healthy sex life, but I'm sorry, no one wants to envision their parents going at it.

Maybe this would be something kept in my father's office downstairs, or in my mother's room off the kitchen. She calls it her office, but as no work gets done in there, I generally refer to it as the sunroom.

Ugh, this house is too damn big for three people. There are too many closets, too many drawers, too many places to stash something you want to keep hidden. I give up when I hear my mother call out that she grabbed dinner from my favorite gourmet shop in town, knowing I've only scratched the surface in terms of my search.

It's nearly a month later when I hit pay dirt. Downstairs in my father's office one afternoon after school, I find a small envelope tucked inside a folder where copies of my social security card, baptismal record and birth certificate are kept. Such an obvious spot that I only gave it a casual leaf-through the last two times I was in here snooping around. I'd even checked behind each and every picture frame, diploma, and outstanding community service plaque on the damn walls, figuring there had to be some top-secret safe to hold this Pandora's box.

There's nothing written on the front. I open it without expectation, sure this is just another dead end, but then come across a picture that stops me in my tracks. It's not that clear. It must have been taken from a distance, or no, with a glass window separating the photographer from the subject—the glare gives it away. My eyes go to the background first, maybe because I can't take it in just yet. It's a hospital room, I think. White walls, stark lighting, no décor. There's a woman on the bed. My mother? No, she's got brown hair. Long hair. Her face is turned to the side and she's looking down at the baby she's holding.

I feel my stomach drop when it starts to settle over me. I sink into the leather desk chair, holding the picture up for closer inspection, but there's not much else to see. I'm desperate to get a clear look at this woman's face, to capture the details of her expression. I want to know if I look like her, but I can barely make out anything from this distant, blurry shot.

I go all forensic scientist on it, digging a magnifying glass from the drawer so I can study every millimeter. There has to be some detail I'm overlooking. A marking on her hospital gown, some sign in the background, a date written on the back. But no, there's nothing to indicate where, when, or why this photograph was taken.

I hear the door open, hear my parents laughing over something as my father takes the one beer he drinks after work from the fridge. I hear the bottle hiss air as he removes the cap, and the clink of the opener as he places it back on the marble countertop. I should just ask them right now, but I don't.

I don't know why I hurry to put everything back where it belongs and close the desk drawer. My parents aren't monsters. They're reasonable and understanding. They would tell me the truth. Wouldn't they?

I join them in the kitchen, ask my dad how his day was, ask my mom how she did in her ongoing quest for world pickleball domination. I joke, I laugh, I eat with them. I act as if everything is all right, that nothing has changed. I pretend.

By the time the weekend has rolled around, I'm at loose ends. I'm frustrated that I've chickened out, and therefore come up empty. My mother joins me on the couch as I'm doing a detailed study of the photo albums that chronicle my early years.

"You were such a beautiful baby," she says as she runs her hand over mine and then gives it a gentle squeeze.

"Did I cry when I was born?" My mother fixes her gaze out the window, but in a way that's wistful. She's not uncomfortable or avoiding the topic. "Of course you did...You screamed bloody murder!"

There's a lock of hair in my baby book. I question it, ask my mother whose hair it is. She cocks a brow when she looks at me smiling. "What do you mean? It's yours."

"It's so dark," I say absently as I rub the short strands between my fingers.

She smiles as she reaches a hand over to touch my ponytail. "You had a tuft of black hair. It was the oddest thing. I never saw a baby born with so much hair."

"Did I look like Dad when I was first born?"

I notice she turns away again before answering me. "The hair, I guess, but who can really tell?" She gets up from the couch and heads to the kitchen. "You can ask Parker if he wants to come for dinner tonight. I'm making salmon."

I shake my head. "Not tonight...I've got homework."

She pauses from taking items from the fridge and turns to me. "It's spring semester of senior year. Can't you ease up a little?" When I don't answer, she presses, "Don't you want to let loose and have some fun with your friends?"

Audrey isn't the total antithesis of motherhood that I'm making her out to be. If I was dabbling in drugs or blowing off school entirely, she'd intervene in a big way. I know that. But her subtle yet relentless *suggestions* grate on my nerves. She wants me to be who she was: the homecoming queen, the *it* girl, the subject of every boy's desire. Take that back. She'd be satisfied if I at least gave off the vibe that I was devoted to Parker the way he seems to be devoted to me.

He's been better this past month. Since that night at Tatiana's party and what passes for a fight between the two of us, he's been true to his word. He hasn't pressured me, and the subject of sex in general has been dropped. In fact, he hasn't laid a hand on me. Quick make-out sessions when we're hanging out at my house or his, or in the car before he drops me home—nothing more. And I've wondered on more than one occasion what's wrong with me, because I'm nothing but relieved.

Prom is in a few months. It's a milestone, but that's not the night where people tend to lose their virginity anymore. For the vast majority of girls I know, that ship has long sailed. I wouldn't want it to be that night anyway. There's too much lead up, drama and expectation. Maybe I should just get it over with now.

But shouldn't it be just a little bit special? Maybe something *is* wrong with me, because I haven't even given the logistics of the big event much thought. And it's not like I'm in a bubble or anything. No, I am faced with witnessing and hearing about everyone else's escapades on a regular basis.

There are only a few bona fide couples in my graduating class—make that my entire high school. Everyone else is just hooking up. Tatiana, for example, is worldly in every way. She spends nearly every school break in some part of Europe, coming back in September to dish about her summer romances. It was Alejandro last summer, Matteo the year before. She has a romantic yet casual attitude towards sex. And while she'll barely give any of the guys in our school the time of day, she's fearless when it comes to going after more mature conquests. I'm too much of a wimp to brave a fraternity party, but I swear, I think half of the Princeton campus would be shocked to know that Tatiana is still sweating out her AP classes in high school. And don't get me started on the obscene flirtation she's got going on with her nutritionist. When I asked if it bothered her that he was married, she scoffed before muttering something about Americans and sexual repression. Did I mention she was born and raised right here in New Jersey?

But one of the couples, they hold my attention. They're both juniors. Her name is Anne. I know her father passed away when she was a freshman, and James, he's a star pitcher on the baseball team. That's all I know for sure, but I daydream up details to fill in the blanks. I see them walk through the hallways holding hands, Anne looking up to him and laughing when he says something funny. Or sometimes I'll spot James waiting at her locker, and I can't look away until I see him smile wide once he catches sight of her. They hang out with a crowd, but there's a bond that is strong and unbreakable between just those two. I imagine she consoles him after a disappointing game, and that he fills a void by tossing a ball around with her younger brothers when they hang out at her house. He could be an abusive monster for all I know, but I can't imagine anything but love and perfection when they have my attention.

Parker holds my hand, he laughs with me and we goof off together, but it's different. I'm playing a role and I suspect he is too. One thing is for certain: I'm not Anne and he's not James.

"Hi."

"Um, hey, what's up?"

When I see the bottle of wine he's holding, I wonder what's going on. Did my mother invite him to dinner after I told her that tonight wasn't good? Would she do that? That would be a new low for Audrey.

"Your parents asked me over for dinner." Taking in my expression, he asks, "Is that all right?"

I force a smile, hoping it doesn't look forced. This isn't his fault. "It's perfect. Come in." I step aside when I realize I'm still blocking his entrance.

"Look who's here," I say to my parents as we make our way into the kitchen.

My dad looks up from his phone, his eyes curious. Nope, he wasn't in on this. "Hello, Parker. How are you?"

"I'm fine, Mr. Hamilton. How was your game Sunday morning? My father and I were just getting started when your foursome was finishing up."

"Can't complain. I won't be wearing the green jacket anytime soon, but I didn't embarrass myself out there. What about you?"

"I shot a personal best."

"Good for you."

I notice my father doesn't ask what Parker's personal best is, while I can tell by Parker's expression that he's damn near bursting at the seams to tell him. I don't think my dad really cares, and he doesn't ask questions just for the sake of bull-shitting.

I also note that he calls my father Mr. Hamilton, and more importantly, calls my mother Mrs. Hamilton when he's in my father's presence. After school, shooting the breeze in my kitchen with my mother while he waits for me, the two of them are on a first-name basis. She's Audrey.

Once we're seated, he tastes the salmon and compliments my mother, jokes about his own mother's failed attempts at cooking an edible meal, and makes a point of mentioning that one of my father's fund managers was quoted in the latest issue of *Forbes*. He's charming. Parents love him. I remind myself that every other girl in my school would kill to be his. And I kind of hate myself in that moment. I have it all. What right do I have to be unhappy when I've had everything pretty much handed to me my entire life?

I come back to the conversation when my father clears his throat. "Honey, Mom was just asking when you should be expecting your acceptance letters."

Parker answers for me. "Technically the schools have until April first, but generally you hear by early March. Well, unless it's an early decision application." He looks back to me. "Did you hear from Princeton yet?"

"No, did you?"

He uses his napkin and then sets it down on the table. "Not yet, but..." *But my father went there, my grandfather went there, my great-grandfather went there. All totaled, they've given a shit ton of money to that school. I'm as good as in and we both know it.* That's what he's thinking, but instead he says, "I'm hoping to see a big fat envelope in our mailbox very soon."

I think to myself that I won't be receiving an envelope, fat or skinny, because I didn't apply there. He knows I'm set on Penn so that I can board Shadow at the campus equestrian center, but he thinks I at least applied to his school of choice. There's a good chance I wouldn't get in—their acceptance rate is ridiculously low—but I'd never go there anyway. It's too close to home. Not like Penn is so far away, but a nearly two-hour drive as opposed to forty minutes gives me a bit of a buffer. It's close enough that I can scoot home for a long weekend if I want, and far away enough to ensure that my mother won't be driving down to take me to lunch too often.

I bet Anne and James are already planning their future, and the idea that they'll be together is a foregone conclusion. He'll have an idea of what schools will be looking to recruit him for baseball, and she will apply to all of them, just to cover their bases. I envision the two of them studying together at night in the library, Anne sitting front and center at all of his home games, and maybe even moving off campus together for their senior year just because they can't stand to be apart.

Then I look to my left and smile because Parker is smiling at me. He takes my hand underneath the table and gives it a gentle squeeze. And in the midst of that loving gesture, all I can think to myself is that I'm so glad we'll be graduating in a few months. He'll be going in one direction, me in another. It's the perfect time to cut ties.

No, I am certainly not Anne, and Parker is not my James.

Chapter Seven

LIAM

"You planning on being a waiter forever?"

I haven't been in the house for ten minutes, and fuckface is already starting in on me. Jeff Opperman, otherwise known as my mother's husband. A fine, upstanding pillar of our seedy community.

Seriously, he has a full-time union job, so that's how he sees himself. And if he was half as kind behind closed doors as he pretends to be to the outside world, then I'd respect him.

I admire every hard-working man who loves and protects his family. Take my Uncle Danny, for example. The way he treats my Aunt Maeve, his daughters, and everyone else in his orbit is something I aspire to. He's humble, keeps his head down, and even though his job does occasionally entail shoveling shit out of horse stalls for spoiled little brats, I see him as a giant among men.

"I don't know, Jeff. It's either that or a bounty hunter...I'm still deciding."

That would have earned me a slap in the face, or, if he was more than a couple of beers in, a punch in the ribs a few years ago, but Jeff hasn't stepped up to me since I turned seventeen. He knows I hit back now, and deep down, bullies are always chickenshit by nature. He used intimidation to keep me in line back then, but he's got nothing to hang over my head anymore. I no longer rely on him for food, clothing or shelter, and that pisses him off to no end.

"Smug little shit. You think you're so smart, don't you?"

I am smart, Jeff. After all, I'm not contaminated by your gene pool. That's what's running through my head as I stand there like a stone.

When stepdaddy dearest doesn't get a reaction out of me, he digs deeper. "I'd pay money to see you hustling around that country club, sucking up to all those rich pricks."

That one hurts. I'll think up a good comeback to that insult a couple of hours from now, but right now I'm cursing myself for being thin-skinned and unprepared. And now that he knows he's hit a nerve, he digs in.

"I asked for my veal chop rare, boy," he booms. Then he changes to a high-pitched, snooty tone. "I'd like the tuna salad. Can you ask the chef if the tuna is organic?"

Did you mean sustainably sourced, dumbass?

His tone changes abruptly when my mother comes in the door carrying grocery bags. "Just say the word, Liam, and I'll get your application in to my boss."

This surprises me, as Jeff doesn't normally make an effort to kiss up to my mother. He must be looking to get laid tonight.

"Thanks, Jeff." I lay it on thick when I add, "You're always looking out for me."

My mother notes the sarcasm in my tone and looks

nervously between me and her man. I love my mother, and the fact that Jeff keeps his fists off her is the one and only reason that I tolerate him. He's emotionally abusive towards her in more subtle ways, but in his eyes, he's justified. I think she believes it too, which is sad more than anything else.

I do love her, but time and time again she's disappointed me. She's stayed with Jeff in exchange for stability, which has cost her in terms of dignity and self-respect. I can't view her as a role model in any way, and I hope to God that my older sister wakes up someday and sees herself as someone who deserves better. But what stings the most is knowing that my mother has kept her mouth shut too many times when he's picked on me for no good reason, and that while I never once hesitated to stand up for her, she wasn't so quick to block his path when he went after me. That's a truth that's hard to acknowledge.

I act as if he isn't even in the room when I go to her and take the bags from her hands. "How are you, Mom?" I ask before kissing her cheek.

"I'm good, sweetie. I'm making lasagna for dinner. Can you stay?"

"Thanks, but I'm working the dinner shift tonight. Tips are good on Saturdays and," I turn to Jeff, "someone has to feed those rich pricks, am I right?"

"Okay," she takes in Jeff's red ears and his grimace, "but promise me you'll come for dinner soon."

"Will do." It's an empty promise and she knows it.

I feel like I can breathe again once Jeff grabs a beer from the fridge and leaves us alone in the kitchen.

"What's new with you?" she asks.

"Nothing much. I have to start up with Mike again soon, getting the boats ready for the season, so I'll be busy."

"Are you keeping the job at the club this summer?"

"If I don't get fired first. They're not too keen on my look."

She shoots me a wide-eyed look of mock horror. "They don't like gorgeous people?"

That earns her a chuckle. "They love gorgeous people, but ones with reasonably short hair and less ink."

"Their loss. Summer might be a bust there anyway."

"Yep. They'll all be heading to their summer spreads. I should ask Lorraine if she can get me a couple of shifts barbacking at Dunes."

"Lucky us," she deadpans. "We get to live by the seashore all year long."

The part of Neptune that my mom and Jeff live in—the town where I grew up—isn't seaside. We're not *far* from the beach, yet we are worlds away from high living on the Jersey Shore. The people from the club who *summer* here wouldn't set foot on a street like this one. Although they live only a few minutes away in posh towns like Avon and Spring Lake, it's completely different.

This part of the shore is where the help lives. The house cleaners, the restaurant waitstaff, the landscapers—my people. And even among us there's a hierarchy. Florists, hairdressers, yoga instructors and caterers are the top tier, while people like me, who clean boats and wash bar glasses, are on the bottom rung of the ladder. My mother and sister are right there beside me. They clean houses for a living. Lorraine, my sister, also juggles a second job waiting tables to support her kid and her lazy-ass boyfriend.

My mother turns back to me after she finishes putting the groceries away. "Was Jeff giving you a hard time before?"

"Just busting on me for being the slacker that I am."

"You've never been a slacker. But do you think maybe he

has," she pinches her thumb and forefinger together, "just a smidgen of a point?"

"Nope. He never makes any sense whatsoever."

Her eyes look tired. "C'mon. Can we just talk about the fact that you're a freaking genius and not living up to your potential?"

"I finished high school."

"With a GED," she counters.

"Makes no difference."

"You should be going to college."

"Is there some trust fund stashed away that I don't know about?"

"Haha...Very funny. But seriously, there must be scholarships or loans you can apply for."

"I'm not going into debt, and I think scholarships are out of the question."

"Because of the GED," she finishes for me. "That's my point."

"I don't need college."

"You do, unless you want to wind up living like this for the rest of your life."

I sit down at the table and open a bag of Jeff's favorite cookies. I should leave just one in the bag to piss him off later on tonight when he goes to stuff his face full of sugar, but I don't even like the taste of them. Only a moron would ruin perfectly good chocolate chip cookies by adding walnuts. And only an asshole like Jeff would like them.

My mother isn't saying anything that I haven't said to myself. I don't want to spend the rest of my life juggling part-time jobs and barely getting by. On the flip side, I don't want to live the way those snobs from the club live either. I just want a comfortable life. One where I can afford a house of my own, nothing too big, and have the luxury of owning a car that won't crap out on me at regular intervals.

Not finishing high school is something I look back on with regret, although I'm too stubborn to admit it to anyone else.

Jeff's worst qualities? When I'm being one hundred percent honest with myself, I can admit that a few have rubbed off on me. I am stubborn, I'm easily offended, and I believe most people act with their own self interests in mind. I suppose I see the world though an *us versus them* lens, although I'm working on becoming a more open-minded person. Most days I fail in this endeavor, but I'd wager Gandhi himself would have a hard time seeing the good in those uppity clowns.

Last weekend I was working the dinner shift after some father-son golf tournament. Dinner wasn't so bad, but the event went late. There was a whole lot of whiskey sipping, cigar smoking and back slapping going on, while the next generation was busy snorting lines in the bathroom.

Most of them sound like pompous idiots dead sober, so can you imagine the nonsense they were spewing after a few bumps? Do they realize how ridiculous they sound? One talking about how much he's making off his crypto investment, another talking shit about how he unloaded some Indian electronic vehicle stock right before it tanked, netting himself *a tidy sum.* Yep, he used those exact words: a tidy sum, and spoke of the transaction as if he was some prescient wunderkind, a regular Oracle of Omaha in the making.

They are liars, posers, foolish boys pretending to be men. They don't know what it means to carry the weight of real responsibility. They don't know what it's like to be afraid.

Chapter Eight

SARAH

I guess he did get the boot from the dining room. He's been working in the stable for the past week, which has Mr. Murphy acting all twitchy, and has me impersonating a dumbstruck weirdo on the verge of a nervous breakdown.

I've stayed away for the past two days following my one and only disastrous attempt to make friends with him. I smiled and said hello when I came upon him in Shadow's stall, and he dismissed me with a smirk, turning his back as he went about mucking while making no effort to avoid me. I backed away like a meek little mouse when some wet hay mixed with dried horse droppings landed on my boot.

What an ass.

Having had two days to stew over it, I practically stomp right in there today, ready to do battle. I'm oddly disappointed when Mr. Murphy greets me with affection instead of his arrogant, nasty nephew.

"Hey there, I thought you'd been abducted by aliens or something. Three days in a row? That's a record for you."

"I was here on Monday, I just...decided not to ride."

He eyes me with curiosity. "All right." He peers behind me, gauging the gray skies. "Are you heading out there now? Looks like we might get a shower."

I look to where his eyes are fixed and see that the overcast sky has turned several shades darker in just the past few minutes. *Crap.* The wind has also picked up. I check the weather app on my phone and reassure him, "Looks like a passing system. I'll just wait it out."

And while I'd normally pass the time talking to Shadow, I'm wary of my nemesis walking in on me in the middle of my horse whisperer routine. I pull today's calculus notes from my backpack instead and sit on the little bench in the corner of the stall. It's a ridiculous plan, as Shadow has his snout right up in my face a moment later. I can't help but nuzzle back, which would probably seem beyond gross to anyone except other like-minded horse people. And giving me a not so subtle hint, he nudges the notebook right off my lap, demanding my attention. I'm thinking Shadow must want a treat when I abandon my notes to go looking for an apple or some oats.

"Is this what you wanted...A big, juicy carrot?"

I'm putting the root end between my teeth as I enter the stall, and nearly lose my lunch when I see him crouched down gathering my notebook from the floor.

He chokes on his laughter when he catches sight of me, eyes wide with amusement. "Holy shit, Neidermeyer. I didn't know people actually did that in real life."

I remove the large phallic symbol from my mouth and clear my throat, trying my best to regain the upper hand. I sound ridiculously snotty to my own ears when I shoot back, "What are you even *talking* about?"

"Um, Neidermeyer?" When he sees that I don't get the reference, he clarifies, "*Animal House*?" I'm still shaking my head, completely baffled, while simultaneously trying my best to act like this entire episode is tiresome. "Never mind," he says with a shrug. He tosses the notebook on the bench and leaves the stall, calling over his shoulder, "Half of your answers are wrong, by the way."

"What?"

He does a poor job of concealing a smirk when he says, "If you're studying for a test, I'd say you've got your work cut out for you."

"And you know this, how?"

"Yeah, that's right, I shovel horse shit for a living so I couldn't possibly know my way around a basic math problem."

"No," I counter cautiously. Even though, seriously, I am kind of wondering how he thinks he's more knowledgeable than I am. His look, the careless attitude—the vibe he gives off doesn't exactly scream academic. "It's just that I'm pretty good at math, and this is anything but basic. It's advanced placement calculus and those answers look right to me."

"Sorry to burst your bubble, sweetheart, but they don't look right to me."

I lift the notebook and flip back to the page that was opened, a piece of dry straw serving as a convenient bookmark. He's making his way back towards the tack room when he hears me mutter, "You don't know what you're talking about."

He lets out a short laugh that comes off as mean-spirited. "No, I probably don't. Good luck on your test, Neidermeyer."

I wind up brushing Shadow for the next twenty minutes, waiting in vain for this drenching rainstorm to let up. It doesn't stop, and Liam doesn't even slow his steps when he passes me, making a run for his car as I walk across the parking lot getting soaked. I think he even stomped extra hard to splash me as he ran past.

And what do I do as soon as soon as I get home? Shower and get into dry, warm clothes? Study for tomorrow's calculus test? Nope. I cue up *Animal House* and then nearly die of embarrassment when I watch that scene he was referring to. And then I laugh, knowing I'm busted, because while Neidermeyer is no doubt an arrogant, sadistic monster, the man does love his horse, and I probably do sound a little bit like him when I'm loving on my Shadow.

I relive that episode in the barn over and over. I reimagine it. This time it's a friendly exchange. He smiles when he sees me feeding Shadow, and then looks at me with soft eyes when he points out the mistakes in my notebook. "It's a common error, Sarah. Everyone puts a 2 in the denominator, but it's B minus A. Look, I'll show you," he whispers as he leans over me and takes the pencil from my hand. It's like that cheesy scene from my mother's favorite movie, except Liam is filling in for Patrick Swayze, and we're proving Rolle's Theorem instead of engaging in foreplay that involves wet clay and a sculpting wheel.

Liam is a nice person in my fairytale version of events, while in reality he reminds me of a caged animal: tense, angry, positioned and ready to attack. Nothing about him is relaxed or easy. His clipped, condescending words are like claws, and his height gives him the advantage of looking down on others with cold, judgmental eyes. Even the way he moves is violent.

Coiled tight and aggravated, as if his body can't contain his rage.

Every word I've used to describe him is negative and ugly, yet I will freely admit that Liam is the most physically beautiful person I've ever laid eyes on. He stands tall and broad and capable, a smoking hot Gulliver next to my Lilliputian frame.

I'm not one to describe myself as the epitome of fierce female empowerment or anything, but I'm not a shrinking violet either. I think one of the reasons he makes me so mad is that I don't like the way I act around him. I feel small, literally and figuratively, and I feel unsure of what to say or how to act. When he was in the confined space of Shadow's stall with me the other day, I could hardly move, or catch my breath for that matter.

And, oh yeah, I only got an eighty-one on that test. The fact that he was right and I was wrong has me burning with indignation while simultaneously fangirling over his intellect.

The next week, I'm careful to sound casual and disinterested when I ask Mr. Murphy why he hasn't been around.

"Is your nephew going to be working in the stables now, or does he still work in the dining room?"

"He's helping me out here and still waiting tables. Doing a little bit of everything, I suppose. Grabbing as many extra shifts as he can."

I try and mask my relief when I respond ever so eloquently, "Oh."

Liam has been missing in action. I was actually weighing the pros and cons of thanking him for trying to help me with those calculus problems, but I'm thinking it's for the best that I haven't run into him these past few days. No doubt he would have fired back with some insult, and really, besides pointing out my errors he didn't help me one bit.

"He's a handful, that one. But Liam is a hard worker, and he's always looking to help his mother out by sending whatever extra he has her way."

I say, "That's kind of him," as I think to myself that it's also shockingly decent.

Yes, I have to remind my idiotic self, Liam has a mother, and he has a life outside of the two barely civil exchanges we've shared. Does that life include a big family with lots of sisters and brothers? Maybe underneath it all he's just a big old softie who lets his little brothers climb all over him and drives his sisters to soccer practice. Is there a girlfriend? I decide the girlfriend thing is fifty-fifty. I have no doubt that girls fawn over Liam, but he seems too hardened for sweet words.

"It's *too* kind, if you ask me. He should be saving for his own future." As Mr. Murphy takes the saddle from me and places it on the rack, he adds, "He should be saving for college."

"Um, yeah...He seems very smart." I laugh when I add, "He barked at me when he saw that my math notes were wrong."

He rolls his eyes. "Sounds like Liam. I'd say he's a know-it-all, but he does know a hell of a lot."

"Why did he leave school?"

"He was accused of plagiarizing, and instead of trying to prove his innocence he quit school in protest."

"Talk about cutting off your nose..."

His expression is somber as he nods. "Spite and pride are proving to be his downfall."

"It's kind of messed up that he was wrongly accused. It *was* a false accusation, right?"

"I'm sure it was. Liam is too high on himself to hand in someone else's work...Probably because he'd judge it as inferior."

I laugh at that one just as my father rounds the corner into the tack room. "I was hoping I'd catch you here."

"Hey, Dad. Did you take a half day or something?"

"Good to see you, Danny." He turns back to me after shaking hands. "Something like that. Mom isn't home and I'm starving. Want to grab a burger with me at The Grill?"

"Sounds good."

"Tell my nephew to mind his manners, Gypsy Girl."

"Liam is working today?" He nods and winks as I breathe deep to steady myself. Tell him to mind his manners? I do my best to shake off the nerves and excitement when I answer, "And risk getting my head bitten off? I think I'll pass."

Chapter Nine

LIAM

"Hi, I'm Liam and I'll be your server. Can I start you with anything to drink?"

The man at the table is smiling like he just heard a really funny joke, while his companion is literally hiding her face behind the menu. Whatever. I'm over it. These people are weird.

"I'll have a Bud, thanks." When the woman doesn't say anything, I ask, "Just water for you?"

If it's not vodka then it's pretty much always water, because why spend money, or God forbid calories, on a beverage if it's not going to get you wasted?

"Um, yeah, water is fine," odd little lady mutters while continuing to study the mid-afternoon pub menu that has all of four choices.

When I drop the man's drink, I'm pleasantly surprised when he tells me he doesn't want the glass. A normal, domestic beer *and* he doesn't need a chilled, frosted pilsner glass? Who is this guy?

"Have you had a chance to decide?"

The guy hands me his menu when he says, "Cheeseburger, medium...Thanks." He casts his eyes on the girl, and when she doesn't pipe up, he looks to stall. "Are you Danny Murphy's nephew?"

I answer that I am, and from the corner of my eye I can see the girl lowering the menu just enough so that she can glare at the man. *What the hell is* she *doing here?*

"Um, hi."

I nod at Tiny and then gesture to the menu. For some reason I'm surprised to see her here, even though she obviously belongs to this country club. I take another quick look between her and the guy, deciding this is a daddy taking his little princess out for a meal kind of thing.

She looks about as uncomfortable as I feel, standing here like a jackass while I wait for her to demonstrate that she is, in fact, capable of speech.

Yes, I know her name is Sarah. I overheard her boyfriend calling out to her as she was leaving the stables one afternoon. He came driving up in his shiny European luxury sedan, hopped out when she walked by his car without taking notice of him, and then called out, "Earth to Sarah," as he waved his arms. He laughed when she finally snapped out of it, and I was smiling too. The few times I've been around her she does seem to be lost in her own head.

Her name is Sarah but I call her Tiny. Maybe I call her something different because Sarah is *his* name for her, and I cannot stand that prick.

And she is tiny for sure. I had to do a double take the first time I saw her in the stable with Uncle Danny. I thought she was a kid, but then quickly determined that aside from her height, there was nothing childlike about her.

Tiny finally pipes up with, "I'll have the same," but when I turn to leave she adds in a small voice, "Can you please ask them to hold the bun?" And just like that, she ruins it. I decide that Tiny is just like the rest of them: diet-obsessed, vapid and ridiculous.

At least she didn't ask me to hand-wrap her burger in lettuce leaves. Yes, that's a regular occurrence around here. So much so that the chicken avocado club can be ordered as *standard*, meaning on toasted artisanal multigrain bread, or you can have it *deconstructed*. I want to hurl every time some prissy bitch orders it that way.

And just when I'm getting ready to write her off, her father says, "Honey, did you ever ask if they have unseeded buns? They might. Or maybe the cook can stick it in a wrap or something."

And now I'm feeling all tender and sappy. "You have an allergy?"

She nods like she's ashamed of the fact. "Sesame seeds."

"Let me ask the chef. I'll be right back."

On my way back to the kitchen I'm asking myself, *What the hell is wrong with you?* but that doesn't stop me from pleading her case to the new guy manning the grill. "She's allergic to seeds," I tell him when he rolls his eyes.

"All of these spoiled brats are allergic to *something*. Peanuts, wheat, strawberries...Who the fuck is allergic to strawberries?"

"Yeah, that's actually a thing." I don't know why I feel the need to school him. "So, you got a bun without seeds?"

"Maybe I was allergic when I was a kid. Yeah, to wheat,

peanuts *and* strawberries. Wanna know what my mom woulda packed in my lunchbox? Fucking peanut butter sandwich with strawberry jelly on wheat bread, that's what. These kids are all pussies today."

The guy is spouting off as if he commando-crawled across the beaches at Normandy, when I'd estimate he's pushing no more than thirty. He is a Gen-X, fellow pussy, but pointing that out would take even more time. "About that bun?"

"I can stick it in a pita. Good enough?"

"Perfect. Two burgers, cheese, medium. One in a pita. Thanks."

I avoid their table, and she doesn't wave me over to further inquire about the great bun dilemma. I only have two other tables, so I'm not exactly busy. Occasionally I look their way, and it's easy to see that she has a good relationship with her dad. I'm genuinely happy for her. She doesn't seem tough enough to live on my side of the tracks, and I'd never wish it on anyone, let alone her.

I know more about her than I let on. I know more than her name, that's for sure.

I know she talks to her horse like he's her best friend, just as I know that for some reason, I don't find it the least bit weird. I know she's smart. I snuck a look in her bag and every book was for an advanced class. Biomechanics, calculus, foreign policy— she's not looking to breeze through her senior year. As I grab their order from the kitchen, I remind myself that I know she has allergies, and as I place their plates on the table, I remind myself of what she doesn't know about her life that I do.

I know she's dating an absolute douchebag, and I know beyond a shadow of a doubt that he's boning someone else on the side.

"Oh, thanks!"

She seems delighted when I place the burger down in front of her, so I give her a gruff, "No big deal," so she doesn't go thinking I'm a nice person, or that I care about her in the least. Because I don't care about her.

Not one bit.

Chapter Ten

SARAH

Last Saturday my parents threw a lavish surprise eighteenth birthday party for me at the club.

I'm not big on surprises.

And it was *quite* the surprise, being that my birthday is in August. Yep, three full months away.

My mother gave me a glass of champagne the second we walked into the room packed with family, my parents' closest friends, and every member of my graduating class. Parker told me later on that I looked horrified when everyone screamed *Surprise!* so I guess I did need those two, three, four glasses of bubbly?

I had fun after the shock wore off, I think. I was definitely tipsy, but still with it enough to know that I was laughing loudly, hamming it up for the photographer with my friends, and dancing to every single song. In short, I was not acting like myself.

I do remember feeling irrationally alarmed when I looked

across the room and saw a big, brooding member of the wait-staff with his eyes fixed on me right at the very moment when Parker picked me up and squeezed me tight.

Looking into my teacup the next morning, I'm wondering if the fragile thread we've been weaving between the two of us still exists.

Liam and I aren't friends. No, I definitely wouldn't go that far. But since that day he waited on me and my dad at the club, he's lightened up. He's now in the habit of cracking a smile when I walk into the stable, and—wait for it—we actually say hello to one another. Once in a blue moon we even make polite conversation. There's no deep dive, we're not braiding each other's hair or anything, but there is—or was—something changing for the better.

Only one way to find out, I decide, and after a greasy bacon and egg breakfast, I head over to the stable in sweats and a hoodie. I don't have the energy to put on my riding clothes, and I have no intention riding today anyway.

But he's not there. He's not there when I pop in after school on Monday, Tuesday or Wednesday either. It takes an iron will to keep myself from asking Mr. Murphy where Liam has been every single day I go without a sighting. I even arrange to meet my parents at the club for a casual dinner on Thursday night, but strike out there as well.

By Friday I'm depleted of any remaining will power or pride. I have my back to Mr. Murphy, trying to sound as casual as possible when I say, "Haven't seen Liam around lately...Is he back to just working in the dining room?"

My body stiffens and my hand stalls mid-brushstroke when he responds, "Aw, you've been looking for me?"

Deep calming breath. "I just haven't seen you around. I was wondering..."

"What exactly were you wondering?"

I can't tell if he's teasing me or not. Liam is never playful from what I've witnessed, and when I turn to face him, the cold look he's shooting my way confirms that this is not a friendly line of questioning.

"I wasn't wondering anything. Forget it."

"Consider yourself forgotten."

When I start laughing, and I mean belly-laughing, he's taken off guard. "Oh-kay. Did you forget to take your meds this morning, Sarah?"

I nod and slap my own forehead. "Yeah, forgot my happy pills today, but you obviously didn't." I laugh, adding, "You're the same old barrel of monkeys you always are."

"Barrel of monkeys?"

"Barrel of monkeys, barrel of laughs...You know, easygoing and fun. That's you."

"Oh, that's me?" He moves into the stall and stands within a foot of me, forcing me to take a small step back. "Maybe it's this place and the people. Did you ever consider that maybe it's impossible to be happy when I'm surrounded by people like you?" I can't do anything but swallow down my discomfort and wait because he's clearly not finished. "I can't act as well as you do. I can't dance around like an idiot and pretend. But I have to hand it to you, you've got skills. Did you have to ice your cheeks from faking that smile so hard last weekend? Looked like a workout."

"You're an asshole." I can feel my cheeks heat when he cracks a smile. "Is it so hard to believe that I *was* happy? Maybe *you* like to stomp around and brood all day, and maybe you don't have any friends or anything to be happy about, but I do."

He still hasn't moved, and he doesn't shift his eyes away from mine. "Whatever you say, Princess."

"Call the rich girl a princess. That's original." I want to slap him as much as I want him to like me, which makes me pathetic.

And just when he's about to lob a comeback, his uncle comes into view. Mr. Murphy glances back and forth between us once, looking concerned. "Did you workout Miss Potter's horse yet?"

With a jaw fixed like stone, he answers back, "I'm on it," and heads to the stall across from mine.

And just to pile more onto this bitter and awkward morning, who comes strolling into what was once my private sanctuary but Parker and Logan. "Are you ready to go?"

Liam slows his steps as he leads the horse back towards the room where the saddles are stored. He's listening, which makes me stiff with discomfort when I ask, "Ready to go where?"

Logan rolls his eyes and Parker looks mildly pissed. He probably asked me yesterday and I nodded without really knowing or caring what I was agreeing to. I'm flighty, everyone knows this. "To my house? You said you'd help set up for tonight."

I want to ask what's happening tonight, but I know I'll come off like a total nutjob. "I know. I just didn't think we needed to start this early."

"The caretaker opened the house this morning but we need to get ice, booze...Lots to do."

Oh, a party at his shore house. It's all coming back to me. "Just give me five. I'll meet you in the car."

Parker looks at his phone as if he's actually prepared to time me, but then takes notice as Logan approaches Liam. "Hey, I know you. You're friends with Mike, aren't you?" When Liam doesn't answer right away, Logan asks, "You worked on my boat last season, am I right?"

Liam shrugs and cocks his head to the side. "Maybe."

"No, it was definitely you. Remember, we hung out at the beach that night after you and Mike finished up?"

"Yeah," Liam nods, slow and deliberate, "I remember now. Sailboat, right?"

Logan smiles more genuinely than I've ever seen him smile before. Even when I watch him interact with his closest friends or with family, Logan's smile has a snake-like quality. "I saw Mike last week. He came over to hang out." Liam looks like he's trying to smile back but just can't fake any enthusiasm whatsoever. And Logan is eager, damn near fawning when he says, "You and Mike should come tonight." When Liam doesn't answer right away, Logan adds, "Penny will definitely be there."

The mention of my bestie's name piques his interest. Wait, is Liam...smiling? "Maybe we'll stop by. Text Mike the address."

What in the ever-loving world is happening right now? But now Penny's voice is in my head. She's yelling over the music at a party, telling me about the hot townie she hooked up with last summer. What did she say about him? That he looked like the guy who played the mean tribute in *The Hunger Games*? I'm frustrated when I can't remember anything else she was babbling about, because now I want to dissect and analyze every last detail.

Parker adds, "Definitely come by. It's gonna be lit."

I mentally cringe, listening as Parker changes his language like a chameleon to suit his audience. *It's gonna be lit*? Last Sunday night when he came over for dinner uninvited *again*, he deemed Audrey's mediocre attempt at chicken piccata *outstanding*.

Logan is typing into his phone and then nods without looking up. "Done." He adds, "See you later," before turning back to Parker. "C'mon, we gotta jet."

"Two minutes," Parker warns me before following Logan outside.

I'm stuck in my thoughts, stroking Shadow. "You'd better jet, Princess," Liam says with a smirk. "Your *friends* are waiting for you."

"You secretly think you're better than everyone, don't you?"

He juts his chin in the direction of the exit. "Than those two? C'mon, Princess, that's not even fair. They've set the bar pretty low, wouldn't you say? Like, in the gutter?"

I take my time, trying to act cool and unaffected as I scramble for something to say that will cut him. "And you hate," I add air quotes, "people like us. Isn't that what you just said?"

"What can I say? Free booze, free weed, and bored girls who suck dick for fun. How can I pass that up? *And* it's gonna be lit, isn't that what the man said?"

"You're disgusting."

He shrugs like my words couldn't possibly touch him, let alone hurt him. "And you're fake."

I've got no comeback for that one.

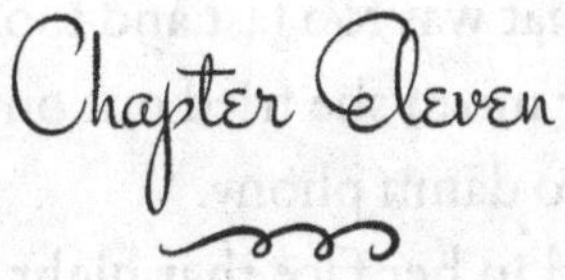

Chapter Eleven

LIAM

Those people are not her friends.

I'm furious after she leaves, after she walks out the door and gets into *his* car. I want to scream at her, *Hey moron, he's fucking your best friend*.

That *one* night we hung out at the beach together? God, that guy Logan is a walking, talking asshole. We've hung out at least half a dozen times, but that's his way of trying to gain the upper hand. *Hmm, you look familiar, but I don't really pay a whole lot of attention to people like you.*

I didn't like it when Mike invited them to our beach last summer. It was an intrusion. Her boyfriend Parker was always along for the ride too, but I'm good at reading people, so I'd bet money he legitimately didn't recognize me just now. It's almost easier to respect him for being dismissive because at least he's not pretending. And he was preoccupied last summer, just like he was preoccupied the night of Sarah's party last week.

Tipsy little Sarah was inside knocking back another glass of obscenely expensive champagne while her boyfriend had his tongue down that girl Penny's throat and his hand up her dress. I saw them when I was hauling trash to the dumpster out back. He had his hand jammed between her legs, his arm thrusting in a way that was too fast and too rough. And she was doing that porn star moan she tried out on me last summer. So eager to please and so damn phony.

I almost laughed in her face that night on the beach, that's how absurd she sounded, but at the same time I felt sorry for her. When she tumbled over me, stood up and wobbled as she went to remove the few remaining scraps she wore, I stopped her. She didn't seem to care that we were only a hundred yards away from the others. She didn't care that we were messing around in sand that was still a little damp and sticky from the last high tide. She didn't even ask if I had a condom. And I didn't care when she got mad, or when she laughed at me as she pulled her clothes back on. I couldn't go through with it. I didn't want to. Right before she stormed off, she turned back, looking to emasculate me when she ran a hand over the front of my jeans to point out that my dick had gone soft. I could have struck back, said something to make her believe she wasn't enough to rouse interest in any man, but I passed. Even acting like a complete and total bitch, there was something in her eyes that told me I'd be kicking a three-legged stray.

Passing them on my way back into the kitchen last weekend, listening in as she whispered, *Yeah, right there*, and then moaning like she was in some dream-like ecstasy, I wanted to call out to her, *Pipe the fuck down, Penny...There's no way in hell that feels good.*

And by then the party was almost over, thank God. The kids were drunk while their parents looked on smiling and laughing. Wistful for the booze-soaked, depraved nights of their own youth, I guess.

I'm surprised I didn't pull a muscle from all the times I shook my head that night. First off, who in their right mind wastes Cristal on a bunch of teenagers? Would any of them even know the difference between Cristal and the cheap shit? I mean, that stuff costs like two hundred a bottle.

It was everything—the entire night was a tribute to waste and excess. I don't claim to know much about flowers, but those vases were packed with branches and blooms that looked exotic. I bet each one of those table centerpieces cost double my shift pay, and there were a *lot* of tables. But the worst was seeing that seafood tower laden with plump hunks of fresh, pristine lobster, knowing it would go largely untouched. The amount of good food dumped in the trash that night was obscene.

I needed three days to cool off before walking back into the barn. My uncle needed the help, but I knew I'd be grinding my molars to dust to keep from lashing out at her.

By the time I do see her again I'm damn near itching to tell her what she's too blind to see, but I don't. If she's that clueless then shame on her, she deserves this life. She'll be like the rest of those ladies, the ones who start nursing cocktails during lunch with their friends so they can be comfortably numb by the time their disinterested husbands come back from the city late at night with the smell of booze on their breath and other women on their skin.

Happy loving couples.

I won't be at their party tonight. I'd rather eat glass. And I feel this evil sort of satisfaction as I lead the horse into the paddock just as their car pulls away. If I know Sarah, and I'm starting to believe that I do, she'll be watching that door open and close, looking for me all night long.

Chapter Twelve

SARAH

I feel physically ill as we make the drive from the club to Parker's shore house.

Liam makes me feel awful, as if my very being is capable of inspiring disgust and loathing in another person. Abhorrent, that's the college board exam word I'm looking for. In his eyes I am abhorrent.

I stew in the backseat of the car wondering why. I've never had an enemy before. Truly, I am not aware of any person in my past or present who has actively disliked me. I'm not saying that people cheer when I walk into a room or anything, but I don't think I've ever felt genuine hatred directed my way.

Hatred is what I seem to inspire in Liam, though.

I want him out of my head, so it's almost a comfort to dive into party planning mode. Parker smiles my way as I'm rolling up an area rug, appreciating when I insist that it's too nice to leave out. The three of us work for two or three hours getting everything ready, and once the keg is icing, the jello shots are chilling in the fridge and the Hastings family's valuables are securely locked away, we relax on the deck. It's still chilly out, but summer is coming and the sun feels good on my face.

I even take the beer Logan hands me, and for once I don't hate the taste of it. It's cold and refreshing, and I'm probably dehydrated after a morning of riding followed by party chores, so the bitter taste doesn't bother me like it usually does. One shot—just to make sure I didn't screw up the recipe—and then the boys drop me off with a warning to be ready in an hour.

People start to roll in at around seven, and by ten o'clock the house is packed. Tatiana hasn't showed up yet, but no one expects her until close to midnight. She insists on making an entrance unless the party is at her house. But Clara and Penny are by my side, and while there's a voice in my head reminding me of how crappy I felt the morning after overdoing it at my birthday party, a louder voice is overruling sensible Sarah.

Screw it, I'm having fun.

And I am having fun. School is winding down, and we're all a little sappy and nostalgic as we acknowledge this bridge we're about to cross over. In a few months, the people I've spent most of my life with, countless hours in and outside of school, will be scattered across different time zones. The realization brings on a closeness that I've never really felt before.

I'll miss Penny, Clara and Tatiana. Although I don't open myself up and expose my innermost thoughts, I do feel close to them and I know I'll miss them. Penny won't be there to make me laugh, or to give me a gentle nudge so that no one teases or rolls their eyes on those frequent occasions when I space out. Clara won't be there to talk me through it when I'm stressed out over grades, tests, or other things that I'm beginning to see as unnecessary worries. And Tatiana won't be there to teach me what I don't know. I shake my head at the outrageous things she does, but from watching her I've been acquiring the kind of knowledge you can't get from books.

The three of us do a shot to our impending graduation, another once Tatiana shows up to toast her acceptance into some prestigious art program in Paris, and another as we pledge to visit each other at our respective colleges regularly.

Borderline euphoric in my buzzed state, I'm still a realist at heart, so I know the pledges and promises are a lie. I don't believe these girls will disappear entirely from my life, but we'll drift apart. Tatiana will be in Europe, and knowing her she may never come back. Clara is heading off to California and Penny will be in Texas. I'll be at Penn and Parker will be at Princeton. Looking around the room at my drunken peers, I decide that I don't really care where the rest of them are heading. Pretending otherwise would be fake on my part, and I've already been accused of harboring that loathsome trait once today.

The damn door has opened and closed like a hundred times so far, and yes, I want to slap my own face for checking to see who's coming and going. I tell myself again that I don't care if he's here or not, but like I said, I'm not so far gone that I don't see the words for what they are: a lie.

"Oh!"

"Get out," Parker barks as he pulls the blanket up to cover me.

"Sorry," Penny whispers as she backs out of the room. When I hear the door close, I push my hair out of my face and attempt to open my eyes. I'm so tired and my mouth is so, so dry.

"How are you doing, angel?" Parker asks as he rolls onto his side to look down at me.

I try to wet my tongue but it feels two sizes too big for my mouth. I manage to answer, "Good, but I need some water."

"On it."

He gets up and walks to the bathroom. He's naked, which compels me to peek underneath the covers to discover that I'm in the same state.

I made a decision. Sometime late last night when Parker told me that he loved me, I decided to end this ridiculous stalemate. I was still ambivalent when it came to Parker, but holding out any longer seemed pointless. I'd have sex eventually, so why not now? Why not tonight?

He comes back into the room and hands me a glass with a pill. "This will make your head feel better."

As he waits for me to swallow it down, I lower my eyes to look at him. He doesn't make an effort to cover himself and I find myself staring. I must still be a little bit drunk because I'm thinking that he's big, and it looks like a long, lazy thing dangling between his legs. I smile, thinking to myself that penises are weird, ugly things. They're nothing like the muscles on a man's body, or the lips that can kiss you senseless or frame a dazzling smile.

It's obvious that he's trimmed the hedges. I'm not really surprised, he's been shaving off his chest hair for as long as I've known him, but Parker's smooth and hairless manscape makes me self-conscious for a fleeting moment. The only reason the idea of waxing isn't entirely foreign to me is because my mother all but insisted upon it. But I don't keep up with any kind of beauty routine, so I can't help but wonder if he's judging me and finding me lacking. One look back up at his face tells me my worries are unfounded.

"That was pretty great last night."

I nod my head and do my best to match his smile.

Was it great? I have no idea. I have nothing to base my opinion on. I just know that I brushed any concerns I had aside last night, told myself it was time and that it was no big deal.

Virginity is such a ridiculous, outdated concept, but despite what people say, there's no doubt in my mind that within the confines of high school, it's still an adjective assigned to us by others or one we assign to ourselves. People still put way too much value on that rite of passage.

People talk about Clara likes she's a little girl, like she's some cute little mascot. The boys don't bother with her in that way, and they don't talk to her using the crude terms they let fly in front of girls like Penny.

With Tatiana it's the opposite. They treat her as a friend, but behind her back the boys shake their heads and say they wouldn't lower themselves to be with her because she has *too* much experience. Personally, I think they're afraid of her experience, afraid she knows more than they do and therefore they couldn't possibly measure up. I overheard Parker saying that he had no desire to go where *so many had gone before*, but in truth, he'd never get the chance because Tatiana would never give any of those boys the time of day.

And then there's Penny. They talk about her like she's a joke. I overheard Logan one afternoon when I went down to meet Parker at the marina. I knew Penny had been with Logan but didn't realize it was a regular thing. He laughed about her, called her sloppy and made some crack about her *weak head skills*, adding that he was surprised, given the fact that she's sucked off half the guys in your grade. I laid into Parker once Logan and the rest of them left, but Parker just shrugged and put his hands up as if to say it was all on her.

Maybe it's no easier on the boys. They act like they know so much, but Tatiana has me convinced that most of them got their limited education from watching porn online. She swears most of them are virgins but are too ashamed to admit it.

I'm suddenly curious and ask Parker, "Was that your first time, too?"

He looks genuinely sad as he averts his gaze and shakes his head. "No, but I wish that it was."

"Who was your first?" When he hesitates, I reassure him, "I'm not mad or anything, just curious. I kind of figured you already…"

"Some girl at sailing camp. It was way before we started up." He lifts the covers and gets back into bed, turning me so that my back is to his front before he wraps an arm around me. "And it was fast and rushed and lame compared to last night. I really do love you, Sarah."

And the rite of passage I dismissed as outdated and laughable? I guess it's more important than I was willing to admit, because his admission brings on a rush of emotion that feels like loss.

"Hey," he whispers into my hair as he pulls me in closer, "are you crying?"

"No," I say in a choked voice as I try to rein my emotions in.

"You are," he says as he rolls me onto my back. "I hope you're not regretting last night."

"I'm not," I try to reassure him, but it's hard to speak past the lump in my throat. "I just…"

I just what? Don't think I was ready? Don't know why I'm such a freak?

"Something has been on your mind. You've been acting weirder than usual for the past couple of weeks."

He gets out of bed and reaches down to grab his clothes from the floor. He's punishing me now, in the subtle way that's his custom. *Weirder than usual.* The dig isn't lost on me. And even though I know I'm being insulted, he's playing on my worst fears: to be viewed as different, peculiar, and therefore unlovable. I'm a smart girl but I can't help it, I fall for it every time.

"I know, Parker. You're right."

My admission stops him in his tracks. And once Parker sees the tears making a hot path down my cheeks, he drops the clothes and crawls back in beside me. "What's going on?"

I proceed to lay out the last six weeks' worth of sadness and frustration for him, hiccuping through this ugly cry that goes on and on. I tell him about the blunt force trauma I endured in that science class, my pathetic detective work, and my inability to confront my parents. It's a full ten or fifteen minutes before I pause, and once I catch my breath, I have to admit that I feel lighter in some way, better.

He grabs an undershirt from a drawer in his nightstand and proceeds to wipe my face. "That's a lot to take in. I wish you would have told me."

"Every time I've tried to talk about it, I just can't get the words out."

"But now I know, so I can help you through it."

"Thanks." I truly am thankful to Parker, thankful for the genuine concern in his eyes.

"I mean it. Talk to me. I'm a good listener."

"I think I'm talked out for the moment. Just getting that off my chest feels so much better, really."

He shifts me down on the bed so we're no longer sitting up, and grazes one hand over my breasts and then down. I can feel him pressing into my side, and when his tongue enters my mouth and his hips begin to rock against me, I get the memo that he's looking for round two. And I'm on board for the wordless, anonymous *help* he wants to give me. I'm looking to forget.

"Let me," he whispers as his mouth leaves mine and makes a slow path southbound.

I am wrung out and defenseless, so that's what I do. I let him.

A few hours later we're sitting in his car, parked in my driveway. It's like he doesn't want to let me go inside, and I'm not eager to break the spell either.

Parker was slow and deliberate, smiling every time he made me blush this morning, pausing to ask me at every turn if I was all right and if I liked what he was doing to me. "Does this feel good?" But I was too ashamed to answer. I don't have that vocabulary or that attitude in my arsenal. Parker got off on that, too. "My sweet Sarah," he called me more than once.

I seriously didn't know if it felt good. I've come by myself, many times, and decided at some point when he had his fingers lodged inside me in what seemed like a never-ending quest to find that elusive spot, that I liked it better when I was alone. Alone in my own bed, alone with my fantasies, and free from being watched. His eyes on me and his expectations were too much. I had to pretend, to make sounds and move my body the way he wanted me to, just so he'd stop. And once he believed I was satisfied, he ripped open another condom and then entered me in a rush. Pump, pump, pump, pump *and*...victory. Sweat dripped off his brow and onto me before he collapsed beside me.

Parker lifts my hand, turns it over and lays a gentle kiss on the inside of my wrist. It seems to come out of nowhere when he asks, "Why would you even consider confronting your parents?"

It takes me a moment to comprehend that he's back to this morning's conversation. "Why? I just...I have to know."

"Do you? I mean, it seems to me like you already know everything there is to know. You were given up for adoption by the woman in that picture. You were adopted by your parents, two wonderful people. And here you are, eighteen years later, living a great life." He turns to me smiling. "Adoption wise, you kind of hit the lottery, wouldn't you say?"

And just like that, Parker kills the warm and fuzzy vibe. Whereas I was starting to feel understood—*seen* by Parker for the first time ever—I'm back to questioning what it is that drew him to me in the first place and what keeps us together now.

I slip my hand out of his grip. "What is that supposed to mean?"

He shakes his head sporting a look that's gentle, as if he's breaking something down for a child. "It's your life, so you're having a hard time being objective. I'm trying to be objective for you. What kind of person would give their newborn away?" Just hearing the word newborn wounds me but he doesn't notice. He keeps going, the question obviously rhetorical. "A single woman, a poor woman, a woman without family to step in and help her out. And that's best-case scenario. I'll bet most of them are in *really* bad situations." He's almost flip when he adds, "There's a good chance that girl didn't even know who the father was. There could have been drugs involved, abuse, mental illness...You name it."

I can't speak past the lump in my throat. Parker has just intimated that my birth mother could be crazy, an addict, without morals, or all of the above. And I feel incensed on behalf of the woman, who probably *is* awful because let's face it, she did hand me over to strangers.

Parker takes my silence as a cue that he's getting somewhere, so he piles on more. "The important thing to focus on is that you were plucked out of that life. You live," he gestures to my front door, "on an estate. Your father runs one of the most successful investment funds in the country. Your mother and father can and *would* provide you anything under the sun. You, Sarah Hamilton, are set for life. I'm just asking why you'd rock the boat?"

It takes me a moment to sort it all out before asking, "If it was you, wouldn't you want to know where you came from?"

"No," he answers decisively. "I'd be content and I'd be grateful."

I'm weary getting out of his car, and thankful my parents aren't around when I come inside. I stayed out all night without calling, but they wouldn't be worried because I was with Parker.

The water runs hotter than I normally like it in the shower, and I stand under the spray until my skin is red. I want to wash every speck of him off me. Every sloppy kiss, every touch, every tactless word.

"I love it, don't you?"

"The color is great. I never would have thought this would look good on me."

My dress just got dropped off from the tailor. My stuff always needs to be altered to accommodate my chest and my hips. Tatiana, Clara, Penny, and even my own mother—everything is made to fit their bodies effortlessly. Slip in, pull up the zipper and you're done. Not me.

"Just two more days. Did you decide how you want to wear your hair?"

"Down?"

My mother comes to stand behind me so we're both looking in the mirror. She pulls my hair up and then lays it back down. "Either way would look great with this neckline." She smooths her hands down my sides and rests them at my waist. "So, are you excited?"

If I was being honest, I'd answer, "Mheh," but that would disappoint her. "I mean, it's not a formal or anything, but I'm sure we'll have a good time."

We don't do prom at my school. That's for less sophisticated folks. They actually put an end to prom a decade ago. There was an incident involving a couple of boys from other schools, boys who were invited as dates. From what I've heard there was a massive brawl—over who or what I don't know—and it was decided that moving forward there would be no outsiders allowed. The administration sells it as a semi-formal group activity. It's not even called a dance. I don't think anyone would even bother with it if not for our parents insisting. It's just another night hanging out with your friends, except dressed up and unable to consume booze. In short, it pales in comparison to the house parties my friends host any given day of the week.

But my mother took me dress shopping, she's planned a cocktail hour at our house for my friends and some of the parents, and she's arranged for a driver to take us there and then deposit me and my friends wherever the after-hours scene takes us.

So I'm stuck, but not for long.

I keep telling myself that I just have to get through this week.

Then I'm going to end this.

Chapter Thirteen

LIAM

"I'll wait for you guys out here."

"C'mon, you won't come inside?"

I'm settled in the back seat of Nicky's car, pretending to read text messages on my phone. "Nope."

Nicky looks over to Mike, gesturing to his brother who's crammed into the back seat next to me. "Me and Derek can do this."

Mike shakes his head. "No, it'll be better if I go in with you." He looks over his shoulder to me, adding, "I wouldn't mind hanging out for a little while, though."

"So hang out. We can leave you here with your buddies."

"Don't be a dick, Liam."

"Me? They called you to be their errand boy. And they just assume you can score drugs. Don't you feel even the slightest bit insulted? You don't even do drugs, you moron."

Mike nods in Nicky's direction. "I see it as helping out my friend's business."

"That's some bullshit. They call and you come running."

Nicky's brother, taking a break from cleaning his finger-nails with his teeth, chuckles and adds, "You're Logan's bitch."

"Fuck off," Mike says as he gets out of the car. Nicky follows. His brother looks to me, shrugs and then follows after them.

I watch them walk up the front stairs. Stairs that lead to a tall set of front doors. That's how you know it's a nice house. Regular houses have one front door, plain and simple. But just about all of the shore houses in this part of Jersey have double doors. There are no chips in the paint, the landscaping has been professionally designed, and the furniture on the front porch probably costs more than my car.

I can't even believe I came along for the ride. Sometimes I want to shake Mike. He has no pride whatsoever. That asshole Logan called Mike an hour ago, and as soon as they got off the phone Mike was tapping out texts, trying to score some coke for his buddies. He doesn't see it the way I do. He thinks they invited him to come to their party. I think they told him he could come, so long as he doesn't come empty handed.

At least Mike didn't lay out the money for it with the expectation that Logan would pay him back. Rich people never expect to pay. Nicky likes to know who his customers are, and he'll make damn sure he gets paid. I don't especially like the guy, but to use his brother's words, at least he's no one's bitch.

When too much time has gone by, I lean my head back against the seat, growing angrier with every passing minute. The door opens, but it's a petite little thing in a short blue dress who emerges, not the three idiots I'm waiting on. She takes the stairs carefully, one at a time, holding onto the railing with both hands. Must be wasted. I keep watching, wondering when—not if—she's going to teeter on those high heels and face-plant onto the lawn.

I almost want to break into a round of applause when she makes it to the landing without incident, but then lower my head in an effort to hide once her face comes into view. She passes our car, teeters down the driveway looking around, and then comes back to sit on the bottom step as she taps into her phone. I sneak a look at her face, but her expression is blank.

The guys finally come out, but my hopes to get out of here unnoticed are shot to hell when Nicky stops to chat her up. I reach over the seat and give the horn a quick tap to let him know I want out of here, but they're ignoring me while paying attention to the hot girl in the tiny dress. Go figure.

"Your ride didn't show?"

"It says a car is twenty minutes away."

"It's not high season yet. Not too many cars around. Sometimes they take the fare even though they're way over on the mainland." She doesn't answer the first time Nicky asks, "You want a ride?"

The second time he asks, she shakes her head and says in a quiet voice, "Thank you, but I don't know you."

The girl said no, he should leave it at that. Getting into a car with strangers would be a dumb-ass thing to do. But no, Mike decides to chime in. "You know me," he says. "I'm friends with Logan and with your boyfriend, Parker. I know Penny, too." He crouches down so he's at eye level with her. "I'm Mike. I'm sure they've mentioned my name."

He sounds ridiculous, and when I see how uncomfortable she looks, I lose what little patience I had. Leaning my head out Nicky's open window, I snap, "We're not going to abduct you, Sarah. Get in. We'll give you a ride."

Yeah, I guess I'm as bad as Mike.

She looks relieved for a split second when she recognizes me but then drops her head into her hands just as quickly. I'm not begging her to get into the car. She can go back inside for all I care.

"Sarah?" Now Parker is coming down the stairs and shooing the guys away.

"Get the hell away from me."

Whoa, Tiny is mad. Take that back—her angry words are delivered without any force. She looks tired more than anything else.

He stands over her, not moving. Barefoot and dressed in jeans and a white linen shirt that's got half of the buttons undone, I can make out his glassy eyes from twenty feet away. Parker's right hand shoots up as he extends his middle finger. I follow to where he's directing the gesture to see Penny at the top of the stairs. Her hair is a mess, she's got mascara smeared across one cheek, and the top of her dress looks like she tried to pull it back on in a hurry.

She calls out in a voice that's barely audible, "Sarah?"

Sarah's jaw is clenched tight when she shakes her head. A moment later she says, "Go back inside, Parker."

When he doesn't move, she nearly rips the strappy heels from her feet, gets up, pushing past her man in the process, and walks over to the car. She opens my door and says, "Move over," without making eye contact.

I do as I'm told, and when I look up I see Parker flicking a cigarette butt into the shrubs before making his way back up the steps. Didn't put up any sort of a fight, which doesn't surprise me one bit.

I steal a quick look over to see her mouth fixed in a firm line, eyes straight ahead.

"You okay?"

"Fine," she answers.

Yeah, our last encounter ended on a sour note.

When Nicky's brother opens the opposite door and gets into the back with us, Sarah has no choice but to perch on my lap. The car is a little piece of crap, and there's barely enough room for one full-grown person in this back seat, let alone three.

She scoots up as far out of my lap as she can possibly get, but it's no use. I shift back trying to create a few inches of space between her ass and my body, but every time Nicky hits a pothole, she slides right back into me.

Nicky seems to be hitting the brakes hard at the stop signs and red lights, and taking off fast when the lights turns green. Sarah's body is stiff and her cheeks are turning red, either from embarrassment or from the effort it's taking to hold herself completely still. I try to catch Nicky's eyes in the rearview mirror, but all I catch is the smirk he's sporting. He's finding this funny.

"Where am I dropping you, sweetheart?" Before she can answer, he says, "No wait, let me guess...Your shore house, right? Which isn't to be confused with your regular house, your ski house or your fancy digs in the city."

Mike says, "Give it a rest, Nicky. You offered her a ride so let's just bring her home." He's been uncharacteristically quiet in the front seat, which tells me he's still pissed that I insisted on leaving the party.

"I didn't offer shit. You and Prince Charming back there offered her the ride." He pulls a U-turn. "I need to meet a guy on Pacific. We'll swing by there on the way. It'll just take a second."

Mike turns his head, gauging to see if Nicky's fucking around or not. We all know what kind of guy you'd meet on

Pacific Avenue, even if it wasn't common knowledge that Nicky deals. Just about all of the streets surrounding the casinos are crime-ridden, but the spot he's threatening to swing by is no joke.

I can see her reflection in the rearview mirror too, and to her credit she doesn't flinch.

"Drop us at my house, Nicky. We're not taking her there."

"It'd do her good to see how the rest of the world lives." When his eyes meet mine in the mirror, he backs off, turning the car to head back to the mainland. "I see how it is, Murphy. You want to collect your reward for coming to the little lady's rescue tonight, don't you?"

I just shake my head and do my best to ignore him. Nicky isn't someone to fear, but he can be unpredictable and I'm not looking to test him. I just want to get Sarah out of his car, drop her home and put this shitty night to bed.

Mike isn't talking to me at the moment, which is comical when I think about it. I gave up a shift, an easy hundred for this. We were supposed to hang out tonight, but no, he had to fuck it all up. And for what, to suck up to some rich douchebags who aren't the least bit amusing? I want to ask him where he's going when he hops out of the car at my house, but I'm not angry enough to leave him behind to make house calls with Nicky and his brother.

Sarah is barefoot when she gets out of the car. She's holding her shoes in one hand and has her arms wrapped around her middle. Her dress has ridden up but she hasn't noticed. I'm not about to point this out to her; she looks uncomfortable enough as it is. I'm hoping she doesn't step on any broken glass but can't take the time to inspect the sidewalk. If I do I'll see what she sees, and I don't want to.

"Wait here," I tell them both as I lift the old-style latch on the chain link gate. I don't know what I'll find inside, but it's Saturday night, so odds are good that my stepfather will be drinking beers on the couch while sporting a wife-beater tank that hugs his flabby middle.

Taking the front steps two at a time, I try to overlook the dried-out, overgrown weeds that pass for a front lawn, the rust from the gutters that left a brown stain trailing down the cheap aluminum siding in several spots, and the garbage cans left out in full view, overflowing with Jeff's empties. I usually tidy up outside, but when I left here the other day I was fuming at my stepdad. I wouldn't clean up his mess on principle. Kind of regretting that decision now.

I clench my teeth, knowing I'm going to do something stupid if he gets in my face right now. I'm already envisioning the scene that's about to unfold when I ask to borrow my mom's car. My mother will say yes, he'll laugh in my face and tell me no, they'll start fighting loud enough to be heard outside and it will go downhill from there. The house is pathetic enough, I don't need her getting a front-row seat to the dysfunction that is my family.

I'm breathing a sigh of relief when I see that Mom is home but not Jeff. My sister is sitting with my mom at the kitchen table drinking wine.

"Where's Andrew?"

I'm in a rush, but I'd never breeze past my nephew without a high five or a hug. I love that kid, and between his loser of a father and his grandpa Jeff, I see myself as the only positive male role model in his life, which is saying something coming from a high school dropout.

"Carl took him fishing."

I'm legit surprised because that's the kind of thing a father *should* do. "Where?"

"Surfcasting down at the beach," Lorraine answers. "This is a nice surprise." She comes over to give me a hug. "What have you been up to?"

I shrug when I tell them, "You know, working and stuff." Looking to my mom, I know my expression is pleading when I ask, "Can I borrow your car for a little while? I have to drop a friend off at home and then I'll be right back. Just for an hour, tops."

"The keys are by the door. And there's no rush...Jeff is working tonight and I'm not in until the afternoon tomorrow."

"So I can drop the car off in the morning on my way to the club?"

"Sure."

I lean down to kiss her cheek. "Thanks, Mom. I'll have Uncle Danny follow me in the morning and I'll bring it back with a full tank."

"Love you, Liam," she says as I'm heading for the door.

"Love you too."

"Hey, did you forget someone?" my sister teases, tapping her cheek.

"Love you too, Lorraine."

I'm back outside with the keys inside of two minutes. I'm about to open the passenger-side door for her but stop myself when I'm halfway around the car. No, I don't want her thinking I'm some knight in shining armor. And I also don't want to get too close again. She smells good. I had to stop myself from leaning in and smelling her neck in the back seat before. The back seat. Now I'm thinking about how she felt sitting on my lap.

Stop it.

When I went to make some room between us, I slid her

forward with my hands on her hips. She's small but she's curvy, and I liked the feel of her in my hands. Liked it a lot.

There's no sense in dwelling on any of it so I swallow it down. Any thoughts I had about being friends with Sarah, let alone being with her, were shot to hell the night of her birthday party. My hands grip the steering wheel hard when I picture his arms wrapped around her and the two of them laughing.

"Where to, Princess?"

I cringe when Mike chuckles—forgot he was even in the back seat. I'm expecting a scowl or some smart-mouthed comeback from her, but I get nothing. I look over to see her still clutching her middle. Sarah didn't look wasted, but right now she looks like she might get sick right here in my mother's car. *Fuck me.*

"I'm taking you home, right? It's in the same direction as the club?"

It's another full minute before she snaps out of the daze she's in and looks my way. "Oh, yeah. I'm about ten minutes from the club. But I, uh, can't go home yet so just take me there."

"Where?"

"The stable."

"I can't."

The snark is full blast when she snaps back, "Yes, Liam, you can."

Chapter Fourteen

LIAM

If it was the middle of the day I'd drop her snarky ass and let her figure it out on her own, but it's dark and her request isn't rational, so I let the sarcasm slide.

"It'll be locked up and deserted by now. I can't just leave you there."

"Why can't you go home?" Mike asks from the back seat.

"My parents are home and they have friends over."

"And?"

Sarah turns around to face him. "And I don't feel like playing twenty questions with them." Looking to me again, her voice is softer when she says, "Really, you can leave me at the club. I'll be fine."

Mike leans forward again, poking his head between us. "Drop me off before you head up that way."

"You ruined my night and now you're bailing?" I make it sound like I'm annoyed, when in reality I can't wait to drop his ass off. I can't be myself with Sarah in front of him. Being that he has no filter whatsoever, I'm surprised he didn't press me on the fact that I called her by name back at the party. As far as he knows, Sarah and I are strangers. I've never mentioned any of our interactions.

Come to think of it, I've never said her name in conversation with anyone ever. Not that Mike or any of my other friends would bring her up. My uncle is the only one who speaks her name, one among the others he mentions when he talks to Aunt Maeve about the goings on at the club. I don't chime in at the dinner table much, so my one-word answers and grunts don't raise any suspicions. Yeah, I pretty much act as if she doesn't exist when nothing could be further from the truth.

She pops into my head at the most random times. Yesterday I was helping my aunt get something from a high shelf in the kitchen, and when she remarked on how tall I was it brought me back to a time in the barn a few weeks ago. Back when Sarah and I were teetering on the verge of something that felt like friendship. It was short lived, but it was nice while it lasted.

"You're a freak of nature," she huffed out as she was jumping up, trying but failing to grab the notebook I was holding up and out of her reach.

"Just admit that I'm a superior mathematician," I teased.

"You're superior, all right...As in, you've got a major superiority complex."

"And?" I goaded.

Out of breath, she held up one hand in surrender—or to shut me up. "And I wouldn't have gotten a five on the AP Calc exam if it wasn't for you. Satisfied?"

I nodded and handed her the notebook. "I'm glad you got a five. That means you can skip it next year, correct?"

"Yes, thank the Lord. It's a prerequisite for biology majors and I'll have enough on my plate as it is."

"Bio is a good major. Gives you a lot of options."

She paused, looking cautious for a moment before saying, "You should go back and finish." When I turned away she put a hand on my shoulder, and her touch felt so good that it scared me off. I had to hold my tongue, keep myself from lashing out at her to mask my discomfort. "You're smarter than I am, Liam, and I'm in the top five in my class. The top ten usually get accepted to ivy league schools...You should be on that path."

I smirked when I said, "Yeah, I'm not exactly ivy league material."

"Hate to break it to you, but you're the very definition of it."

"Doesn't matter."

I don't share with her that I've already finished high school, or that I'm signed up to take the college entrance exams at the end of this month like the juniors in her high school who got a late start or did crappy on their first few attempts.

I don't want to tell this girl I got my GED even though there's nothing wrong with it for other people. Seriously, it's not an easy test if you're not a student, and most people who go that route had a tough time in school. I helped Lorraine study for it a few years ago and she needed a second go at it before she passed by the skin of her teeth. But for me? For me it's an embarrassment, and a constant reminder that I have a tendency to get in my own way, or self-sabotage, as my well-meaning high school guidance counselor put it.

Sarah let it drop, thankfully, but that conversation has been playing over in my mind in the weeks since. After dropping Mike off, I toy with the idea of telling her my plan, but I don't want her thinking she's had any influence over me, positive or otherwise.

She breaks into my stubborn inner monologue, looking out the passenger-side window when she says, "Aren't you going to ask me what happened?"

"Doesn't take a genius to figure that one out."

"Did you know?"

I want to tell her that everyone with eyes, ears or half a brain knew, but I like her too much to kick her while she's down. "He's an asshole and she's a bitch. It's no reflection on you."

"That's just it....Penny isn't a bitch. She's been my best friend since fourth grade."

She won't appreciate my advice to be a little more selective when picking friends, so I keep that to myself. But I do ask, "What about him?" because I can't help it, I'm too curious.

She nods. "Parker is an asshole."

We drive in comfortable silence and eventually pass over into the part of Jersey that's all rolling green hills and grand estates hidden behind stone walls and tall trees. "Where are we headed?"

"The stable." When I don't respond she says, "Please just take me there. I'll hide out for an hour or two and then call for a ride."

"I'm not letting you call a car service to pick you up. It's dark and totally deserted at night."

"I'm not going home." She looks to me with sad, tired eyes. "I seriously can't deal with them right now."

"Your dad seems like a good guy."

She's twirling a piece of hair when she answers absently, "He is a good person. I always got the feeling he didn't really like Parker. He never said it outright, but I could tell."

"Then he's a good judge of character, too."

"Unlike yours truly?"

I can't help but crack a smile when I answer, "I wasn't going to say it, Sarah."

She shifts her body, turning to face me. "What's gotten into you? Why are you being so nice to me?"

"You *want* me to be mean?"

"No, you idiot. I just feel like you're giving me whiplash. You're either decent towards me or you're cruel. I don't like your mood swings."

"It's no picnic having my moods either, if that makes you feel any better...Although I'm sure it doesn't." She doesn't respond. "I'm sorry, all right?"

"Is it me? Something I did?"

I swallow my pride and answer her truthfully. "It's me. Half the time when I'm shooting my mouth off I'm just mad at myself, no one else."

"Your uncle told me why you dropped out of school in tenth grade." When I look over to her with wide eyes, she looks afraid. "Don't get mad at him. It was me...I was being nosey."

Fucking Danny.

Gotta say, I'm surprised. He's not one to blab or talk behind other peoples' backs. My dropping out was a colossal disappointment, I knew that, but it must still be eating at him if he's confiding in a kid at the horse stable.

Mr. Pippens. Just picturing his face has me gripping the steering wheel hard. I'm talking out loud but not really even talking to Sarah once I start down memory lane. "I bet the teachers at your school would never accuse a student of plagiarizing an essay."

"They would if it was warranted. But they wouldn't do it

without just cause. They'd get their ass handed to them if they were wrong."

"Mr. Pippens didn't give it a second thought before calling me a liar."

"That's so unfair. And I don't know what happened, but I'd bet everything I have that you wouldn't cheat on an assignment. You'd have no need to cheat."

"You know the worst part?"

"Tell me."

"He made a grammatical error in his critique. The dumbass wrote, 'Checking your work, this essay is nothing more than plagiarized garbage.'

When she doesn't respond, I clarify. "The *essay* didn't check the work. That's a dangling participle!"

"*That* is the part of the story that got you riled up?"

"The point is, he can't even write a grammatically correct accusation. Do you not get the irony?"

"That's beside the point and you know it. The point is that he shamed you, and it must have hurt."

"People look at you, they judge where you come from, what clothes you wear, the car you drive." I look down to the console separating me from Sarah. The console that pops open if my elbow isn't resting against it. The one with faded and torn leather marring its surface. This car is a piece of crap. "Sometimes I feel trapped, do you understand?"

"I think so."

"And that essay he tore up in front of me? I worked on it for two weeks, edited it so many times I could probably still recite it word for word."

"What was it about?"

"My father, and a trip he took me on when I was around nine or ten years old."

"Are you close to your dad?" she asks.

I keep my eyes on the road when I answer, "I haven't seen him since that day."

"Oh." She looks wounded on my behalf.

"It's fine. Don't go feeling sorry for me. It makes me mad." I say that last part as a joke but it falls flat.

"I don't know who my father is, or my mother for that matter."

I pull into the parking lot and cut the engine, legitimately surprised. "*What* now?"

She pulls on the hem of her dress in an effort to smooth it down, obvious in her discomfort. "Yeah, I just found out I'm adopted."

"Shit. Your parents just told you now?"

"They didn't tell me. I found out on my own."

"And what did they say when you asked them about it?"

"I haven't...asked them about it."

I can't help but shake my head. "Seriously? Why not?"

"I don't know. I've stopped and started a few times but the words just get trapped in my throat. I know that sounds stupid—"

"No, it doesn't. Everyone acts like they'd know what to say, how to handle every situation the right way, but that's bullshit. You can only do that from the cheap seats as a spectator. When it's you, when it's *your* life, then it's not so cut and dry. I have about ten different conversations I've rehearsed in my head, but I'm tongue-tied and too chickenshit to say anything when I'm finally face to face with them."

"Them?"

"My stepfather, my mother, my father *if* we ever cross paths again." I look to her and smile. "I've got quite a list."

"You don't give the impression of being afraid of anyone."

"I didn't say I was afraid of them, just that I can't seem to speak my mind when it matters most."

"Got it."

I look down at my phone and she mistakes it for impatience. "Seriously, you can leave me here."

"So you've told me...several times." I shrug, feeling more relaxed than I have in a long time. "I've got nowhere to be. When will the coast be clear at your house?"

"Twelve-thirty? Maybe one just to be safe?"

I reach behind me to the backseat and grab her a sweatshirt. "Here, you look cold."

"Thanks," she says as she pulls it over her head. It's swimming on her, which for some reason makes her look ridiculously cute. "Wanna sneak in and check on Shadow with me? I know where your uncle hides the spare key."

"Lead the way."

"No," she hisses just as I'm about to flip on the lights. "Leave that."

Not only did she know where my uncle keeps a key hidden, but she also knows where a spare flashlight is stashed.

"Here," she whispers as it clicks on and casts a glow across the barn. "This is enough light."

It's barely enough to see a hand in front of your face at first, but within a minute or two my eyes adjust. "Do you creep in here late at night on a regular basis?"

"No," she says. "I'm just observant," she flashes me a smile, "and crafty. I saw your uncle give that key to one of the stable hands a few weeks ago, and he just used that flashlight the other day to show me something on Shadow's left rear hoof."

"Crafty, huh?"

Turning to nuzzle her horse, she murmurs, "Isn't that right? Yes Shadow, yes it is."

"You two have a very close bond." She thinks I'm teasing when I'm not. "I mean it. Your horse connects with you. It's not like that with most of the other owners." Before thinking it through I speak the memory out loud. "There was this one day you looked really sad, and Shadow came to you and nudged you before laying his head in your lap. Like, he instinctively knew you were down in the dumps and was looking to comfort you."

"So, let me get this straight. You're saying that in between bouts of scowling at me you took note of my emotional state?"

"I—"

She cuts me off even though I had nothing to add to that one syllable. "Don't. I was just kidding."

But she wasn't kidding, and I feel pretty disgusted with myself acknowledging that I was gloating—maybe even basking in her misery—and knowing I could cut her down to size with just one look.

"I was acting like an asshole after your birthday party because I was jealous." I look up, away, around—anywhere to avoid her eyes. I never let my guard down, and I'm not comfortable feeling so exposed.

"I'm the one who was acting like an idiot. Dancing around, hamming it up for the cameras..."

"You looked like you were having fun, but I knew...I mean, I *know* what he's like, and I was angry that you couldn't see it too."

"It's sad, but I was already wishing the summer away, looking forward to breaking up with him before leaving for school."

It's quiet for a full minute or two until I ask, "When do you leave?"

"Orientation is August twenty-third."

"So you have two months."

She nods, and I catch the trace of a smile before she turns away slowly. "Looks like my calendar is wide open now."

Is this an invitation? I decide that it is. I take a step back, rest my head and then slide down the wall until my ass hits the ground. She looks at me, looks at the spot on the floor next to me, and then takes a few steps to close the distance. "It's a good thing your uncle is such a neat freak," she says as she slowly slides down and plops her butt next to mine.

"He doesn't clean the floor. You have me to thank for the pristine condition of this place."

"Gracias."

"De nada, señorita."

I can't see her rolling her eyes, but I'm pretty sure she is. "Don't tell me, you speak like three foreign languages, right?"

"English only. Sorry 'bout that."

"Same here. It makes me feel unworldly."

"You're right. It does."

When she turns my way and goes to swat me, I grab her wrist, hold it as I rub my thumb over the spot where her pulse beats. She's nervous. I want to tell her that I am, too. I don't know if I'm making a misstep, don't if I should release my hold on her. I don't know what I'm doing.

Sarah watches my thumb move back and forth. "I can't stop thinking about you," she whispers.

"Same."

Her eyes are soft when they meet mine. "You think about me?"

"Yeah," I confess. "I think about you a lot."

SARAH

Someone is knocking on the door downstairs but I'm not getting up to check. I just don't care what's going on outside my little bubble right now. I want to stay this in good memory for as long as I can before facing reality.

My fingers trace over my lips and I smile thinking back on our kiss. Liam looked tense in that moment before he closed the small distance between us and kissed me. It was a quick kiss but not rushed. It was soft and gentle. When Liam pulled back and looked at me to gauge my reaction, I wonder what he saw on my face. I was happy but he must have only seen the tears forming in my eyes.

"I won't do it again," he whispered, lowering his head. I was confused for a split second, wondering what was going on when he turned away from me and rested his head back against the wall.

"Liam," I whispered, "look at me." He wouldn't though, so I moved from where I was sitting next to him and planted myself in his lap. "I liked the kiss." He wouldn't look at me until I took his face in my hands and gently turned him. "I wanted it."

"You're crying."

I smiled, batting that one hot tear from my cheek. "I've been doing a lot of that lately."

"I'm sorry I've been such an ass to you, Sarah."

"I know."

Fully in the memory, I see his face, inches from mine. So close that I can see the indecision in his eyes. He wants to bridge the gap again but he's nervous. Me? *I* make him nervous? It doesn't seem possible, but I can see that's what is holding him back. "Kiss me again," I tell him, and he does.

This kiss is soft too, but now he's holding me close, moving his hands to make a slow path up to my shoulders and then back down, skimming over my arms until he hits the curve of my hips. The kiss goes on as his hands move, sticking to that safe path. I pull back just to get the sweatshirt that's swimming on me off and over my head, and as I toss it aside, I find him staring at what I've revealed.

I'm nervous about going any further with him, but I want to at the same time. I've thought about Liam, dreamed about the moment we're currently in more times than I could count on all my fingers and toes, but didn't figure that my heart would be hammering in my chest, or that he'd look as unsure as I am. But my fear dissipates when he kisses me again and keeps his hands resting on my hips. This, I decide, is better.

Slow, careful, deliberate.

I don't know if the tide is going to change after this spell is broken. Past experience tells me that Liam may scowl at me the next time we cross paths and make me regret this. I pray that's not the case, but I'm not giving myself over to anyone just yet. Parker taught me a valuable lesson last night.

It's the memory of Parker that brings me back to my senses —that and the sound of Penny's voice coming from downstairs.

"Thanks, Audrey. I feel as bad as I probably look right now." My mother says something but her voice is muffled compared to Penny's. "Maybe I should bring one up for Sarah, too." And in response to what my mother says next, she replies, "No, don't worry, Sarah didn't overdo it last night. She's not as stupid as I am."

I'm not ready to face her when she knocks a minute later, so I bury myself back under the covers and turn to face the wall.

I can hear her sigh when she comes in, her steps as she crosses my room, and the sound the glasses make when she rests them on my nightstand. I can also hear her breath hitch when the mattress dips under her weight. She's curled herself up right next to me, and I begin to cry when she wraps one arm around me. Penny is crying too, and neither one of us speaks for what feels like an eternity as she keeps hold of me.

I don't know how to hate her.

"I'm so sorry, Sarah. There's nothing I can say in my defense, I know that. And I know I sound like an absolute fraud when I say that I never meant to hurt you, but I didn't." She sniffles and catches her breath before saying, "It's like there's this disconnect between what I was doing and reality. I wouldn't let myself think about how awful I was or who I was hurting." She pauses and then says, "If it makes you feel any better, no one is talking to me. Not Tatiana, Clara, Logan...basically no one in the universe."

She doesn't mention Parker's name, but I'm pretty sure

he's not standing by her side through all this. That's not his style.

It's like Penny has read my thoughts when she adds, "Parker practically spat on me when he came back inside last night, like this is all my fault."

When I roll over to face her, I can see Penny's face is puffy and red, and her eyes are bloodshot. For a split second I'm happy to see her suffering, but that feeling doesn't last. There's no way to feel victorious here.

"My closest friend with my boyfriend...Why?" Her face is blank. She has no answer for me. "Penny, you have to give me something here. What happened? *When* did it happen?" Penny takes a deep breath, but before she starts in I feel the need to warn her, "The truth. Don't you dare lie to me. I'll never forgive you if you lie to me right now."

She nods and swallows. "Ninth grade. It was at that sailing camp we used to go to in Maine. The one where the boys stayed on one side of the lake and the girls' camp was on the other."

"Freshman year? The summer before or the summer after?"

"After."

Parker's words repeat in my head. *It was at sailing camp...it was awkward and rushed and lame.* "Wait...so *you* were his first? His first time was with you?"

"Yeah...My first, too." She rolls onto her back and stares up at the ceiling. "And it's not exactly the touching kind of memory you read about in those Nicholas Sparks books." She lets out a sad laugh when she says, "Parker wouldn't even look at me the next day."

"Was that it? I mean, did it stop for a while?"

"I wish." She turns back and props herself up on her elbow

to look down at me. "And I mean that. If I could go back and do it all over again, I never would have been with him that first time."

"Did he push you to do it?"

"Not really. I swear, I think he was more scared than I was. And I think he kind of hated me for it afterwards. The other boys knew, which was horrible. On Friday nights they held these campfires...The boy and girl groups mixed together. At the next one, every boy was laughing at me. Parker was smirking but I could tell he didn't like the attention either. And of course the other girls found out soon enough. It was near the end of the summer, thank God, because I was a pariah those last two weeks."

"And when you came back?"

"I guess Parker had some epiphany that this could work to his advantage. He'd go from totally ignoring me at school during the day, to sneaking me onto his boat after practices and at night."

"Penny..."

"And you're going to find this out, so let me just get it out before I'm too embarrassed."

I'm bracing for something really horrible, so when she says, "I've been with Logan, too," I'm relieved.

"I knew you were hooking up with Logan."

"You did?"

"Everyone knows."

"He doesn't really acknowledge me that way either, so I didn't think anyone knew."

"How did that work? You and Logan and Parker are always sailing together." When she doesn't answer, I ask, "Wait...they both..."

"Yeah. I was with both of them. I told myself we were all

like, more worldly than the rest of you, more mature, but that was a crock of shit. I was a joke to them. One afternoon I actually heard Logan tell someone that I was a slut. And I don't know," she starts to cry, "I don't know why I stayed down below deck and kept my mouth shut."

"Penny."

She cuts me off even though I had nothing more to say. "I'm not telling you all this so that you feel bad or take pity on me or anything. I just need you to hear me out."

"I'm listening."

"I've been staying quiet all this time. I stood by and watched last year when Parker started paying attention to you. God, it made me so mad. You got the kind words, you got all the good stuff. I'd hang back and watch him stare at you in class or try to flirt with you. You barely acknowledged him and he just kept at it, trying to," she shakes her head and lets out a breath, "woo you right in front of me."

"You were jealous?"

"Yes, no...I don't even know. I just couldn't figure out what you had that I hadn't already given him."

I'm talking to myself when I say, "I can't believe this has been going on behind my back for a year and I never caught on."

"It wasn't all the time. He hasn't touched me since—"

I roll over on my side and push her shoulder. "He touched you last night!"

Penny looks scared. "I know." She grabs for my hands and holds them in hers. "But please believe me when I tell you that I was beyond drunk. It's no excuse but I've been avoiding him since that night when I walked in on you two a few weeks ago."

The memory of it, and the realization that I gave Parker a piece of myself—that I trusted him—makes me physically sick.

I'm weak as I push her off and whip the covers back. I need to lock myself in my bathroom for a few minutes. I need to wash my face, wash all of this off. Studying myself in the mirror, I tell the girl looking back at me to get a grip. *You don't even like him.* I even start to tell myself that Penny did me a favor, but stop short of finishing that one.

Does anyone even like me? If my boyfriend fed me all those cheap lines, lied to my face for the better part of a year, and my best friend acted like everything was all good while screwing him behind my back—what does that say about me?

Penny gives a weak knock on the door before asking, "Do you want me to go?"

But I don't want her to go. No, I want her to explain this shit to me. Opening the door, I fix her with a look that's probably murderous. "Did you two laugh at me behind my back? Was I a joke to you?"

"No! Never! I swear to you...It's like it was two universes. You and Parker were the real life version, and me...*I* was the joke."

I shuffle back over to my bed and sit with my back up against the headboard, gesturing for her to join me. "Why would he bother with me then?"

"He really does like you, Sarah." When I let out a cheerless laugh she adds, "I'm not looking to plead his case or anything, I'm just telling you that he sees you differently than the way he sees me. He'll always comment on how smart you are, and he brags to people about how you're going to an ivy league school for sure. God, he talks about your riding, your perfect parents, the fact that he's already like a member of your family...He's pretty much nauseating when it comes to you."

"I didn't mean it when I told him I loved him. I wish I never said it back to him."

"Are you going to talk to him when he calls?"

"No. There's nothing to say. I don't want his cheap words."

"Or mine," she mutters. I don't respond. A minute passes before she says, "Can I ask you something?" I look her in the eye, noncommittal, because let's face it, I owe her *nothing*. "Are you friends with that kid Mike? I saw you get in their car last night."

"I just met him last night but I'm friends with Liam."

"Where did you meet him?"

"At the club. He works there and he helps his uncle out in the stable sometimes."

"I know."

"You know him?"

She averts her eyes, and in that moment I'm brought back to a night a few months ago, a party. *The hot guy from the shore.* Did she say *his* name? And now I'm mad. "Were you with Liam, too?"

"It was nothing."

"You say that a lot...You realize that, don't you?"

"We kissed. It was nothing. He hates me anyway, so you've got nothing to worry about there."

"Get out."

"Sarah, wait."

"Leave." When she doesn't move from the bed I physically push her off, and have a fleeting sense of satisfaction when I hear her land with a thump. I roll over after whispering, "Please, I just want you to go."

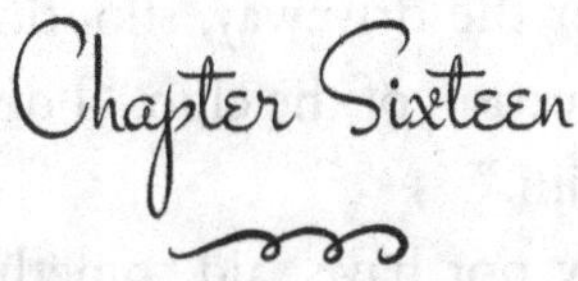

Chapter Sixteen

LIAM

I woke up with a smile on my face this morning, but by the time I'm out of the shower and heading back towards my mother's to drop off her car, the doubt is creeping in and pushing out the good memories from last night.

She won't be the same Sarah today.

I'm working on some of the equipment today, golf carts and maintenance vehicles, but chances are that I'll run into her. And I want to see her, I absolutely do, but I'm wary of how it's going to be between us. Last night was the very definition of a rebound situation. She was hurt, maybe even looking to get back at her guy, and I was the convenient option—that's all.

And I don't care. That's what I'm telling myself because I just can't. I can't care, can't get hung up on some girl I've got no shot with, can't get sidetracked.

Can't set myself up for a giant letdown.

"Everything all right?" my uncle asks, gesturing to the fingernail I'm gnawing down to the quick.

"Uh huh," I mumble, hardly acknowledging him as I mentally beat myself up for taking this extra shift.

"What did Jeff just say to you?"

I turn to Uncle Danny, confused. "Huh?"

He backs out of the driveway, shooting Jeff a look as we head back in the direction of the club. "I don't know why your mother stays with him."

Jeff may or may not have said something shitty to me; I wasn't even listening. There are times when I actively ignore him because nothing pisses him off more, but today I was truly lost in my own head. "I don't know what he said. I like to pretend he doesn't exist."

"You know, your mother had so much promise. Maybe that's why I'm so hard on you. She was my responsibility—"

"You were only a kid yourself."

"I didn't push her. She could have gone to college, Liam. She was so intelligent, but I was too busy with my own life." He glances over at me before looking back to the road. "I look at my little sister now and I'm filled with regret. I feel responsible."

"But you're not responsible. She made her choices. She *chose* Jeff." I can't help but laugh before adding, "Keep in mind, she chose that loser more than once." I cut him off before he can speak again. "And I know where this is going...You're not responsible for me either. I made choices, and I know some of them weren't so great, but it's my life and I'll be fine. It pisses me off when you look at me that way, like you're disappointed."

"I'm not disappointed in you. I'm sad more than anything. I want to see one of us Murphys succeed."

"I see *you* as a success."

"I don't see myself as a failure, don't get me wrong. But I

was the first one here, and you make sacrifices to pave the way for the ones who come after. That's how it's supposed to be, each generation more successful than the one before it."

"And you see me, Lorraine, and my mother taking this family in reverse, is that it?"

He shakes his head, looking tired even though it's not much past eight in the morning. "When my mother died and your mom was sent to live with me and Maeve, she was a teenager full of spit and vinegar. She was torn away from everything familiar, put on a plane, dumped with a much older brother she hardly knew. She was so angry, and looking back on it now, I guess she had every right to be. It was hard going to a new school, being teased about her brogue." He looks to me. "Do you know she stopped speaking entirely? The kids in class would laugh when she'd answer a question, so she just stopped speaking all together. I was twenty-five at the time. You think I knew what the hell to do when the school counselor called?"

"She never told me that. And I don't hear any trace of a brogue in her speech. It's hard to believe she was even born there."

"I'd hear her sitting in front of the television for hours, imitating the actors' American accents. And she'd catch herself, shaking her head and repeating the word when she'd do something wrong, like annunciating the syllables in certain words like we do back home."

"Veh-jeh-tah-bulls."

"Exactly. But she went months without saying much of anything. She refused to give more than a one-word answer until she believed she had the hang of it. And in the meantime, she dropped out of school, took a menial job cleaning houses, and—"

"End of story, right? She's still stuck in place."

"It's more than that. She's stuck with *him*. Without an education, you're trapped. She can't walk away."

"That's some bullshit. She could have walked away from him many times, but she chose him and she chose to stay."

"Agree to disagree…She had two children to feed."

"Don't go rewriting history now. She had *one* child at the time. She left him to shack up with loser number two and then got pregnant with me. When he took off, that's when she went crawling back to Jeff. And he never lets her forget that he took her back, or that he raised some other guy's kid."

"He didn't have a hand in raising you."

I don't say that he did use his hands—used them to beat the shit out of me on a regular basis. I've never spoken of it, and I'm sure my mother hasn't aired our dirty laundry either.

We're silent for the rest of the ride to work. No one would accuse me of shying away from conflict—most people would say I actively seek it out—but not with my uncle. He's actually the one person in this world whose opinion matters. Sounds sad and pathetic, but I want him to be proud of me someday.

"We're good?" my uncle looks to me and asks as we pull into the lot.

"Always, Uncle Dan…We'll always be ok."

I walk a few paces behind him, my thoughts shifting back to Sarah. Did she show up early to ride this morning? Did she come early hoping she'd run into me? Not likely, given that I only dropped her off a few hours ago. I smile thinking about that last parting kiss, then decide it's better if we run into each other later on today, or better yet, tomorrow.

I'm the only one who can repair the golf-ball picker, so I guess you could say I've become indispensable around here. Being the go-to guy for the greenskeeper at the golf club is not among my life goals, so I'm happy to get back to repairing the paddock fence a couple of hours later.

If I have to be at this godforsaken place, I prefer working in the stables over the clubhouse or golf course for many reasons, but one cute reason in particular. I check my phone as I head back, and feel a smile forming on my face when I see it's just past noon. I'm quick to school that smile, though, and pair it with my version of a pep talk. *Calm down, you idiot. Last night was no big deal. Don't seem too eager or she'll think you're a loser.*

But it's not Sarah waiting for me when I round the corner, it's two guys in button-down shirts, pressed pants, and deck shoes that look like they've never gotten wet. Casual Sunday morning attire around these parts. They stand like sentinels at the stable doors, looking past my uncle to study me.

"Can I help you, Mr. Thomson?"

I've heard the name but never met the club's director. He looks to my uncle. "We're just here to speak to your nephew."

"About what?"

"It's ok, Uncle Dan, I can handle this."

But when Thomson gestures for me to follow him and his sidekick, my uncle isn't having it. "Mr. Thomson, if you head back to the clubhouse I'm coming along, so maybe you just want to have this discussion here so we can get on with our workday."

He shoots my uncle a look that's part condescending, part annoyed, but then settles back on me. "There's been a report of some items missing from the kitchen and your name came up."

When my uncle goes to protest I wave him off and step forward. "Items missing from the kitchen? What are you talking about?"

"Inventory from the cold case...Quite a lot, in fact."

His guy takes one step towards me. "I'm here to escort you off the premises."

When he lays a hand on my upper arm, I hear my uncle make a clicking sound with his tongue, the same one he makes to calm his jittery horses. I am so mad that I'm sure my face is burning red, but the subtle reminder of my uncle's steady presence quells the urge I have to knock this uppity fool on his ass.

"Wait...Are you accusing me of stealing?"

With that, my uncle steps between us. "This is ridiculous!"

"Mr. Murphy, please understand, this has nothing to do with you."

"This is my nephew, so if you're accusing him of something you'd better explain yourself to me right now."

Thomson puffs up his chest. "I actually don't have to explain anything, but your nephew was spotted taking a few cases of premium lobster tails from the cold storage box, along with God knows what else. Do you know how much that lobster retails for?" He doesn't wait for an answer before directing his eyes my way. "It's enough to warrant a felony charge."

"Fuck. You. I didn't steal anything."

"Care to tell me where you were last night?"

A dead calm has come over me, so I don't raise my voice when I answer, "I'm not telling you shit, old man."

I'm thinking this day can't get any worse when I hear her voice from behind me.

"What's up?"

Those two words are delivered clipped and ice cold, so I assume that Sarah just heard everything.

Fantastic.

All that righteous anger bleeds out of me as a deep-rooted

sense of shame takes hold. Why on earth do I feel ashamed when I didn't do a damn thing wrong?

When no one answers her, she sets her sights on Thomson. "Where's your proof? Where's the evidence?"

"Sarah, not now."

"Not now, my ass!" Turning back to them, she points her finger at them and says, "You better have something rock solid before you start throwing accusations around, do you understand? Our attorney will rip you both a new one if you say one more slanderous word against this man."

The sidekick guy smiles at her in a way that's meant to placate. "Miss Hamilton, there's video footage."

I take a minute to let that one settle in before unleashing on the guy. "Bullshit! There's no video footage of *me* because *I* didn't steal anything!"

"What is going on?"

And now her father is here…Awesome.

"I don't need your help, Sarah. *Please,* just go." And I know that my eyes must be pleading with her as I make the request because Sarah shakes her head as she wipes at her watery eyes, but then does as I ask and heads out.

"Mr. Hamilton, we have a credible accusation that this employee has been stealing from the club. He cannot stay on the premises and if he doesn't leave I'll have no choice but to call the police."

"He's leaving right now," my uncle shoots back, "and I can assure you I'll be right behind him. Who the hell do you think you are?"

"Uncle Dan—"

"Not a word," he warns me. Tossing me the keys to his truck, he says, "Go home. *My* home," he clarifies. "I'll get this sorted."

And I don't need to be told twice because I want out of there. Sarah is gone when I leave the stable, thank the Lord, and in my periphery I can see her dad talking to those two assholes before they drive off in a golf cart. Batman and Robin are in a rush, no doubt, off to solve some other first-world problems.

Just as I'm about to get in the truck, though, I turn back. I feel the need to make sure my Uncle Dan knows that I am one hundred percent innocent. I also don't want him doing something stupid on my account. He loves his job. I don't want him quitting.

Rounding the corner, I stop in my tracks when I hear him talking to Sarah's father. Standing off to the side, I listen in, and want to put my fist through the wall by the time they're done.

"He's a handful, I'll give him that, but he's no criminal, Mr. Hamilton. Liam would never steal."

"They said there's footage of your nephew wearing a hoodie in the parking lot putting a large box into his car."

"Footage of *someone* putting a case of lobster tails into *some* car. It wasn't him."

"Did they give your nephew a chance to explain?"

My uncle lets out a sigh. "You don't know Liam. He's proud. Too proud to plead his case. He told Thomson he didn't do it, but wouldn't answer any of their other questions, so they fired him."

"Thomson said an anonymous tip came in. Someone called to report that an employee was stealing from the club and selling stock to a local restaurant. To the restaurant where Liam just happens to cover some shifts as a bar back. You have to admit, Danny, that doesn't sound good."

My uncle shoots back, "It sounds awfully *convenient* to me.

I'm not blind where my nephew is concerned, but I'm also not blind to the fact that he's an easy target. Some of the kids at this club have more motive to steal than he does."

"What are you implying?"

"Not implying, stating facts. Liam doesn't do drugs or have other expensive habits like some of the members' children."

There's silence for a moment before my uncle adds, "I believe Liam. If they fire him, I'll be handing in my resignation immediately."

"Give me a few days, Danny. Let me look into this."

I want to tell Mr. Hamilton not to bother, or really, I want to tell him to take his concern and shove it. *Let me look into it... Give me a few days.* You and the rest of them can fuck right off.

I hate these people.

Each and every one of them.

Chapter Seventeen

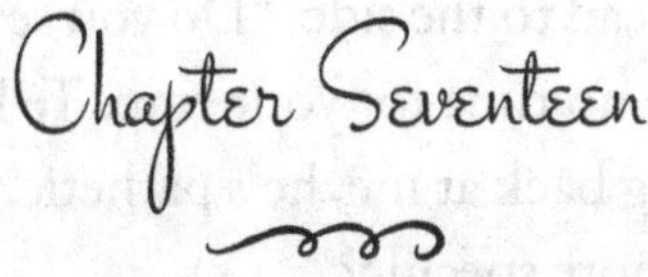

SARAH

I am fit to be tied.

I had no intention of ever speaking to Parker again, but he's given me no choice.

No, I don't know Liam all that well, but I would bet my life that he's innocent.

I march right past Penny, ignoring her weak but surprised greeting. I can feel her eyes on me as I make my way to the landing next to where Logan's sailboat is docked. There are other people working on their boats and a junior sailing class is in session, but I don't care who's watching or listening.

"Parker?" I call his name louder when I get no response, and it's another full minute before Logan makes his way topside while buttoning up his rumpled oxford shirt.

"Can I help you with something?" Polite words, but oh so rude and condescending the way they're delivered by this entitled ass.

"I'm looking for Parker."

He purses his lips and nods as if he's giving my words serious consideration. "Kind of got the gist of that from you shrieking his name."

I ignore the dig. "Is he here?"

He cocks his head to the side. "Do you see him here?"

"Logan, I have no time for your crap. Tell Parker that if this is his way of getting back at me, he's pathetic."

"Can you be more specific?"

"An anonymous tip to the club's director about stolen goods? Setting an innocent person up for a felony charge? Remind him that making a false police report is *also* a felony." Cocking my head to the side, I add, "Will you pass that along, Logan?"

"Sarah, I seriously have no idea what you're babbling about."

"Sure you don't."

"Believe whatever you want, I could care less."

I stumble over a nail on my way back down the gangway and hear Logan chuckle. If I'd face planted I would have made his day. Why did I ever waste one minute of my time hanging out with these people?

"Wait," Penny pleads, catching up to me in the parking lot. "Sarah, please don't cut me off. You...You're my only friend."

Her skin is mottled red, the way you look after you've been crying for a seriously long time, but I still can't help but lash out at her. I'm mad on Liam's behalf, and I am so jealous that Penny had something with Liam, too. "What are you even doing here, Penny? Looking to get back in with Parker now that I'm officially out of the picture? Do you realize how sad that is? How pathetic you are?"

Her mouth opens and closes before she whispers, "No. I'm just here to clear my stuff out. I don't want to sail anymore."

"Well, good luck with that."

The words are bitchy and mean, and I can feel my stomach twisting with guilt before I can cross the lot and lock myself into my car. I settle in and look back to where we were just standing. Penny is still there, eyes cast down to where she's kicking pebbles with her foot. I remind myself of what she's done, fight the urge I have to console her.

There's no going back. Yes, she was my one true friend, but that was then and this is now.

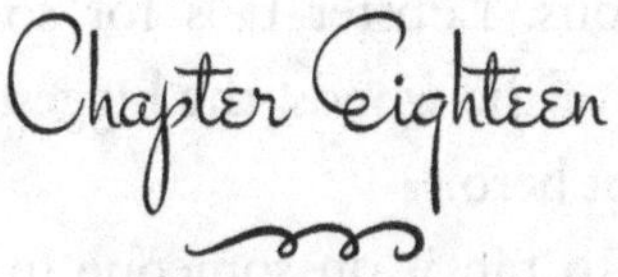

Chapter Eighteen

LIAM

When Mike called and told me what he overheard at the boathouse, I already had a good idea of who was behind this.

He taped them, so I got to hear everything. It was no consolation to hear Parker express just the slightest bit of remorse when one of his buddies told him I was probably going to be charged with a felony. When he said *No way*, his friend explained that, *Apparently, a case of lobster tails is expensive.*

But these kids wouldn't know that. They'd have no idea that a few cases of Maine lobster would put you well over the limit for felony burglary in the state of New Jersey—a low-level felony, but a felony nonetheless.

"Losing his job is one thing, I don't want him going to jail. I mean, I'm not a dick," he said in his own defense.

As if falsely accusing someone of a crime isn't bad enough, as if that alone doesn't make you a pathetic excuse for a human being. Yes, Parker, you are a dick.

I guess people like Logan and Parker would never even think to take a ride to the store to buy lobster tails. And they'd probably gag on the flash-frozen crap people like us splurge on at Costco for the really big occasions, like weddings, Communions or graduations. Lobster tails for some random house party? In my neck of the woods, the biggest events warrant no more than a six-foot hero.

The plan was to pin it on someone in the kitchen. They weren't picky, anyone would do. Just drop an accusation and lead Thomson to the tapes that would show a hooded guy putting the loot into the back of a shitty, late-model car in the restaurant's staff parking lot. People like Parker ask dumb people—my best friend comes to mind—to do their dirty work, so who knows, for fifty bucks maybe one of the guys in the kitchen did lift the stuff and then name me.

I could picture Thomson and his boy doing a more thorough inventory at this very moment, with my ever-expanding rap sheet in hand. From what I heard on Mike's phone, basically everything they served was courtesy of mummy and daddies' club. Cases of mini-beef Wellington appetizers, jars of olives and two cases of jumbo shrimp will be listed among the missing. I can't even imagine what was stolen from the liquor storage. That alone would land someone in jail.

When my name came up, Logan said something like: *Don't fret, she's just taking a walk on the wild side, she'll be back.* Even better, Parker answered that he didn't want Sarah back because she's a frigid bitch, but he already has an internship lined up with her dad this summer, and *that loser isn't fucking it up for me.* I'll go ahead and assume that I'm the loser.

How do they even know we were together last night? I have no clue and decide that I don't care. I'm actually glad he knows.

The only other thing that brightened my day was Sarah's blind faith in my innocence, even before she heard from Penny. I'm thinking Penny was looking to redeem herself when she tipped Mike off to what was going on.

I smile until I remember we're not currently on speaking terms.

When I saw the unknown number I wasn't even going to answer, and then I had to fight my instinct to hang up when I first heard her voice.

Shame is powerful. In my case, it's so powerful that it can trigger that fight or flight response. No, I don't have to be chased by a hungry lion or have a loaded gun pointed my way. Sometimes all it takes is a curious look that lasts a beat too long.

And what happened this afternoon? That was a pile on. I was red-faced and shaking off the overwhelming urge to cry like a little kid, talking myself down, reminding myself that I didn't do what they'd accused me of as I was driving back to my uncle's house with a white-knuckle grip on the steering wheel.

Makes me the crazy one, right? To think so little of yourself that you have to *remind* yourself you're not guilty? It sounds batshit when I think about it like that.

It burned when Sarah called me out, and it still burns because I know she's right.

She's furious that I won't defend myself to my manager or the assholes on the club's board.

I know they haven't gone to the police yet so they probably aren't planning on it, and I'm not interested in *clearing my good name*. Her words, not mine.

"It's like tenth grade all over again. You really showed them back then, didn't you?

"What are you talking about?"

"You're shooting yourself in the foot, cutting off your nose to spite your face, whatever...Defend yourself, Liam! Don't let them get away with this!"

"It makes no difference."

"What?" She's speechless for a moment. "Did you just say that it makes no difference? That being accused of a crime you didn't commit is no biggie, like, just your average Saturday night?" Before I can come up with a comeback, she unleashes. "So I guess it also makes no difference that you chose to drop out of school? That you could have graduated with honors and gotten a scholarship, but instead you've got nothing to show for yourself now? Holy crap, Liam...It matters!"

"I may not be on my way to an ivy league school, Princess, but that doesn't mean I've got nothing."

"Do *not* turn this back on me. Don't imply I'm calling you nothing, or that I somehow see you as inferior. I don't and you know that. I just want you to stand up for yourself and take what you've earned. I don't want the club to get away with this, the same way I still want that sack of shit teacher to pay for what he did to you!"

Sarah isn't wrong, but that righteous indignation sits lodged in my chest, burning hot. I guess I haven't changed much because I'd still rather the whole world believe a lie about me than beg them to see the truth.

But instead of sitting home stewing—my default response—I'm driving to her. I need to apologize, to tell her how much it means to me that she believes me, proof or no proof. Sarah is in my corner, and I want her to stay there.

Chapter Nineteen

SARAH

Her ring rapping against my window startles us both. "Get out of the car, Sarah!" When I turn to her, stunned, she barks, "Now!"

I lower the window halfway. "What is the *matter* with you?"

She just interrupted Liam and I making up after an argument, and her timing sucks, because things were just getting good.

Her eyes cut to Liam with disgust. "Isn't that the boy they caught stealing from the club?"

"Who told you that, Audrey?"

She pauses, doesn't like it when I address her that way—the way my friends do. She knows I'm mocking her and she's smart enough to recognize that maybe she is the slightest bit ridiculous with that nauseating little ritual she encourages.

"Did your fellow Stepford wives fill you in on the hot gossip?"

At least she has the decency to pull me aside after I get out and stand toe to toe with her, but I'm sure Liam can still hear her stage whisper, and that makes me madder than hell. "Sarah, your father told me what's going on. *He* said Liam was caught on camera. And who knows how much he stole from the kitchen before he was caught? There are full cases of vodka and champagne missing from the bar storage area, too. Did you know *that*?" She tips her head in his direction. "Your friend seems to be quite the entrepreneur."

"Oh my God!" I scream. "You are *so* clueless!"

"Hey, hey...What the hell is going on?" My father looks to me. "You owe your mother an apology."

"She owes *me* an apology, she owes *Liam* an apology, she owes the whole *world* an apology for kissing up to those snooty morons at the club!"

My father places his body between us, one hand on each of us like he's separating Frazier and Ali. "Enough! Both of you, inside."

And when I see that Liam is now out of his car, watching this all go down with a crushed look on his face, I want to die. If I were him I'd want to spit in my parents' faces, but his voice is calm when he nods and says, "Go inside, Sarah."

Tears choke my throat when I whisper, "No."

"Go." His voice is gentle when he adds, "I'll call you later."

Once the door clicks behind me I turn on her. "Liquor has been going missing from the club for years. Where do you think everyone gets the booze for our parties? But the board members just noticed bottles missing *now*? Right, totally plausible. I get it, Mom. It's all about you... Liam reflects poorly on *you*. That's what this is really about. You're mortified, admit it."

"He's trash! Is it so wrong that I want better for you?" My father gently takes her arm to stop her from saying more.

"You call him trash but you don't know the first thing about him. Meanwhile, you think Parker and his friends are good, upstanding citizens when nothing could be further from the truth. It's sad, not to mention laughable, that you're so caught up in this bullshit world."

"Oh, that's rich. You seem to enjoy the many perks this bullshit world has afforded you."

"I never asked you for anything."

"You never *had* to ask! You've been given everything! Every, single, thing!"

"That's enough! Both of you, please stop." Looking to my mother, he says, "Let's take a minute to calm down," and turning to me he says, "Go upstairs, ok?"

I'm about to do just that when he adds, "And Sarah, I never want to hear you speak to your mother that way again, is that understood?"

Flip and inconsiderate, I shrug as I turn back and waltz past them. Stopping to grab my keys, I turn them over in my hand, see the logo for my shiny new import, and then drop them back on the entryway table. I don't want her thinking I need one single thing from them.

Down the road I'll look back on this exact moment and regret it. I'll wish I could take back the words. But that's a fool's game because once spoken, there's no going back. And there are no words of apology that will ever erase the hurt I cause when I land my parting shot.

"Well, you're not my father and she is *not* my mother, so that won't be too difficult."

Chapter Twenty

LIAM

"You're sure you want to do this?"

"You've asked me three times already and we haven't even left New Jersey."

"You don't look sure, that's all."

"I'll never be sure, might as well just go for it, right? I mean, when will it ever be the *right* time?" She turns to face me. "But can you swing this? Tell me the truth."

"Got no job, remember? I'm free as a bird." I squeeze her hand when I see she's now looking out the passenger-side window. "Hey, I was going for humor. And I do still have my shifts at Dunes, as far as I know, so I'm good. And by the way, none of this is on you."

"It's *all* on me. My club, my friends, my boyfriend—"

"Ex, correct?"

She laughs for the first time. "Oh, you can't *get* more ex than he is." The smile drops as she looks down to her lap. "But I am sorry, Liam. I'm sorry they did this to you. And sorry most of all for what my mother said back there. I don't know why I feel the need to defend her right now but she's not an awful person. I seriously can't believe she said all that crap."

Not an awful person? I'm thinking to myself that her mother is one class-A bitch, but don't voice that opinion. "I don't really care what she thinks."

"You absolutely shouldn't, but when people judge you, it hurts. You can say that it doesn't, but it does."

"It's not the first time and it won't be the last."

She looks to me and nods, and I'm grateful for her honesty. There's certainly no need to sugar coat it.

"Are you sure—"

I cut her off when I can sense she's about to ask the same question for the umpteenth time. "Yes, I'm in. I love road trips."

She smirks. "Been on a lot of spontaneous road trips, have you?"

"This is actually my second one, and I've got high expectations. The last one was a bust."

I'm not sure if she remembers what trip I'm referring to until she says, "I'm hoping you can write an essay with a happy ending this time."

When we pass a sign for a service station, she says, "Mind if we stop? I could use some caffeine."

"Sure."

"Should I call home?" she asks, looking uncertain.

"Uh," I look to the dashboard clock, "we haven't been gone that long, but maybe you should. Your father looked all right but your mom looked pretty rattled when you all went back inside the house."

"She deserves to sweat it out for a little while longer."

"What happened in there? I mean, I could see she wasn't

too happy with me dropping you off, but how did it go from that to the epic quest we're on now?"

Sarah is looking to reassure me when she says, "It has nothing to do with you," but she's not convincing.

I'd say it had everything to do with me. I practically jumped out of my skin when her mother banged on the window and then screeched like a banshee until Sarah got out of the car.

It's weird. They're not biologically connected, but they do share a lot of the same mannerisms. When they were facing off in the driveway, they looked like mirror images of one another with their fingers pointed in accusation and heads cocked to the side. They don't share any physical traits, but there are similarities that I wouldn't dare point out to her right now.

"I overheard my parents talking once. Apparently, my grandparents didn't think my father was good enough for my mother. Which is hilarious, being that he basically saved their house from foreclosure a few years after they were married."

"Your father wasn't good enough?" I laugh. "I don't stand a chance then, do I?"

"My grandparents wanted their only daughter married off to someone from an established family, and from money, of course."

I nod as if I'm in total agreement. "Of course."

"My father's star was already on the rise but they turned their nose up at him because he was from Queens, can you imagine?"

"I've never been to Queens."

"My dad's parents passed away a while ago, so we haven't been there in years, but I used to love visiting. The area he's from basically has every nationality represented within a square mile. They seriously have the best restaurants."

"Do you have cousins?"

"My parents are both only children like yours truly."

"Actually, we're not sure if you're an only child or not." And I regret the words as soon as they're spoken because Sarah goes pale as I cut the engine.

"I didn't even consider that. Oh my God, I probably do have siblings. Shit, I can't just crash into her life! What if her kids hate me?"

"Hold up. This is just a fact-finding mission, right? We'll see where the road takes us. Nothing is written in stone."

I fill up while she's in the convenience store. Staring at my pre-paid debit card, I estimate that I've got around twelve hundred dollars between what's left on here and the money stashed at my uncle's house. I won't be getting any more paychecks from the club, so I'll really be missing the cash I make from the bar.

"I'll be back for my shift on Friday, so it's just Wednesday I need covered." I give Sarah the *just a minute* sign when she gets back in the car and goes to hand me a cup. "No, that was just some bullshit. Some assholes from the country club stole some shit for one of their house parties and tried to pin in on the staff. Wait, did someone come around asking?"

We hang up after I assure my sister that all is good and my name is cleared. It *will* be cleared but I'm not getting into the whole story while Sarah is sitting a foot away from me looking like she's on the verge of tears again.

"What happened?"

"Lorraine said two guys came to Dunes asking about the missing stuff and the manager told them off when they implied he was buying stolen goods." I look to her smiling. "Guess what is not, and has never been on the menu at Dunes?"

Sarah rolls her eyes but then she's smiling like a loon. "Lobster?"

I nod as we pull back out onto the highway. "Parker isn't the sharpest tool in the shed, is he?"

"No, but he's got life skills for sure. He can charm and weasel his way out of many situations. Take yours, for example. He won't get in trouble unless we take him on."

There's expectation in her tone, but I am so done with this. "I know what you're thinking but you're wrong. I'm not bowing down or backing down from him. Fighting over this is like giving oxygen to a fire, you make it more than it is, and I'm just over it."

"I'm not going to badger you because I can kind of see you point, but I want you vindicated. I want them to apologize."

"Who...Parker, or Mr. Thomson and the rest of the board?"

"All of them."

"Thomson already knows he was wrong. I'd like him to apologize to my uncle but I won't be holding my breath on that one. And Parker? He knows I think he's a piece of shit. I'm satisfied with that."

She's chewing on her thumbnail when she mutters, "My parents owe you a massive apology."

"Uh..."

They certainly do.

I thought her father was different, but I read him wrong. In the end, money sticks with money. Her mom? I don't see her opinion of me changing and I don't care. I smile to myself thinking about the look on her face this morning.

"What are you thinking about right now?"

"Oh, just that your mom was probably appalled by my vehicle. She's going to want to take you somewhere to get decontaminated when we get back."

Sarah throws her head back and laughs. "Oh, she wouldn't

step foot in this car…Definitely gives off the hillbilly vibe." She quickly amends, "No offense."

I lift my elbow off the center console and let the top rise up like Count Dracula's coffin at daybreak. "I kind of hated this car myself until I found out it's a classic." In response to her dubious expression, I add, "No shit, I've been stopped at red lights and had people ask if I was willing to sell."

"For real?"

"They don't make these anymore, sweetheart. They're getting to be a collector's item. Car buffs are all over the internet trying to get their hands on this model. This wouldn't go for as much as an El Camino, but '79 was the last year Ford produced Rancheros, so they're rare."

"So this car is over forty years old? How is that even possible?"

I caress the scuffed dashboard. "Lots of tender loving care."

"So you can fix this car if it breaks down, right?"

"Don't worry, she's in mint condition. Mint-ish, I should say. And yes, I can fix it most of the time."

"Does it come naturally to you? Mechanics, I mean?"

I shake my head because I already know where this is going. "Are you about to extol the benefits of me going to college and majoring in Engineering?"

"Damn, am I that obvious?"

"Yeah," I look away from the road to her, "you are."

"I'm sorry, I just…"

"I have a plan, Sarah. I'm not some aimless guy planning to scrape by for the rest of my life."

"So let's hear it." She rests her head back and closes her eyes for a moment. "It'll take my mind off what's potentially at the end of this road we're on."

I'm about to assure her that all will be good in the end,

nothing to worry about, but that's a crock. And while I'm not exactly beaming with pride about my plans, distracting Sarah wins out over my discomfort.

"I took the college boards in May, and—"

"Wait," she perks up, turning to face me, "you're going to graduate?"

"I took the GED last year. Technically, I graduated from high school before you did."

"OK," she nods her head to encourage me, "go on."

"I'm signing up for community college in September, then after I get my associates degree I'm hoping to get a scholarship so I can finish college somewhere far, far away from here."

"You don't like it here?"

"I don't hate it. I like living by the water, I like spending time with my family...I just can't stand my mom's husband. He's," I consider the best way to describe Jeff and what he means to me, "like this constant, nagging presence in my life. An absolute zero who wants to convince me I'm even more of a loser than he is."

She rests one hand on top of where mine sits on the gearshift. "I can't imagine what that's like. My parents certainly aren't perfect but they've always made me feel like *I* was perfect in their eyes."

"I'm thinking you were very...wanted."

"I guess so. I mean, why else would you adopt unless you wanted a child?"

"Well, Jeff wanted to legally adopt me when I was around twelve, so not all adoptions are the same."

"I'm guessing he didn't because your name is Murphy."

"I don't have my biological father's name either," I fix her with a look, "which is fine by me. When Jeff came up with his asinine idea, I begged my mom not to do it. I threatened to run away. He's so lazy, I doubt he ever would have mustered up the effort to get it done anyway."

"Your uncle was probably more of a father figure to you than either one of them, so it's fitting that you're a Murphy."

"Exactly."

There is no other name I'd accept as my own. I don't tell Sarah how often I've wished that Dan and Maeve were my real parents and that I grew up in their house. I love my mother and I love Lorraine, but my life would have been so different.

"Now that I know her name, I can't help but imagine what my life would have been like if…"

I fill in the void. "The great what if…You'll never know. And speaking of knowing her name, what else did you dig up?"

She opens her phone's picture app. "Not much else. Only her name is listed on the birth certificate with her date of birth. She was twenty years old."

"She didn't name the father?"

Sarah looks straight ahead and shakes her head.

"All right. Grace Dawson, twenty years old when the lovely Sarah was born, last known address in Durham, North Carolina. So what does that tell us?"

"Maybe she went to Duke?"

"A definite possibility."

"But NC State, UNC and Wake Forest are all nearby, too. And there's a good chance she wasn't in school."

"True. And if she wasn't in school, there's a decent chance she'll still be in the area."

"Ugh," she groans, "I'm probably taking you on a wild goose chase, aren't I?"

"A fact-finding mission. Even if she's not there, we'll get a lead."

"Maybe this is a mistake."

"What?"

"I'm just saying that when I turn eighteen in August I'll have legal access to the adoption records. Maybe I should just wait."

"Hold up. You're not eighteen yet?" She starts to giggle. "I believe I *worked* your eighteenth birthday party."

"Audrey thought it would be best to surprise me a few months early because I never would have been on board with a party, and she also figured most of my friends would have left for college by the time my actual birthday rolled around in August."

"That's weird. You do realize that, don't you?"

"Yes, but she definitely achieved the element of surprise."

"It's like throwing a graduation party at the end of junior year."

"Or an anniversary party before you get married."

"Or a funeral before you croak."

Now we're both laughing, which is obviously better than the alternative.

"Thinking back on it, you did look kind of sick when you first walked into all that hoopla."

Sarah nods. "I was baffled, then pissed. She ambushed me like that last year, too." Looking to her lap, she says, "I don't like extra attention aimed my way, and she knows that. She's not mean and she doesn't do it to torture me, but it can feel that way. I think my mother really believes she's helping me to," Sarah air quotes, "come out of my shell." Looking my way she adds, "But I'm not a social butterfly like her. That woman can work a room, and people have always just gravitated towards her. She's interesting, she can be funny...I don't know, people naturally like her. We're different."

"You don't think people like you?"

Sarah levels me with a look. "Well, I thought Penny was a genuine friend...and I took Parker at his word, too. And up until last year, Penny was my *only* friend."

"Usually I'd say one good friend is worth a hundred acquaintances, but in Penny's case..."

"Yeah."

"Tell me about the seventeenth birthday bash. Wait, no, let me guess...A spa day with your besties? A weekend jaunt to Paris for some shopping? I'm sure no expense was spared."

"Stop it, you jackass." She's smiling, so I know my teasing didn't go too far. "My mother let me know about it two weeks before, which is definitely why she took the surprise route this time around." Her eyes are wicked when she says, "I basically made her life a living hell for two weeks."

"How so?"

"It wasn't intentional. I was legitimately freaking out. You don't take an introverted kid and invite a bunch of girls and trap them on a bus with you for twelve hours straight...Girls who didn't even acknowledge me up until then."

"Sounds pretty awkward."

"I was back and forth between being sick to my stomach and wanting to kill her."

"How did it turn out?"

She shrugs. "While I'd love to say she was one hundred percent wrong, it did kind of set me up with a few more friends for my senior year. And Tatiana, Clara, Penny and I are," she stops herself, "I mean, we *were* tight." She rubs her temples, working out what she's about to say. "Aside from wanting Parker to evaporate these past few months, I felt like a," she looks unsure of her next words, "social success this past year. Does that make sense?"

"Social success? I don't know. Sometimes I think girls put

more weight on stuff like that. I'm definitely not someone who's ever been at the center of it, but I've never wanted to be."

"But that's what I've always told myself, too. Do you think that's more of a defense mechanism than the truth?"

I mull that one over for a bit. "I don't like what I see when I look at the quote-unquote popular kids, in your crowd or in mine. I feel, I don't know, older than them, or alien. But I see your point, that you kind of put them down in your mind so that you don't have to think about why you're not one of them. Still, I've always had Mike and that's enough for me."

"What's his story?"

"He's a good friend. He can be a dumbass sometimes, like when he sucks up to people like Logan. He doesn't recognize when he's being used, which doesn't make *him* a bad person. Let's just say he's way more optimistic and trusting than yours truly."

"So he's your ride or die?"

I never liked that expression. "Are those the only two viable options?"

She shrugs. "It's just nice when you have someone you can depend on."

"Yeah...I can depend on him."

We're quiet most of the way through Virginia, and Sarah nods off for a bit. She's awake when I come out from paying for gas and gets out of the car to stretch while I'm filling the tank.

"Some co-pilot I am," she says on a yawn.

"Right? For all I know we could be heading towards California right now." I look her way just as she's reaching up overhead, which makes her cropped shirt ride up to the point where her entire torso is exposed, right up to where the band of her white bra is resting. The sight makes me disoriented for a second. When I cough she looks to me with concern, but I recover well. "Who needs you when I've got my phone?"

"My dad always says stuff like, 'When I was your age we'd have a map stretched out across the entire front seat.'"

"I have to agree that we do have it pretty easy as far as navigation goes."

"Where are we, anyway?"

"We just crossed over into North Carolina. Says we have around an hour to go." She looks green all of a sudden. "You all right?"

"I didn't think we were so close."

"Yeah."

"Should I use the bathroom here?" Sarah looks behind her to the convenience mart, which is pretty rundown.

"If you aren't desperate, we'll definitely be able to find a place when we get there."

"Someplace slightly cleaner, maybe better lit?"

"Yeah, this does give off a *Deliverance* vibe."

"Never saw that one."

"Me neither. I just know it's a cultural reference for a place you don't want to be."

"I'd ask if you want me to take the wheel but I can't drive shift."

"My uncle swears everyone should have that in their life skills toolbox, but since there are hardly any manual cars around I look at it as more of a lost art than a necessary skill. And it works to my advantage because no one can ask to borrow this beauty."

"You're a glass half-full kinda guy after all."

"Ha...You're the first person to accuse me of that."

Chapter Twenty-One

SARAH

I've been watching the dashboard clock count down to our ETA the way I imagine a special forces operative watches the timer on a detonator.

What was I thinking, just taking off without a plan? This is crazy. I set off like a badass, intent on getting answers, and now I'm praying to God this woman who gave birth to me doesn't answer when we arrive on her doorstep.

"Darling Drive," he says as we take the exit for Durham off the highway. "I'd say it's definitely a nice place but I live on Misty Harbor Lane and I'm not that close to the water."

"Yeah, let's hope for a darling, though, ok?"

"Oh, I'm 'a hoping, I'm 'a praying..."

I can feel my heart begin to race when we pull up outside a townhouse that sits amid several identical two-story structures. He must sense my unease because he reaches over and takes my hand, stroking his thumb over the top. It's soothing, and makes me realize that Liam is, if nothing else, my friend.

"Thanks."

"For what?"

"For coming along on this crazy ride, and for...everything."

"You got it." He looks away when he adds, "No place else I'd rather be."

"So, what do you think of this place?"

"Looks like it could be students, but there's a mix," he says, taking note as a middle-aged couple walks by holding hands. After waiting a beat during which I make no move to get out of the car, he says, "Shall we?"

"Yeah, I guess." But when we get to the door, I can't do it. "You knock, all right? And you ask for her. I mean, she knows she had a daughter, so if you knock we won't get a door slammed in our faces."

"Let's expect a positive reception."

"Expect the best, prepare for the worst."

Liam pats my head like I'm his puppy. "That's the spirit, Tiny."

I break into a cold sweat when the door opens and a girl answers. She's young, looks to be around nine-ish, and I instinctively move my body halfway behind Liam, hiding myself from someone who very well may be my little sister.

Liam says, "Hi, we're looking for someone named Grace Dawson. Does she live here?"

The little girl looks him up and down and then slams the door as she hollers, "Mom, there's someone at the door!"

"Oh my God," I whisper-scream as Liam takes hold of my wrist to keep me from bolting.

"Relax, Sarah. It's going to be ok."

And for some reason I believe him, so I'm standing in the same spot when a beautiful but tired-looking woman holding a sleeping infant opens the door.

Liam speaks softly when he says, "Sorry for bothering you."

"It's fine." She shakes her head looking behind her with a smile. "I've told her a thousand times not to open the door to strangers, but she's got a mind of her own. What can I do for you?"

Liam is about to answer when I pipe up, "Are you Grace Dawson?"

"No," the woman answers, her expression curious.

"Oh, sorry," I say, tugging on Liam's sleeve, fully aware that I'm acting like a lunatic but unable to calm myself. "Let's get going."

"Whoa, hold up," he says before turning back to the woman. "We just had this listed as a last known address, but to be honest, it's from a long time ago."

She takes us in for a moment, and ultimately decides we pass the *probably not serial killers* test. "We've been here for around eighteen months. My husband is in grad school. It's a pretty transient place."

Liam says, "Lots of students, I bet."

"Students, younger faculty," she answers, nodding.

"Any idea who rents the place out? Maybe they'd be able to help."

"Hang on a sec." She turns her head, "Maeve, get mommy's phone from the kitchen counter, ok?"

Liam smiles. "My aunt's name is Maeve."

To which she says, "My mother's name, too." After scrolling for a minute, she holds the phone towards us, and I momentarily break out of my coma to take a picture of the contact for a realty company.

"Thank you."

I'm sure it's all in my head, but it's as if this stranger knows why we're looking for Grace Dawson when she gives me a soft smile. "I hope you find her."

Liam is all business when we get back in the car. "Hey, it's almost five. Let's call just in case the office is about to close."

I can see that it's only a few blocks away. "Wait, it's like two minutes from here. Let's just go."

He pats my knee. "Get 'er done...That's my girl."

My girl? I like the sound of that, but make a joke to avoid what's sure to be an awkward moment. "You are such a nerd."

I spend the next couple of minutes navigating him towards the address, which is another identical looking townhouse. The only difference is a sign that reads: *Fulton Realty* in the front window.

I'm not half as nervous now, and I know it's because that somewhere deep-down, I'm hoping to hit a dead end, and I'd say the odds are pretty low that Fulton Realty is going to give us any meaningful intel.

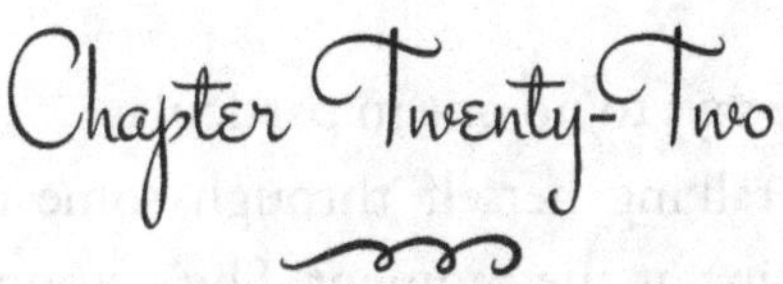

LIAM

"I don't know about you, but I think the fact that she left a forwarding address is a really good sign."

Sarah is looking green again. She was back to easy-breezy when we knocked on the realtor's door, to the point that she was cracking jokes while the realtor did us a solid by agreeing to go through her father's files.

"He has records on his tenants from that far back?" she asked, her voice suddenly high-pitched and wary.

Our new friend rolled her eyes. "You should see his house. He has every National Geographic magazine from 1968 to the present. I shouldn't complain because he's still sharp as a tack, but it's...a lot."

While she went back to look through the file cabinets, Sarah started pacing the room while wringing her hands.

"Don't stress, all right? Even if we hit the jackpot, doesn't mean we have to go."

She's clearly relived I offered up that alternative. Her tone is a tad too hopeful when she asks, "And I'm sure you have to get back for work, right?"

"Like I said, I'm technically down to one job, and no, I don't have to be back at Dunes until my shift on Friday. I have time."

"Right," she says to no one in particular.

I bet she's talking herself through some deep breathing meditation routine at the moment. She's stopped pacing, but her breaths are going in deep and coming out in a controlled, slow manner. I'm about to comment on it but decide it's best to let her be.

And whatever she did must have worked, because she surprises me when the woman comes out with a slim manila envelope. Sarah is typing something into her phone, barely listening to the woman at first, but I nod attentively as she tells us what she's found. And we both close in when she produces a handwritten note from Grace Dawson to her father, thanking him for being such a good landlord—odd—but then there's a line at the end with the explicit instruction to give this forwarding address to anyone who comes looking for her. The word anyone is underlined twice.

Her mother wants to be found.

Sarah's eyes well as the realization hits her, too. She looks to me with a watery smile. "Have you ever been to Hopwood, Pennsylvania?"

Back in the car, she puts her hand on mine. "Seriously, it's another seven hours. I can't ask you to do this for me."

"You didn't ask, I offered. Really," I say when she doesn't look convinced, "I'm not even tired. I'm hungry, but I'm fine to keep driving."

So after taking the realtor's advice to stop at a place that makes the *best barbecue in the country,* we get back in the car to plot our next move.

"You can't tell me you're not tired after that feast."

In truth, I'd like to pass out because I'm so stuffed, but I lie. "I'm fine. That was great, and thanks for treating."

Sarah waves me off. "You haven't let me chip in for gas, so we're still not even close to even."

Now I'll feel the need to be all gentleman-like and insist on filling the tank for the rest of the trip, whereas I might have let her chip in, seeing as we're heading pretty far west from home.

I change the subject to get my mind off my pitiful finances. "Those ribs were awesome, but would you tag them as *best in the country?*"

I think everyone from Texas, Louisiana, Georgia, the Carolinas—"

"Like everyone in the South, you're saying."

"Yes. They *all* think they have the best barbecue."

"Just like New Yorkers think they have the only edible pizza on the East Coast?"

"Exactly. They're so obnoxious about their pizza."

"And their bagels...Don't even get me started."

She winces. "I'm going to concede that one point to them. They do have better bagels. There's something about the water. It's like a proven fact."

"I've never had one but I'm gonna call bullshit."

"You've never had a New York bagel, so you can't weigh in."

"You've been to New York, does the water taste different?"

"Uh, wait, you've never been to New York? Like *never*?" I guess I should be embarrassed by my lack of world experience, but in front of her, I'm not. When I shake my head, she says, "Then that *has* to be our next epic adventure. As soon as we get back we're riding the train into Manhattan, having bagels for breakfast and pizza for lunch."

"I'm in. Um, speaking of getting home, are you going to check in with them? It's getting dark, so maybe..."

"Yeah, I guess I should."

"I'm going to stretch, maybe take a walk around the block."

She nods, so I know she's grateful for the privacy. I'm doing this for her, but it's also for me. If my name comes up— which I'm sure it will—I don't want to hear what her parents have to say. I've already been shit on enough times this week.

She's leaning on the hood, typing into her phone when I come back ten minutes later. Acting like there's nothing to report, she says, "So if you're truly up for this, it's a seven-hour drive, which will land us in Pennsylvania at around four in the morning."

"Sounds like a plan. We can park a little ways from the address and close our eyes until the sun comes up."

"Or grab a coffee and hold off on wrecking this woman's life until at least seven-thirty or eight."

"See, you're always coming up with good ideas."

I start the car and get myself off the local streets before I ask how it went.

"Um, my mother was kind of frantic when I said I'd be home tomorrow, but my dad was ok about it."

"That's it? Did thy ask where you were, what you're doing, who you're with?"

She looks at me and ticks off one finger for each as she answers, "Yes, yes and yes."

"I'm kind of dying of suspense, but talk when you're ready."

"I cut to the chase. Told them I was sorry for what I said as

I was walking out the door." She senses me turning my head in question and raises her palm in a *don't ask* gesture. "It was a rotten thing to say. Anyway, I told them I've known about being adopted for a few months and I was pretty mad they've kept it from me. I also told them where we are, and they kind of put two and two together."

"What did they say?"

"My mother was crying so hard I could barely understand what she was saying." And Sarah is speaking through her own tears when she says, "I know they're both sorry. I'm not even mad at them. I mean, I guess I am, but I don't want them thinking I'm looking for my real parents so that I can ditch them." Looking to me, she emphasizes, "They *are* my real parents."

"Did you tell them that?"

"More or less. I told them this is something I have to do, and it's something I want to do on my own."

"And they were ok with me...with you?"

"I know my father doesn't dislike you." When she sees me raise an eyebrow, she says, "He's on your side, I know it. He has a lot of respect for your uncle, and he knows you had nothing to do with stealing from the club. When I asked him what was happening, he brushed me off, said we'd talk when I get home. My mom *was* crying in the background, so..."

"Honestly, I couldn't care less if your dad thinks I'm innocent, or anyone else for that matter."

"I care. I care what my parents think, what Thomson believes...I care what the world thinks about you."

"But don't you get it? Why am I even *in* this position? I have to prove my innocence? No one would ever *dare* accuse a kid like Parker of theft. Parker, or Logan? They'd have to walk right by Thomson with a case of lobster in hand, and even then, he'd probably assume they were authorized to take it. People like me, though...the help? It's just assumed that we're guilty." Now I'm riled up, so I press the point. "Someone has to *prove* Parker is guilty, because he's presumed innocent, while *I* have to prove I'm innocent. It's fucked up."

"I agree with you."

"And what's more? Those jackasses at the club will conveniently forget about this little dust up once they find out who stole all that stuff."

"I'm not like them."

"I know you're not. And I'm just pissed off, I didn't mean to raise my voice like that."

"It's all right." She looks to me with eyes that softens my hard edges. "I can take it."

Chapter Twenty-Three

SARAH

"So, we have two options, we can head back exactly the way we came, then veer west when we hit Pennsylvania, or we can take the scenic route and drive through West Virginia. It's basically the same in terms of time."

"You're driving, so what's your preference?" I ask him.

"I've never ventured past Ocean City, Maryland, so any direction we take will be a new adventure for me."

It hits me again, same as when he told me without a hint of shame that he'd never been to New York, which is just a quick forty-minute ride on the train. It highlights our differences. It's not normal, but I tell myself it's not ridiculously abnormal either. It's just that *my* life isn't normal. To have just about every page in your passport stamped by the age of seventeen is weird.

"I can practically hear those gears grinding," he says with a chuckle. "Don't feel bad, Tiny. I'll get to all those great places you've already seen someday."

"Well, I've never been to West Virginia, so let's take the scenic route."

He shoots me a warm look. "West Virginia, here we come."

"Poor West Virginia, our trip reviews will be highlighting a series of drive-through windows and restrooms."

"And we're going to be in the pitch dark for most of it." He taps his phone to look at the list of directions. "Make that all of it." Pulling out of the lot, he says, "Adios, North Carolina, it's been real."

"Do you need some coffee before we get back on the highway?"

"I don't drink coffee, but I'll stop for a soda in an hour or two."

"So tell me about Ocean City, Maryland."

He side eyes me. "Have you ever been?" and then nods in a knowing way when I shake my head. "Too low-brow, am I right?"

I brush him off, when in reality, it is probably the last place on Earth I could picture my family vacationing. "We have a perfectly beautiful beach close to home, don't we?"

"I was just teasing." He looks out his window for a beat. "Or maybe avoiding the topic...Not sure which."

"If you don't want to talk about it, it's fine."

"Ah, fuck it, who cares. It's a tale as old as time. Deadbeat dad calls on occasion, always promising to come see his kid but flaking out whenever plans are made. Then shows up one day out of the blue and says, 'How'd you like to take a trip with your Dad?' At first I was like, 'No thanks, I'm good'." He catches my eye before looking back to the road. "Mind you, I'm ten years old and I've met the guy twice. I wasn't really eager to jump in a stranger's car."

"Your mom was cool with him taking you?"

He nods. "She's a pretty relaxed individual, but I get your point."

"So what was the conversation like? Was it awkward as hell?"

"No, I don't remember feeling awkward, but I do recall wanting to make a very good impression on him."

"So he'd stick around?"

"Or maybe realize what he'd been missing out on...Who knows? So I told him I was making straight A's, that I won the science fair for my grade that year...I was selling myself big time."

"What was his reaction?"

"He told me those were his genes at work." Smirking, Liam says, "Apparently he was top of his class in *every* subject, the best pitcher his hometown had ever seen, fastest runner on his track team...You get the idea. And I'm mesmerized, like, he's my new hero, you know?"

I'm thinking Liam's father is an ass, but I keep that to myself. "I'm sure there's some truth to the intelligence part, because you're smart, but he sounds like," I look to him with an apology in my eyes, "a child."

I'm relieved when he seems to agree. "Yeah, it took me a few years to work that out."

He's quiet, and I study his profile, silently willing him to go on. I want more, I want to know everything, so I feel rewarded a moment later when he decides to go on. "The whole way down he's talking about the ferris wheel, the great candy shops and ice cream parlors on the boardwalk. And the guy is always talking in superlatives." He puts on a voice that's not his own. "It's *the* best. No, you *think* you've had ice cream before, but you've probably only had store-bought crap. The place *I'm* bringing you to has *actual* peaches in their peach ice cream."

He frowns. "I was trying to act interested, but even back then I was thinking: *Big deal, I've had homemade peach ice cream before.* Every sentence started with *I* or *my*, and everything was the *best*, the *fastest* or the *biggest*."

"So what was it like?"

He shrugs. "Well, it *looks* like an awesome place. The boardwalk has loads of places to eat, good junk like cotton candy, ice cream, hot dogs—"

"Ugh, I'm still too full to hear about food."

"Truth. I could barf just thinking about eating right now." He's still smiling when he says, "From a kid's perspective, the place looked magical, but it was March and nothing was open."

My eyes go wide. "He took you off-season?" And now my heart is breaking, picturing Liam as a kid, walking down a deserted boardwalk on a gray, blustery day with every storefront shuttered.

"Yep, Mr. Rhodes Scholar didn't figure the beachside attractions would be closed for business in the winter."

"Jeez."

"I know, right? And by the time I could look back on it, really examine it, you know?" He looks to me and nods. "Then I felt sorry for the guy. Which is pretty generous of me if I do say so myself, being as I spent most of our father-son bonding trip holed up in a booth in a bar while he played pool."

I have a clear visual in my head of the scene, and it's so sad that I ache for him. I don't look directly at him, but rest my left hand on top of his and gaze at the way my fingers naturally fall into the gaps between his much larger hand. Liam flips his hand over after a moment, inviting me, I think, to fully slip into his hold. When I do, I feel him let out the breath he's been holding as I do the same.

"I want to read that essay someday."

"He tore it up."

"What?"

"The teacher tore it up in front of my entire class. But I dug it out of the garbage, remnants of kids gum and God knows what else on it, and I taped that sucker back together. I'm not even sure why I kept it."

"I'm glad you did."

"Why? I mean, does it matter? And couldn't one argue that it's better to let go of the painful shit from our pasts?"

I see his point, but I'm kind of desperate to know as much as I can about Liam. I've never been as close to anyone—my friends, my one crappy excuse for a boyfriend, my parents—as I feel to him, a guy I've known for a ridiculously short period of time.

"Your father, for as absent as he was, is a major part of your story. Maybe he's not a part of your life, but he's a part of your history the same way Grace is a part of mine. Even if I never get to meet her." After a quiet moment, I add, "I want to read it so I can know you better. I think you're pretty fascinating."

He doesn't answer, but doesn't let go of my hand either.

"I don't like this," he says as we pull into a truck stop.

"It looks all right," I say, even though the area does look sketchy. It's three hours into our drive now, and I have one seriously full bladder. "I don't think I can hold off much longer, Liam."

"Fine. Wait," he commands when I go to exit the car in a hurry. "I'm coming inside with you and parking my ass right outside the door to the ladies' room." I roll my eyes even though I'm grateful, and sort of happily dumbstruck over his desire to protect me.

"Stay close to me," he says, taking my hand as we enter the convenience mart. The fluorescent lights are harsh, highlighting the haggard face of the woman working the register, a teenager who looks at items in the snack aisle while surreptitiously casing the store, and an older trucker fixing himself a coffee.

And I take the quickest pee ever, hovering over a seat that looks like urine droplets from dozens of different women have been intermingling on its surface for weeks. There are small mounds of wet toilet paper strewn about, with one used sanitary napkin barely wadded up with paper before being tossed to the ground. People can be so gross.

I make the universal facial expression for *eww* as I exit and make eye contact with Liam, and he just shakes his head laughing. Tipping my chin in the direction of the mens' room, I say, "You'll see. I am not being a princess right now."

"Can't be that bad. Stay put, I'll be thirty seconds, tops."

"Aye, aye, Captain." I do wander back into the food mart, grabbing a seltzer for myself and a soda for him.

Maybe fifteen seconds have passed when he's right behind me. "I told you to stay put!"

"I'm like, twenty paces from where you left me. I'm not exactly roaming around taking in the scenery. So, what's your poison?" I ask, holding up a ginger ale in one hand and one of those energy drinks that look like they would rot your insides in the other.

"Water is good...Maybe some licorice, too." He answers my question before I can even ask. "I'm not tired."

After grabbing chips, licorice, gummy bears, and two bottles of water, we get back in the car and take a moment to look at the GPS and sort out the rest of our journey.

"Once we get on I-79 we've got around two hours to go. That should land us there at—"

I jump in my seat when some dude raps on my window and makes a gesture for me to lower it down. And I don't know why, but I do it on command. That's the female gender's downfall, I think. We're too polite.

"Nice car," the guy says, looking to Liam. "My brother collects 'em."

"Cool," Liam answers back without any enthusiasm.

"Ever be looking to sell it?"

"Never," he says, "but thanks. You have a good night."

He rolls up my window from his side, shaking his head once the guy is a few feet away.

"Rules of the road...No talking to anyone you encounter at a truck stop after dark. Can we agree on that?"

I'm in full agreement on that one, so I nod my head. "I don't know why I did that."

"You trust people, I don't."

"Well, I didn't exactly believe you talking about this car like it's a sought-after classic, but your buddy there just proved me wrong."

He laughs. "*And* you went and showed off the power window feature. Now he knows this is the high-end model."

"Well, like you said, it's not, and never will be for sale," I lovingly caress the dashboard the same way he did yesterday, "so he can't get his hands on this baby."

"Unless he follows us into the night, shoots out the back tires, carves us to bits and effectively takes ownership the hard way."

"Damn, you watch a little too much true crime television or something?"

"Never. I imagine that crap would give you nightmares, not to mention a tragically skewed view of the world."

"Tragically skewed," I pause and then settle back into the seat as I rest my bare feet on the dashboard, "you have an awesome vocabulary."

"That turns you on?"

"Oh yeah, baby. Big time. Go on, slay me with your description of West Virginia."

"No joke? Before the sun completely set I thought it was one of the most beautiful...No," he pauses to laugh, "*majestic* sights I've ever seen. Who knew? They're just mountains, right?"

"Same. It's so vast, so beautiful. It's like when you see a field of tulips or hear birds calling to one another in the morning. This kind of beauty affirms my belief in God." I inwardly cringe for a moment, hoping I didn't just come off like a weirdo or a sap. Clearing my throat, I ask him, "Hey, are we in the Blue Ridge Mountains or the Appalachians?"

"At the risk of ruining your high opinion of me, I have no idea which mountain range we're in."

I look to him, wide-eyed. "Liam Murphy doesn't know something? I'm appalled. No wait, I now have a tragically skewed opinion of you."

"You, are a wiseass."

"Admit it, Murphy, you love it."

"I certainly don't hate it."

And I'll take that with a smile because he's letting me in slowly, letting me discover him, piece by fascinating piece.

Chapter Twenty-Four

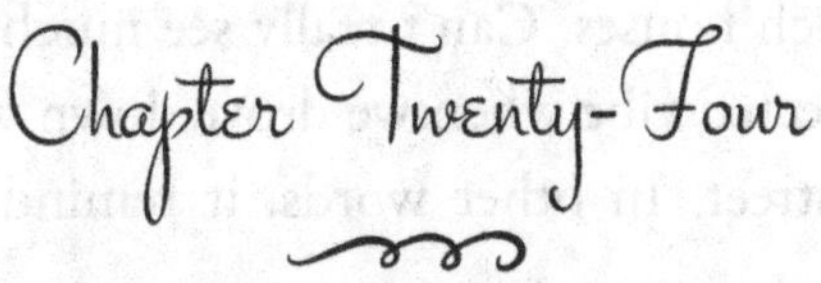

LIAM

"Look alive, Sarah." I toot the horn as she rubs the sleep from her eyes. "Welcome to Pennsylvania."

My plan was to just keep driving, to find a spot close to the address and get some shut eye until daybreak, but I thought she might freak if her first sight was this lady's house number.

As she combs both hands through her hair, she says, "Sorry. How long have I been asleep for?"

"Not too long, two hours maybe? Seriously, you can close your eyes again. Says we'll be arriving in twenty minutes but we can't be knocking on the door for a few more hours anyway."

"No, I'm up. I'm good," she says, fishing a ponytail holder out of her shorts pocket. Pulling down the mirror, she asks, "Think we could scout out a restroom before we get there?"

"Absolutely."

I'm doing my best to be upbeat and cheery, because I sense Sarah might be starting to freak out.

She looks grateful when she smiles back at me, which

almost makes me tear up with the satisfaction of being, I don't know, worthwhile in her eyes. Fatigue, that's what I blame for the sappy state I'm currently in.

And it reads three a.m. when we finally pull down a street with small ranch houses. Can't really see much, but the town gave off a neglected vibe when we drove down what seemed to be the main street. In other words, it reminds me of home sweet home.

After about twenty minutes of frenetic, random commentary, I'm wishing I left Sarah sleeping before. "C'mere," I say as I lean back while pulling her into me and wrapping my arms around her front, "I need to shut my eyes for a few minutes."

"Oh, of course," she chirps, nestling right into me. "Get some rest."

"Hey there, buddy."

I startle to the muffled sound of a guy's voice and a light tap on my window. Damn, I was just in the middle of an extremely good dream, and as I sit up, I realize the dream was so good that I'm poking Sarah with some morning wood.

It takes me a minute to shift her off me, orient myself and lower my window. "Hey."

This guy looks super awake and super friendly. "You two lost or something?"

"Uh, no, just um…" *Should I get into it with this guy?* "Just looking for someone who maybe used to live around here."

Sarah rouses from her slumber and starts looking all freaked out and afraid when she catches sight of the guy.

He ducks down and looks across to her. "It's ok, hun." Looking back to me, he says, "Well, I've lived in this town my whole entire life, so if this person exists, I'll know 'em."

I give Sarah a moment to take the lead, but she stays quiet. "Grace Dawson? Does that name sound familiar?"

"I'll say!" And with that, a woman comes out the front door holding an infant with three other kids trailing behind. He calls over to her, "These two are looking for Grace Dawson."

I'm expecting him to wink or something, like there's a punchline coming, because now the two of them are smiling—like super happy, spanning the width of your face grins. And when I look to Sarah, I can see that her eyes are now fixed on the woman's belly, where upon further inspection, you can see that she's expecting.

"Oh my God," Sarah whispers, and I'm kind of shitting my pants now, too. My words from yesterday come back to haunt me: *You might not be an only child.*

I whisper, "She's too young, Sarah."

"How do *you* know?"

As I ponder that rhetorical question, I notice that two sets of hands are now pressed up against Sarah's window, taking her in like she's an exhibit at the zoo, another kid is clamoring to be picked up by this dude I presume is her dad, and the baby is starting to cry.

"Come on out," the mom gestures with that super friendly smile. "You two look like you could use some breakfast."

The mom ushers the kids away from the car so we can get out, and I'm thinking we must look a little shell-shocked, like we're aliens who've been kindly invited to disembark from the safety of the mothership.

Shifting her baby to the other hip, she offers Sarah her hand. "I'm Sienna," looking to the guy, she adds, "and this is my husband, Garth." Sarah lets out a relieved breath, which doesn't go unnoticed. "Grace is one of my very dear friends."

To which her husband adds, "Grace is the best. She was our English teacher in high school. I still call her Miss Dawson sometimes...Force of habit."

When an uncomfortable ten seconds pass while Sarah continues to imitate a statue, I pipe up. "Nice to meet you. I'm Liam Murphy and this is Sarah Hamilton."

The little boy who's now holding onto his mother's hand plucks his thumb out of his mouth to say, "You big and you tiny."

I fist bump him, soggy fingers and all, when I say, "That's what I call her...Tiny."

I'm glad to see that's Sarah's got the start of a smile going, and that she accepts when the woman asks her if we want to come inside for a minute.

Holy domestic bliss. That's what I'm thinking when we walk into their home. It smells like something really good is baking in the oven, there are toys everywhere, and the vibe is just so...home, sweet home. Taking it in, I chuckle when I see there's a sign with that very saying hanging above the mantle.

"Your home is beautiful," Sarah says, her tone indicating that she's loosening up, thank the Lord.

"Thanks," the mom says as she deftly steps over toys and a pile of books on her way to the kitchen. "Have a seat. These will be ready," she opens the oven and takes a whiff, "right now. Perfect!" Turning to a cutie who looks to be around three or four, she says, "Rose, grab some of that honey butter we made from the fridge, ok?"

I'm about to thank her and tell her she doesn't have to feed us, but the words die on my lips when I smell those muffins. And she makes her own honey butter? Sign. Me. Up.

"Oh, we're ok, you don't have to go to any trouble." And

the fact that I want to pinch and simultaneously shush Sarah speaks to how hungry I am.

"No, it's our pleasure. Any friends of Grace's are welcome here."

Her husband asks, "Are you—," but clams up when his wife shoots him a look that says: *stop talking*.

"So," I ask, "does Grace live here anymore?"

"Um, she sold us this house two years ago." But when the woman sees Sarah lower her head in response to this, she adds, "But she's not far from here."

"She's in Pittsburgh, hardly more than an hour north of here. She moved up there with—"

Again he gets the *shut your pie hole* look. Although I have to hand it to the wife, she delivers it with a whole lot of warmth, considering she's telling him to shut up.

"Did it take you long to get here?" the lady asks Sarah.

"Kinda."

I expand on her one-word answer. "The first address we had was in North Carolina, and from there we got this address."

"Hold up," the guy says, "so you've been on the road for like fourteen hours?"

I try and calculate it in my head. "Something like that."

"Do you want to sleep for a little bit? I'll call Grace. I know she'll be down here in a snap."

"No!" Sarah says this so loud that everyone whips around to look at her, and the baby, who was whimpering before, is now wailing. She's wide-eyed and sweating, looking around and clearly embarrassed.

Taking her hand in mine, I look to them both. "That's all right. We need to keep heading back up north, so maybe you could just give us her address?"

The woman, Sienna, smiles in an apologetic way and nods. "Sure. Garth, my hands are full. Can you text them the address."

The guy seems too easy-going to be crafty, so it's not lost on me when Sienna gestures her chin towards the cell phone on the table as he's reaching for the pencil tucked behind his ear. She wants a record of Sarah's phone number. It comes off like snooping, and I'm not sure I appreciate the intrusion, but I hold off just as I'm about to push the pencil and paper option. For some reason I trust them.

We say our goodbyes and head back to the car with a bag full of baked treats and bottles of water. Pulling away, I decide it's good that we're leaving a trail of breadcrumbs for Grace, just like Grace did for Sarah.

Chapter Twenty-Five

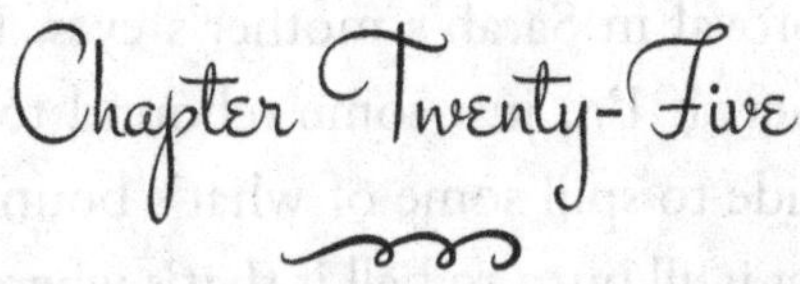

LIAM

"Thoughts?"

She answers, "They seemed really nice, right?"

"I may be biased because those were the best muffins I've ever tasted, but yeah, they were both very kind. Were you panicking there for a second—"

"Thinking I had four siblings? Oh, yeah."

"Aw, it's cute how you can finish my sentences." I'm teasing, but I've noticed that she does seem to have this weird ability to sense what I'm about to say.

She puts her hand to her forehead like she's channeling the realm from beyond. "I believe you're thinking something along the lines of: *It's a lot of work being friends with this girl.* Am I right?"

When I don't answer immediately, she looks to me with a cautious expression. "We *are* friends, aren't we?"

"Um, more or less." I can see this hurts her, which wasn't my intention. "I should say we're more *and* we're less."

And maybe it's simply pure exhaustion leading me down this road to my own ruin, because I just don't have the energy to tap dance around what we're doing. Between being accused of a felony, losing that crappy job, the pain on my uncle's face and the disapproval in Sarah's mother's eyes, I am all out of patience and tact. If I'm just some rebound to her, I need to know. So I decide to spill some of what's bouncing around in my head, and let it all burn to hell if that's where we're heading anyway.

"We're more because I want a repeat of the other night. I want to kiss you and I like how it feels when your hand is in mine." I pause before I say what might hurt her, or sever this still-fragile bond between us. "But we're less. I haven't spent much time with you and I don't know much about you."

"I'd say you know more about me than most people on the planet. Besides Parker, you're the only other person I told about being adopted. That says a lot, don't you think?"

"Yeah, can't say I like being lumped together with him in your circle of trust."

"If it makes you feel any better, I basically blurted it out when I was at my lowest."

"Same situation here, right?"

"What do you mean?"

I shake my head because Sarah is a smart girl. Does she really need me to spell this out for her? "It doesn't get much lower than finding out your boyfriend has been cheating on you...with your best friend. What role am I playing in this story?"

She side eyes me. "Are you looking for reassurance? You know I have feelings for you."

"How would I know that?"

"Um, because I said those *exact* words to you the other

night in the stable?" She pokes my side. When I glance over, I catch the blush creeping up her neck as she turns to face forward. "I also like how my hand feels in yours...A lot."

"Good."

And with that, she rests her hand on top of mine like she did last night. I'm thinking I like this a lot, too, when she lobs one at me.

"Who was your first?"

I cough to clear my already clear airway. "What?"

"You heard me. The other night I told you that I regret being with Parker." She slowly bangs head back against headrest once, then twice. Keeping her eyes fixed straight ahead, she says, "I can't believe he'll forever be a part of my history. Parker Hastings will always be my first."

"And now you want to know mine?"

"Just proving that you *do* know a whole lot more about me than I know about you, *friend*." Sarah shakes her head. "But you're right, it's none of my business. Sorry."

We're both quiet for a few minutes until I speak. "It's not a good story."

"It's a very personal question...Too personal." She waves me off with her hand. "Disregard." I'm weighing the pros and cons of sharing this long-buried secret when she asks, "Would you just tell me if it was Penny?"

"Penny?" I flat out scoff when I deny it. "No." The memory of that girl's drunken smirk surfaces then evaporates. "Did she tell you we slept together? If so, she's a liar, although that's already been well established."

"To be fair, Penny only said you hooked up. And, uh, I know she was interested in history repeating itself. She was going on and on about you at a party one night, but I didn't put two and two together until the other day."

"We didn't. I stopped her. She was bossy, and just... She assumed I'd be into it because of who she is, because she's rich or something. Like I should feel privileged or some shit." When Sarah doesn't say anything, I add, "I actually wound up feeling sorry for her. After what I witnessed the rest of last summer and then more recently, I realized she's got a pretty low opinion of herself."

"Agreed."

"But she's trying to redeem herself, I guess."

"You mean telling Mike about what they did?"

"Yeah. Mike wouldn't have been able to get them on tape if Penny hadn't tipped him off."

"I guess, but I still see it as a cheap way to try and make it up to me. I'm not feeling the love and forgiveness vibe just yet."

"No judgement here. I have loads of people on my own personal shit list." And I guess I do want to expose her to the ugly side of my life, because I press on when she's no longer asking me anything. "So, you wanted to know about my first time?"

"I want to know everything about you."

Her hand is still resting above mine on the gearshift, and it feels good, like something I need. I definitely need something to tell this story I've never told before.

Buckle up, Sarah.

"My sister—"

"Lorraine?"

Nodding, my voice suddenly isn't much above a whisper when I tell her, "She had this friend, Denise. An idiot who did my sister the solid of introducing her to her baby daddy, another sub-par individual." She's turned in her seat, her full attention on me now, so I make a joke to ease my discomfort. "Notice I don't use the word *loser* because it's been lobbed my way one too many times." Sarah doesn't laugh, just nods in a way that encourages me to go on. "It's like Lorraine is my mom reincarnated. Same patterns, same life path."

I'm wishing she'd chime in, but she stays quiet, gives me room to loop back around to where I started. "So her friend would stay over a lot, and..."

She gives me some time and then offers, "You hooked up with her?"

"Uh, she hooked up with me. Snuck into my bed."

"How long ago was this?"

I pause like I'm trying to recall, when I remember every sickening detail of that first time. "I was thirteen, I think?"

Sarah leans forward slightly. "And how old was she?"

"Older." I laugh even though there's nothing remotely funny linked to my very fucked up coming of age. But I need to ease the tension, to ease the embarrassment the memory triggers, to ease this sudden urge I have to punch the windshield. "I'd like to say I was smooth, that I had some moves, but I really—"

Her voice is soft when she repeats her question, "How old was she?"

"Nineteen."

Sarah shifts slowly, facing front again. "Did you realize what was happening?"

I shrug. "I caught on pretty fast."

"Don't do that."

"Do what? I know where you're heading and it wasn't like that. I was into it."

She can see right through this bullshit revisionist history I'm attempting to spin on the fly. "Liam, it *was* like that. If a much, *much* older guy snuck into bed with me and gave me my first sexual experience, it would be a crime, not the awkward fling you're making it out to be."

It's like she's letting the air out of a balloon, and I'm grateful for it, for her. Sarah's not looking at me with judgement or pity. She's just being present while I work this out on my own. "Believe me, I know that...I know it wasn't right."

She gives my hand a gentle squeeze. "Were you scared?"

"Yeah," I admit, my eyes fixed on the road.

"Have you ever told your sister? Does she know?"

"I never told Lorraine."

"You should tell your sister."

"What's the point? Denise moved, hasn't been around in a long time. I'll never cross paths with her again. And I'm certainly not looking to star in my own real-life version of Law and Order, so what's done is done."

"I'm not trying to tell you what to do, I just—"

"Don't. I've put Denise in a drawer with all the other shitty life experiences I've had, and I've closed it. I'm done. I know your concern comes from a good place, but leave it alone, all right?"

She nods as I take the exit to fill the tank up, again. I'm sweating, regretting what I told her as we come to a stop. Sarah says, "So, topic change, if that's all right with you."

"Please."

Anything to take my mind off Denise and the fact that I'm about to drop yet another fifty or so on gas right now.

"I'm thinking maybe we go home and I'll save the big reunion for another day."

I check my phone. "Really? We only have twenty or thirty minutes to go."

"I have a feeling Sienna was on the horn the second we

rounded the corner. I'm picturing some weepy woman standing on her front porch waiting for us. I just can't do it."

I hand her my phone. "Plug in your address. You're the captain of this adventure. I'm just driving." When she cocks her head and raises an eyebrow, I say, "I'm serious. You want to go home, we go home."

"That option doesn't sound very enticing either."

"Let me go inside and pay the guy. You mull it over for a second. And um..."

"What?"

"I'm not looking to please your parents whatsoever, but do you think maybe you should check in again? You know, proof of life so they don't think you've been abducted?"

She nods. "Here, take your phone. Maybe you should check in with your family, too."

I should definitely let Uncle Dan know I'm alive and well. I'm at the point where I only pop in and out of my mother's house when I need to. I don't live with her and Jeff anymore, and I never will again.

Chapter Twenty-Six

LIAM

I'm feeling chipper as I make my way outside balancing a coffee, a water, and two hot dogs that came right off the gas station's grill. I smile when she takes the coffee from me but looks at the hot dogs as if they're vile things.

More for me.

I pull over next to the air pump and unwrap my feast. "There's a third option," I say around a mouthful.

"What's that?"

"We could check out Pittsburgh like two tourists. Tool around for the entire day and then do a stealth drive-by later on tonight."

"What's that grin for?" Cautiously, she asks, "Did you just hear what I heard?"

"That the club will be compensating me for lost wages?"

"With some extra to smooth over the false accusation part, too. Pretty sweet, huh?"

"I'm taking the money from those assholes, but there is no

smoothing over happening here. They can cut me a check for five grand, but let's face it, they're not sorry, and that amount of money means nothing to them. It's probably the annual dues for one pompous jackass's membership."

"My dad said it's being upped to ten grand. I'm not trying to get you to like him or anything, but he told the board you already had an attorney, and that the guilty party had been identified and you were ready to name them to the police. And *ten* grand," she pauses to take a healthy gulp of her coffee, "is more along the lines of what we pay in annual membership dues."

"Ten grand for one year?"

"Yes," she answers, looking embarrassed. "And that doesn't even count towards the stable fees."

"Ten grand will more than cover my tuition at OCC for the year."

"So that's good, right?"

"Yeah."

"You could still name them, too."

"I'll take the ten grand and walk away for good." Nudging her knee with my own, I say, "Really, I'm good with that. It'll be like giving them the finger every time I walk into class this year."

"That's a healthy way to look at it, I guess." Looking to the greasy napkin in my lap, she says, "Healthier than what you just ate."

"They're actually better than decent, but definitely not healthy."

"I can't believe you were even hungry. You had like four of those muffins."

"I wasn't hungry. It's the smell that gets you. The hot dogs are positioned right next to the coffee machine, so I was smelling them while I was getting you your fix. It's all your fault."

"Sure, Liam." She's smiling again, and I'm so glad the topic and the mood has shifted. Very glad about the ten grand, too. "So, Ocean City Community College? You'll be close to home."

"For the time being. It's practical. I can stay with my aunt and uncle, work around twenty hours a week, sock away some money for living expenses for when I—"

"Snag that full ride."

"Exactly." The thought of having some extra money for the first time in my life has me feeling relieved and happy. "I guess I'll have to open a real bank account."

"You don't have one?" She cocks her head to the side. "But you have a credit card, right?"

I fully expected the surprise she's trying to mask right now. I'd wager Sarah not only has a bank account in her name, but also stocks, bonds, and a trust fund to boot.

"No. I buy those prepaid ones from the convenience store because so many places don't even take dollar bills anymore." I side eye her to add, "Which is nuts, in my opinion." Sarah still can't wrap her mind around this alien concept, so I spell it out. "I cash my checks and put it with the money I make from my other side jobs."

"So you take your paycheck, exchange it for cash, then buy a debit card so you'll have spending cash? Where do you even cash checks?"

"Check cashing shops."

"I've never seen one."

"Yeah, they don't have stores with bullet-proof glass in your neighborhood." I continue, not the slightest bit embarrassed, knowing Sarah is soaking this education up and I'm her professor in *Life 101*. "There are some big-box stores where you can do it, but people pay their utility bills there too, so the lines can get crazy long. It's a toss-up," I shrug like the badass I am not, "but time is money, so when it's long lines versus safety, I'll pick the guy behind the bullet-proof glass any day of the week." I say that last bit with a chuckle but she doesn't acknowledge my stab at levity.

"I realize my system is ass backwards." My mood takes a nosedive when I think of him, and I shift uncomfortably as the truth comes spilling out on its own. "When Jeff raided the coffee can I kept stashed in the back of my closet, that's when I moved out."

She doesn't answer, and I'm all right with her knowing the ugly. Is my life enviable? Absolutely not. But I'm not hiding or apologizing for anything. And just because Jeff is a modern-day version of Fagin, that doesn't mean my part of town is full of losers with questionable morals. Mike, for example, has awesome parents. And Lorraine, despite her faults, is a good mother to my nephew.

Reaching over to grab a wayward crumb off my lap, she says, "There's a fourth option."

"I'm listening."

"We could run away from home for a while." Something in my expression has her back peddling fast. "Forget it. I know you probably need to get back. I just had a crazy thought."

"No, I want to hear your crazy thought."

"I was thinking we could go to Ocean City. Find a place to stay tonight." Before I can protest, she says, "I have my credit card and my parents will be footing the bill. Seriously, Liam," she sniffs her own armpit, "I need a shower."

"I wanted to ask Sienna and..."

"Garth," she supplies when I can't remember the name.

"Yeah, I wanted to root around for a toothbrush while I was in the bathroom."

"I did," she says before breaking out into a fit of giggles. She then digs into her pocket and produces a kids'-sized brush with some blue paste mashed into the bristles. It's wrapped in soggy toilet paper, and I still want to get my hands on it.

"Thief! Here I am being accused of a crime, while I've been sitting next to a mastermind this entire time."

"What's that saying about desperate times?" She carefully extracts the damp paper from the brush and leans out her window to pour some water over it before handing it to me. "I don't mind sharing."

"Obviously," I say, taking it from her. "We're sharing with one of those poor kids you stole from."

"They were adorable, weren't they?"

I finish brushing and nod before rinsing my mouth and spitting out the window. "Yeah, but four kids with one on the way? I think I'd lose my mind."

Sarah shrugs. "They sure seemed happy to me."

"No doubt about it."

"There was something so—"

"Warm about their house?" Now I'm finishing *her* sentences.

"Yes! Like you could physically *feel* the love wafting through the place."

I nod when she does. The way those two were around one another, so comfortable and so obviously...in love, made me choke up at one point. I don't know if she caught what I did, but when we were leaving I turned back for one last look, and saw Garth giving Sienna a peck on the cheek and a playful swat on the butt before he went on to kiss each and every one of the kids, her belly being where the last kiss landed. To someone who grew up in a home like mine, their life looked idyllic.

She shifts to me excitedly. "So, what do you think about that detour?"

I'm thinking she wants to make it better, to ease some of the hurts from my past. I don't need that, I want to tell her. But she looks so hopeful, and I'm not looking to part ways with Sarah or go back to real life just yet, so I tell her, "I'm in."

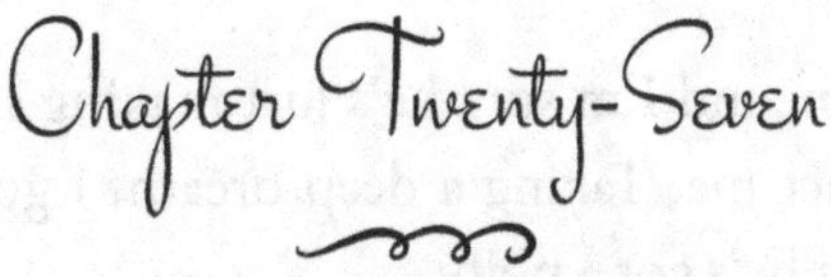

Chapter Twenty-Seven

SARAH

Liam is just about to pull out of the gas station and head off in a different direction when I blurt out, "Wait!"

I'm wringing my hands and taking deep breaths, which is the polar opposite of his cool, calm demeanor. He pulls over again and turns to face me, no question or expectation in his expression.

"I'm just thinking it's silly...I mean, we're here already, right?"

"I can't make this decision for you, Sarah. But we *are* here. Want to get a little closer and see how you feel then?"

"Yes." I hardly recognize my own tremulous voice when I look down to see that I'm wiping two sweaty palms down my thighs. "Let's just drive by. Maybe we'll park far enough away and just walk around for a bit. Then we'll get back on the road and head to the beach."

"You still want to?"

"Hell yes."

A few minutes later he comments, "It's weird how you can tell wealthier neighborhoods from poor ones by how many trees there are. I mean, not in rural areas, but by us it's so obvious."

It's random, and I'm sure he's just making small talk in an effort to distract me. Taking a deep breath, I go along with it and decide that he's got a point.

"On the street where I grew up, a lot of the yards have been paved over with concrete to make room for cars, and the few trees that are still there are kind of scrubby. Head towards my aunt and uncle's place, though, and you see the landscape gradually changing. And forget it once you make it to your neighborhood...It's all rolling green hills and loads of trees and flowers. Driving to work at the club in the spring, it was like this explosion of color every time."

My mother loves gardening. And while she doesn't do the heavy work herself, she did sketch out our landscape's design, and went head to head with the gardeners when their boss didn't agree with some of her choices. I know what Liam means, because sometimes when I'm coming up our *long-ass driveway*, as he calls it, I'm struck by the blaze of colors. And the way she mapped it out, there are pops of color that start in the spring and don't end until the beginning of December. It's like a rotating surprise, one shrub drops its flowers just as another one starts to bloom. But I'm not about to praise her horticultural skills right now, so when he asks what's on my mind, I don't think it through before saying, "Have you ever seen the cherry blossoms in DC?"

He smiles when I stop abruptly. "It's fine, really. Like I said, I'll get to all those places. Go on, Sarah, tell me about the trees."

I take a minute to come up with words that are good enough, ones he might use to describe such a sight. I've been fortunate enough to see them in our country, as well as in Japan one year. "It seems endless, this loop that goes on and on, with clusters of trees that are nearly drooping under the weight of all those delicate pink flowers. When you're walking under the canopy of them, it's magical. It's like being in a dream." I laugh to cover my embarrassment.

"When do they bloom?"

"This year we went in late March. My mother was actually tracking the forecast and booked it last-minute."

For a moment I'm bracing for a snarky comeback, something along the lines of: *Must be nice, Princess,* but I can't really say I'm surprised when he says, "Yeah, I could see the weather making it difficult to plan in advance. Sounds like a great trip."

I look over to him, studying him while his eyes are on the road, all sorts of crazy thoughts flashing through my mind. I want to see DC with Liam, backpack across Europe with him, hike the Appalachian Trail, camping out and sleeping under the stars with him all along the way.

My mind goes back to early yesterday morning when we were parked outside of Garth and Sienna's house. Poor thing. He was breathing deep within five minutes, but I was too nervous and jumpy to sleep at first. The weight of his arm holding me close to his body left me feeling so content, so safe. And when he moved in his sleep and his hand slid lower, resting along my hip, I raised up a silent prayer that Liam felt the same as me. I want Liam to be mine.

Liam clears his throat, signaling with his finger to a street sign that reads Maple Lane.

"Is this the one?"

He nods as he looks at the houses on one side of the street, then the other. "I'm thinking her house will be around halfway down the block. What say you, Miss Hamilton?"

"Can we park and, I don't know, walk around for a bit?"

"No drive-by?"

"Your car stands out," I feel the need to reassure him, "in a good way, of course."

"How do you think they described us?" He doesn't wait for me to answer before saying, "I'm guessing it was something along the lines of: guy who appears freakishly tall when standing next to his Christmas elf-sized companion, driving a 1970's classic in pristine condition."

"Or, two kids with questionable hygiene habits driving a car right out of the Smithsonian."

He sniffs his armpit like I did before and declares, "Yep. That description fits, too."

We exit the car and cross the street, acting casual, trying not to call attention to ourselves in this quiet as a morgue suburban enclave.

"That's the house number, right?" I whisper as we pass by. He nods, and I'm thinking to myself that we must look so obvious. But there's no one around, and no cars are parked in front of the garage door. "Doesn't look like anyone's home."

"Nope," he agrees. "Want to get a closer look?"

I surprise myself when I nod and cross the street as if there's a magnetic force drawing me closer. It's modest-sized, but pretty and well-maintained. There are a few stone steps leading up to the pathway, and I keep going without giving a thought as to what my plan is.

It's not until a woman walks outside, nervously wiping her hands on her jeans, that I stop. She takes me in, swallows and then says my name in a soft voice. When I don't answer, she asks, "Are you Sarah?"

I can't speak. Taking in this woman with her long brown hair, and brown eyes like my own, I don't feel as if I'm looking at a mirror image or anything, but I am sure, beyond a shadow of a doubt, that I've found her.

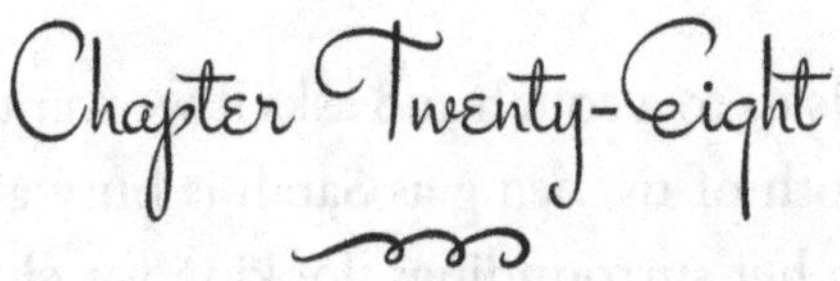

Chapter Twenty-Eight

LIAM

This is her mother, no doubt about it.

Sarah hasn't moved for a solid minute. The woman looked nervous when she first greeted Sarah by the door, but she's composed now, smiling at Sarah in an encouraging way when she holds her hand out, palm up. It's the same move you'd use when approaching a skittish animal, a gesture used to encourage trust, the equivalent of saying: *I won't bite.*

And Sarah responds much the way a wounded animal would. She takes one tentative step closer, then stops and looks back to me. I want to jump in there so badly and broker this summit, ease away the awkwardness and pain for Sarah, but I can't.

"I'm Grace Dawson, Sarah. I'm happy you're here."

Grace is an even keel, thank God. She doesn't go overboard with the weepy, emotional reunion drama I'd been fearing. No, she's patient, knows what she's doing. She's done this before. I don't mean she's met a child she gave up for adoption before—

that would be...something—more that she's skilled at the art of putting people at ease.

I take Sarah's hand and give it a gentle squeeze. My eyes ask, *Do you want to go in,* to which she gives a barely perceptible nod.

Grace leads us to a couch and asks if we want some iced tea. I accept for both of us, being as Sarah is busy at the moment. She's studying her surroundings, looking for clues and details, trying to figure out who this person is.

Looking to me, she whispers, "Are you all right?" That question tells me all I need to know about the state Sarah's in. She's *not* all right. And who would be?

Grace comes back in balancing a cutting board on her forearm while holding two glasses. When she puts it down, Sarah looks at her, perplexed, and says, "You made a charcuterie board?"

And when Grace begins to laugh, Sarah joins in.

It is the *best* sound.

"I know," she says, "I'm ridiculous!"

"No!" Sarah is smiling back at her, still laughing. "I like charcuterie!"

Grace takes a very deep breath and sits on a chair that's close, but not right next to Sarah's spot on the couch. "When Sienna called this morning I was shocked, and then I was a nervous wreck. I wasn't expecting you yet."

"Yet?"

She leans over and tentatively rests one hand over Sarah's. "I've *always* hoped you'd come, but I wasn't expecting you until after you turned eighteen in August. I mean, that is, if you ever did come. I wasn't assuming that you would...come."

As if Grace has just noticed I'm also in the room, she looks to me with hopeful eyes, and I introduce myself. And I don't know what it is about this chick, but she gives off something, a calming, nurturing vibe. I'm not making sense in my own head, but I feel like I don't have to worry because she's around. I'm thinking Grace Dawson can handle this.

Sarah takes a piece of cheese off the board, but I can tell she's too nervous to eat. I, however, am not. Grace gestures to the board again. "I needed something to do with my hands for the past two hours. Making rosettes out of salami slices is more helpful than you'd think."

Just when she's about to say something else, the doorbell rings. Grace gets up, looks to Sarah apologetically and says, "Let me just get rid of whoever this is."

Looking cool as a cucumber, Sarah reassures her, "It's ok, really," but then looks to me with bugged-out eyes once Grace is out of sight. "What do you think?"

I offer, "She seems really nice?"

"Aunt Gracie!"

"Libs! Oh my God, I totally forgot about today. I'm such an idiot."

A voice says, "Are you all right, Grace? You look pale."

"Wait, Libby...Now isn't the best—"

"Who are *you*?"

This kid wearing a dancing leotard in a neon tie-dyed print has barged into the house and she's looking right at me. "Um, I'm Liam."

"Nice to meet you, Liam," she says.

"Dial the flirt down a notch," Grace says with a smile. There's a woman with her when she comes back into the living room.

And then we're both baffled and blurting out, "Sienna?"

"No," the woman answers with a smile, while the little girl simultaneously says, "That's my aunt. My mom is Sky."

"Skylar Hale," she comes closer, "and this is my daughter, Olivia."

Before either of us can get in a hello, or wrap our heads around the confusion, Olivia launches into a commentary on how her last name used to be different from Sky's, *but*, she emphasizes, *not anymore!* Sarah is smiling, while Grace and her friend are looking like they've tried to stop this crazy train before, but have concluded it's best just to let her run out of steam on her own.

"I was the bridesmaid. Do you know what that is?" she asks Sarah.

And Sarah must be feeling more herself, because she plays along. "Kind of, but I've never *been* a bridesmaid."

"Oh, it's a *big* job."

"Olivia," her mom says with a subtle warning in her tone.

But this kid is on a roll and Sarah's not helping, as she's nodding her head, encouraging her to go on. "I had to pick out dresses, I had to throw a party." And she's a pistol, looking to Sarah as if she's got to break it down for her when she clarifies, "It's called a bridal shower."

"Oh, that sounds like fun."

"It was *so* much fun." Looking between me and Sarah, she asks, "Is he your boyfriend?"

"All right, Libs," Grace comes over and puts a hand on her shoulder.

Olivia looks up at her. "What?"

"Maybe we can do your dance lesson a little later? I didn't realize Sarah and Liam were coming, so—"

"They can watch me," she says, starting up a routine that has so many spins it's giving me motion sickness just watching.

"We can leave and come back later," Sarah offers, but Grace is shaking her head and Olivia's mom is doing the same.

"Libs, let's give them some peace and quiet. We'll go to the store and grab some ice cream for Dad, ok? He's opening the pool up later on, remember?"

"Liam and...What's your name again?"

"Sarah," she answers, laughing.

"You can also call her Tiny. That's her nickname."

"It is not!" Sarah looks offended but I know she's not. Pointing her thumb my way, she says to Olivia, "He just calls me that because he's a freaky tall giant."

"You've got two names? Sarah *and* Tiny? That's weird."

I side-eye her, teasing. "C'mon, we've been here for five minutes, and so far I've heard you called three different names. What's that about?"

This kid full-on flutters her eyelashes when she smiles back at me and says, "You're right! I'm Libs, Libby and Olivia."

"So you have three names, you win."

"Nope," Sarah tosses out. "We're tied. My parents call me Bug sometimes because I used to love ladybugs."

"I love ladybugs, too!"

"Libs, Libby, Olivia Hale...Time to go." Her mother gives her a look that leaves no wiggle room when she tells her, "Say goodbye to Liam and Sarah."

"Bye," she says, sulking, but then turns back as they get to the door. "Wait! You wanna come over to my pool later on? My dad is opening it up and it's really nice, and I can swim backstroke and front stroke, and—"

"Bye," her mother calls out right before the door closes shut.

I laugh when I can still hear her pleading with her mom outside. "She's a cutie."

Grace looks towards where they just exited. "Olivia is such a good kid, but my Lord, once she gets going she's like a top that can't stop spinning. Thank goodness she does so well in school, or else her teachers would probably be calling her a problem child instead of spirited and precocious."

"You were her mother's teacher?" In response to her surprised look, I add, "Sienna and Garth told us."

Now she gets it. "Yes, I taught Sienna, Garth and Skylar. Were you freaking out when Skylar walked in? Sorry I didn't prepare you for that."

"Mono—" Sarah stops herself, amends what she's going to say. "Identical twins, I'm assuming?"

Grace nods, studying Sarah. "Yes, monozygotic, as you were about to say."

"Grace, can I use your bathroom?"

"Sure, it's right off the kitchen," she points the way, "in there."

When I come out, they're still making small talk, so I take that as a good sign. "Maybe I'll take a walk around the neighborhood for a little while, give you two a chance to talk?"

And I breathe out a sigh of relief when Sarah nods, looking relaxed.

Chapter Twenty-Nine

SARAH

"Are you ok?" she asks me once Liam leaves.

"Kind of," I answer honestly. I should be freaking out, but I feel calmer now, much calmer than I did half an hour ago.

Grace has a steady, calming presence, and doesn't press me to talk. I have so many questions, so many that I don't even know how to begin.

"You can ask me anything, you know."

"I don't even know where to start."

"Then why don't I just tell you about myself, give you an abridged version of my life story, and you stop me whenever you have a question. Would that be all right?"

"That sounds good."

Grace tells me some basics, like she was born and raised in a suburb outside of Philadelphia. I stop her right away and ask how many siblings she has, and learn that she has one brother who lives out in southern California now. I ask about her parents and she tells me they divorced when she was a teenager.

She shakes her head as if she's still slightly mortified when she tells me that her father remarried a much younger woman and had twins with her. Smiling, she also tells me her mother kind of loves it that people mistake her dad for the twins' grandfather.

"Do they know...about me?"

She nods. "I just told them," she takes a moment to think, "around two years ago." In response to the wide-eyed stare I'm probably sporting, she says, "I didn't tell a soul, for so many years. Not until I met Owen."

"Owen?"

You can tell this person makes her happy by the way she answers, "My husband. We got married last year."

"Congratulations."

I'm pretty sure I'm not smiling the way one should when they're bestowing good wishes on another person, even though I'm not upset in any way. Like, I'm not upset she moved on with her life, but I feel kind of seasick all of a sudden.

Reaching over to get my glass, I gulp down a good amount of iced tea, then sit with both hands in my lap, not knowing what to do with myself. I have an urge to move, yet I'm frozen.

"Wow, I skipped ahead, like, more than fifteen years. Let me back up. So I went to school in North Carolina, and I met your father in September of my junior year." She cocks her head to the side. "Are you heading off to college this year?"

Your father. The words trigger an image of my father's smiling face—my real father, my dad—and I'm overcome with guilt. God, they must have been so hurt by what I said, by what I did. Suddenly I want to cry. I want to call them and take it all back. I want them both to hug me and tell me it's all right, that I'm forgiven.

I answer her question as if I'm a computer spitting out

data, "Penn." And while I'm aware that I should be expounding on these awesome one-word responses I'm giving her, nothing else comes to me as those two words echo in my head. *Your father.*

I'm thankful Grace keeps the conversation flowing, as I'm currently pretty much useless in that department. "Congratulations to you. That's quite an achievement."

I shrug because college seems so unimportant right now. The fact that I'll be embarking on a new chapter hasn't registered. Seriously, since the adoption bomb dropped, I haven't thought about college much at all.

"My parents never came out and said it, but the fact that I got rejected from Duke hit them both hard. I was a colossal disappointment."

This revelation brings me back to the present. "I'm sure you weren't."

"If you knew your grandparents—" Her face pales. "*My* parents. I shouldn't have called them that."

And then it's me comforting her. "Don't feel bad, please. I'm sure we're both going to be tripping over our words. Let's just speak freely, ok?"

She reaches over again and takes my hand in hers. "Thank you for saying that. I'm doing my best not to offend you or scare you off, and I'm petrified that I'm going to do both."

My eyes water as I squeeze Grace's hand. "Keep going...I want to know more."

"Your father's name is Damien, Damien Erikson."

I repeat the name in my head, once, twice, then let out the breath I'd been holding.

"There was no name on the birth certificate, and I regret that. Damien was a United States Marine. He was on an extended leave when we met and was sent back overseas six weeks later."

"Is he alive?"

She shakes her head slowly, watching me. "I need you to know that I loved him very much and he loved me. Probably sounds ridiculous to you, being that it was only six weeks, but a lot can happen in a short period of time." My mind goes to Liam and I nod my head, understanding completely. "When I found out I was pregnant I was scared out of my mind, but I also knew he was a good person, a good man. Never in a million years did I think he would abandon me."

We both look up when we hear knocking at the door. "Liam," I say, realizing he left here a while ago.

"Hey," he says. "Everything good here?"

"I'm sorry I left you out there wandering around."

"Don't be sorry. My hunk of rust has *another* admirer." That earns him a smile from me. He reaches over and grazes his thumb over my cheek, studying my eyes, I think, to see if I'm drowning and in need of a save. Understanding passes between us, relief in his eyes before he shifts his gaze to Grace. "I guess Sienna described my car to her sister, and it turns out that her husband is a car buff."

"Leo," Grace says. "He's a fan of all things motor-related."

"Anyway, he lives just two blocks down. Is it ok if I take a quick walk over there to check out his garage?" He looks to me intently. "It's just to give the two of you some time. I don't have to go. It's not important."

"Go," I wave him off. "We're good."

And once he's gone, I sit back down, eager for her to jump right back into it. "So, he was deployed when you found out you were pregnant..."

"And I wrote to him, but," she swallows, "he stopped

writing back. I kept the faith for as long as I could, but I was crushed. I doubted everything we'd had, everything he'd said to me, every promise we'd made to one another." Grace looks drained, as if the memory of that time still hurts her deep in her soul, while I'm hanging on every word, desperate to know how the story ends. "I wasn't the next of kin. Officially, I was nothing." She looks off into the distance. "It was months before I heard Damien had been killed in the line of duty."

I feel my arms wrap around my own middle, my body rocking back and forth slowly as I absorb the blow. Grace comes to sit beside me on the couch and wraps one arm around my shoulder. "I'm so sorry to have to tell you that. And I've been sorry for years that I didn't honor him by putting his name on the birth certificate. At the time it was more red tape than I was capable of handling. I had to supply a death certificate, which...I didn't even know where to start."

Shifting to face her, and maybe to break the gentle hold she has on me, I ask the one thing that I *need* to know, "Did you ever consider...keeping me?"

"After I gave you up, after it was done? *All* I thought about was keeping you. For nearly eighteen years it's felt like an ache that won't ever go away. But at the time? I was devoting all of my energy to keeping everything a secret. I was nineteen when I found out I was pregnant, twenty when you were born...Not much older than you are now."

I nod as I try to picture myself in the same predicament, but I can't. I can't imagine being so careless, I can't imagine being so numb and thoughtless.

"I spent years being so angry at myself, looking back on that time and wondering why I was so weak. I wasn't some poor kid raised in dire circumstances. I had family, I had friends I could have leaned on, I had financial resources. But I chose to go it alone, and I've paid for that decision every day since."

"But it made your life a lot easier, didn't it?" I don't mean for it to come out sounding accusatory, but then again, maybe I do.

Her one-shouldered shrug is weak. "I was able to go back to school and finish my degree, I didn't have to deal with my parents' disappointment...So in some ways, yes, it definitely did." She looks physically drained when she adds, "Fall classes started exactly two weeks after you were born, and my body didn't get the memo that I wasn't a new mother nursing her baby. It's not something Mother Nature lets you forget. I had to wear a pad all the time that first month because I was rushing around campus in a daze, still bleeding, and I always had a stash of tissues on hand and a clean shirt stuffed in my bag in case my breasts started to leak."

She stands up and walks a few paces. She's not facing me, but I can see her hand go up to wipe at her eyes, and her voice sounds choked when she continues. "Not once did someone ask what was wrong. I'd just gone through the most colossal event a woman will *ever* experience, yet the world kept on spinning as if nothing had happened."

"Did you have a chance to change your mind?"

She turns back to face me. "I did. It may have been one month or three months or six. I couldn't even tell you. I didn't even read the fine print."

"But you said you regretted it right after."

"I don't expect you to understand. It's been years and I still don't know if I fully understand. Looking back on it, I think the only way I could survive it was to cut myself off from my emotions. I turned on autopilot and cruised through my last two years of school, and then through the next ten years after that."

Trying to wrap my head around it all, I get up and excuse myself to use the bathroom. I need a break from this, but at the same time, I know I may never get the answers I need if I don't keep asking, pushing, listening. After today, this woman may never want to see me again.

And there's a chance I'll never want to see her.

Chapter Thirty

LIAM

I interrupt him mid-sentence. "Leo, I think I ought to be getting back. This has been amazing, really, but I need to go check on her."

"Understood." He shakes my hand, firm and with eye contact, same way my uncle shakes hands. Jeff has never shaken my hand, but I'd imagine his would either be flimsy, or the kind where you're aiming to crush bones. "If you're ever back this way, definitely stop in." He looks to where his wife has appeared in the driveway. "No one wants to listen to me talk shop around here."

"That's a lie," Skylar says, looking to me. "Olivia and I listen to him blather on *all* the time. I can talk carburetors and pistons like nobody's business."

"Yeah, *all* the time," little Olivia parrots as she starts using chalk in the driveway to write her name. Scratch that, she's writing *my* name in big bubble letters.

"Thanks again."

Skylar catches on to what Olivia's doing and gives me an apologetic smile as she mouthes the words, *Run for your life!*

"Hey, you said you were gonna go in the pool," she calls after me.

To which Skylar says, "He actually did *not* promise to go in the pool."

"I have to go now, but I'll take a raincheck."

The kid looks at me like I'm loony. "What's that supposed to mean?"

"It means I'll go in the pool the next time we're here."

I hold back from saying that I might not ever come back here. Sarah maybe, but me? I don't know where I stand. There's a decent chance we'll disintegrate once we cross back over the state line and arrive on reality's doorstep. I'd say we're standing on a pretty shaky foundation at the moment.

I tell myself we've kissed and that's all, but the kind of kissing we've done is different. It's more. I held back like a jerk when she asked if we were friends, but she is my friend. She's someone I've confided in, and by holding her close and comforting her, she's given me the kind of comfort I didn't even know I needed. But even if we do firmly establish ourselves as something more than friends, Sarah is leaving once the summer ends. That's a fact.

I take a deep breath before knocking on the door again, and when Grace greets me she looks wrung out, with tears threatening. "Is Sarah ok?"

"Um, she's been in the bathroom for a while?"

When I knock on that door, Sarah says, "Just gimme a minute."

"It's me," I tell her, and the lock clicks a second later. She's leaning her butt against the sink, her face looking much like Grace's. "How are you doing?"

"I'm fine."

"You sure?"

Sarah lets out a breath that goes on and on. "It's just that," she meets my eyes, "it's a lot, you know?"

"Like I said, you're the captain of this ship. You want to go, just say the word."

She reaches back and turns the faucet on to muffle her voice. "I feel like I should be mad at her, like, to tell her she was weak, and, you know what? It worked out fine because I have parents who are better than you ever would have been." I say nothing to this, even when she looks to gauge my reaction. "But that's out of loyalty to my mother and father, and because I feel guilty for the way I left yesterday. I'm not mad at the woman." She looks up at the ceiling. "Ugh, I don't know what to think."

"You don't have to *think* or *feel* or *be* one way or another. You're just learning her story and she's learning yours. And there's no pressure here, got it? She'll understand if you want to leave now and take some time to think about everything, talk another time, meet up or never meet again...Whatever."

"No." Shaking her head, she looks like she just ran a marathon but she's pushing herself to do it all over again. "I might not ever get this chance again."

And we're both surprised when we exit the bathroom and find another person standing toe to toe with Grace, holding both of her hands in his. Grace takes a step back from him when she notices us, and he looks right at Sarah with kind eyes. "Hi, I'm Owen. I'm—"

"Grace's husband." Poised, polite Sarah is back in action. Taking his outstretched hand, she introduces herself, and introduces me as her boyfriend while she's at it.

This is my boyfriend, Liam.

I'm dumbstruck in a good way for a second there. She whips her head back to me, looking to see if I'm horrified by this, so I reach for her hand and give it a squeeze to let her know how I feel.

What a simple word, a word I tagged as stupid and corny before, but I've just been proven wrong because I'm smiling for no other reason than that corny word. I've never been anyone's boyfriend, never believed I was truly special to anyone before, and the idea that Sarah sees me as worthy fills me with something that's good and painful at the same time.

Thankfully Grace and her man are focused on Sarah now, and not scrutinizing me. I can't imagine I look even remotely normal at the moment.

"We're so glad you came," he says, his eyes lingering on Sarah. Shaking his head, he says, "Wow. You look so much like hi—"

"Owen," she interrupts him softly, and shakes her head to stop him from talking.

"Sorry," he says, looking from Grace to Sarah. Changing tack, he says, "Leo and Skylar told me you guys have been on the road for days? Is that right?"

"Not that long," Sarah answers. "We left New Jersey just yesterday."

I add, "But we've covered," I count in my head, "seven states since yesterday, if you count the District of Columbia."

At this point, I don't know if I should chime in on anything, and I hope Sarah's not mad that I'm making small talk. I have no right to feel the way I do about Grace, but I like her. I like her husband, too, even though I've known him for less than three minutes. Their house, their friends, the way they look at one another—there's something about their life that's enviable.

"Man, that's a lot of ground to cover in two days." Focusing on me, he asks, "How are you even standing upright?" Glancing at Sarah, he says, "I'm assuming he was driving. I only know the basics about cars, but I'm guessing that's a stick shift parked outside."

"That's totally sexist," Grace says.

"It is." He apologizes to Sarah and then says, "I can't drive one of those either."

"Have you slept at all?" Grace asks, looking back and forth between me and Sarah.

"We actually got a few hours after we pulled up outside your old address at three in the morning."

"Yeah," Sarah says, "Garth woke us up this morning."

"Oh my God, he leaves for work at the crack of dawn!"

"The whole house was awake," Sarah says with a smile.

I laugh when I add, "And there are a lot of them."

"I can't even imagine what that scene was like," Owen says. "He told me they wake up *every* day, like a clock minus the alarm, just to see him off to work."

The way he says that last part tells me that maybe Owen envies their life the way I envy his.

And just like that—Sarah, Grace and Owen talking about people who are not them—it's back to good.

Grace says, "I guess the upside is that you couldn't be woken up by a nicer person than Garth."

"Makes me feel kind of bad," Sarah looks back to me as she pulls that crusty thing from her front pocket, "that we stole from them."

Grace and Owen are cracking up, and then we are too. A minute later, Owen says, "The washer and dryer are right there," he says, pointing down a hallway, "and there are bathrobes hanging in the guest bathroom. Why don't Grace and I leave for a bit so you two can get freshened up, and we'll come back in an hour or so with lunch." He looks between Grace, Sarah, and then me when he asks, "Does that sound all right?"

A shower sounds like heaven, forget all right. And that meat and cheese board didn't do it for me—I am starving—but I can't weigh in on this. We're all waiting on Sarah...and waiting, and waiting. I can sense that Grace is just about to squash the plan when Sarah says, "That sounds great."

Owen grabs his keys from the counter. "Is there something in particular you're in the mood for?"

"Anything is good," Sarah answers.

"But she can't have sesame seeds."

Sarah looks to me, grateful. "I'm allergic," she tells Grace.

"Got it," she replies, blinking back more tears. "Please, make yourselves at home."

We both collapse onto the couch side by side when they leave, exhausted, relieved, and God knows what else.

"I wish I felt...comfortable, you know?"

"We literally *just* met them. It's early days."

She looks down at the coffee staining her shirt, then points to what is likely hot dog grease on mine. "I thought the washing machine suggestion was weird, but..."

Letting out a tired breath, I smile. "We probably look like—"

"Two homeless vagabonds?"

"I was going to call us dirty dishes left in the sink for days... Same thing."

I tell her to go shower first, that I need to check in with my sister and let her know I'll be back by tomorrow night for my shift. "Wait. Do you think we'll be back by tomorrow night?"

"Oh, yeah," she nods emphatically. "I'm thinking later on today we hit the road."

"I'm fine with whatever. You want to stay, we stay. You want to head to Ocean City, we'll go. But I don't want you doing that for me."

She winces. "Are you sure? You wouldn't mind if we put that on the list of future epic quests?"

"Not even a little."

And that is no lie. Truth is, I could go the rest of my life without seeing my father again, let alone reenacting that god-awful trip.

"I'm throwing my stuff in the machine, you start it up once you get your stuff in there." She walks back out a minute later and throws me a robe. "Here you go."

"This will be another first for me."

"No spa days in your past?"

"Not a one."

I almost fall asleep on the couch waiting for her to finish up in the bathroom. "Oh," she drags the sound out on a breath. "That shower was amazing. They have those jets that hit you from every angle. I want one of those when I grow up."

"I'm surprised you don't have one." I hold my hands up in defense when she narrows her eyes at me. "I'm serious. Your house looks like it would have every luxury feature that exists."

"My house is nice, don't get me wrong, but my dad is frugal in some ways."

"You have a horse."

"I said in *some* ways. And he doesn't give a passing thought to what boarding a horse costs, but if my mother were to suggest, say, renovating a perfectly good bathroom to install a steam shower like the one they have? It would be a hard no. There would have to be a good reason, and I'm not saying my mom couldn't convince him with some nonsense about needing extra jets for an achy shoulder or something, but he's got his ways. He's sensible and more down to Earth than you think."

She has no idea what I think. I think her father may have been a regular Joe back in the day, but he's far removed from that life now. He probably wouldn't step foot back in a place like Queens unless his life depended on it. People like him don't mix with people like me.

Try as he might to come off like a good guy, I think Sarah's father is one of *them*, and he will not be cool with Liam Murphy hanging around his precious daughter.

Chapter Thirty-One

SARAH

"Hi, Mom."

"Sarah," she says my name on a relieved sigh. "Where are you? Are you all right?"

"I'm fine, Mom."

There's a reason I'm tagging *Mom* onto everything I say. I could have just said *Hi* and *I'm fine*, but I want to let Audrey Hamilton know that she—and no one else—is my mother. I know she's probably been going through a hell she doesn't deserve these past two days, and I don't want to pile any more pain onto her shoulders. I want to ease it.

"I met her." My words hang in the air until I add, "Grace Dawson."

"You found her?"

"Yeah, just this morning. I met her husband, too. They live in Pittsburgh."

"I thought, well, it doesn't matter..."

"She left a forwarding address in North Carolina, then

another in a different part of Pennsylvania. I guess that's where she went after she graduated."

"So you've been driving all this time?"

"Liam's been doing all of the driving."

"Sarah?" My body is tensing, already angry at what she's about to say. I'm expecting an insult disguised as a warning to *watch out for boys like him,* so I'm taken off guard when she says, "I'm sorry."

"You and Dad should have told me."

"We did, when you were too little to understand, and we always planned to be more open with you about it, but then..."

"What?"

"Then it just seemed so much easier, and less confusing for you."

"But you had to know at some point that I'd find out on my own."

"This isn't an excuse, and I don't really expect you to understand, but sometimes it's just easier to put troubling things out of your mind." She pauses, then says, "It was me, Sarah. Your father wanted to make it very clear when you were twelve, thirteen...but I pushed back. 'Next year, she's not ready,' I'd tell him, when it was me who wasn't ready."

"Why, though?"

She doesn't answer and I don't say anything to fill the void. I'm fighting a war with myself at the moment. Mad at her, but also reasonable enough to imagine that the child you've raised since day one meeting the woman who gave birth to her cannot be easy.

"Mom, I'm going to call you back later when we get on the road."

"You're still there...with her?"

"Grace and Owen just went out to get us all something to eat, but I'm thinking we'll probably head out later on today."

"Grace and Owen," she repeats. Her voice sounds wrung out and spent when she says, "Wait...Your father is here and he wants to talk to you."

Guilt washes over me again. Troubling things? Yes, I'd like to put the last conversation I had with my parents far, far out of my mind. "Hey, Dad."

"Are you all right?"

"Dad, I'm fine. It's actually been...good so far. Weird and uncomfortable, but good."

"We really are sorry." His voice sounds choked when he says, "We should have told you all along."

And now I'm crying while trying to speak, but the tears fall like a watershed. Liam appears beside me with tissues, and he's rubbing my back. It's a full minute before I can clear my throat well enough to say, "Nothing changes, you know that, right? You're my father and Mom is my mother. Always."

"We love you, Bug."

"I love you, too. I'm going to call you later when we get on the road, all right?"

My mother is back on the line now. "We'll be up, so please call no matter what time it is."

"I will, Mom."

Turning to Liam after catching my breath, I say, "Nice bathrobe," and we both start to laugh. Well, he laughs. What I'm doing is more like a combination of hiccupping and crying.

"I'd ask how you are, but..."

Taking another tissue from the box he's set before me, I proceed to blow what seems like a gallon of liquid from my nose. "Gross."

"Feels good though, doesn't it?"

My head hurts, my skin feels so hot that I'm sure it's a blotchy mess, and I'm so, so tired, but he's right, I do feel better. "Big fan of the ugly cry?"

"I don't think I've ever had one, but it looks cathartic. I'm kinda jealous."

"I needed that, but maybe I should jump back in the shower, or put ice on my face or something."

"Nah, you look fine. And," he looks right at me, "I'd imagine Grace is in the same state you're in right now."

"Do you think it was bad to just roll up on her doorstep like we did?"

"She did get a couple of hours notice, so no, I don't think it was a bad idea. She was definitely expecting you, and, I'd even say, looking forward to meeting you."

"I still feel like I have a million questions."

"So you'll ask them. I put the clothes in the dryer but we've got about twenty minutes to go. Hopefully they stall a bit so we're not sitting here in their bathrobes when they get back."

"Right? Way to make an awkward day even more awkward."

"Grace is pretty cool, though, don't you think?" he asks me. "I thought the more likely scenario would be something more in line with a dumpster fire, but so far, so good." He leans back so he can make eye contact. "What's your opinion of her?"

"I want to..." I shake my head, choked with tears.

"Come here," he whispers as he pulls me in close. "You're doing great," he says as he strokes his hand up and down the length of my back. *Keep doing that*, I want to tell him as I melt into his body. I am boneless, and his touch feels like it's the only thing holding me together at this point.

I ease back a bit and take a very deep breath. "What I was

going to say is that I have this overwhelming urge to tell her, 'I love you,' and that would be bananas, wouldn't it?"

He shrugs. "Maybe when love is something you feel deep inside, you should trust that it's true. When you look at a person and that's the thought that springs to mind, why question it so much?"

"Wise words."

"It's no joke. Hate is a visceral feeling, why not love?"

"I guess because those three words can be thrown around when they're not true."

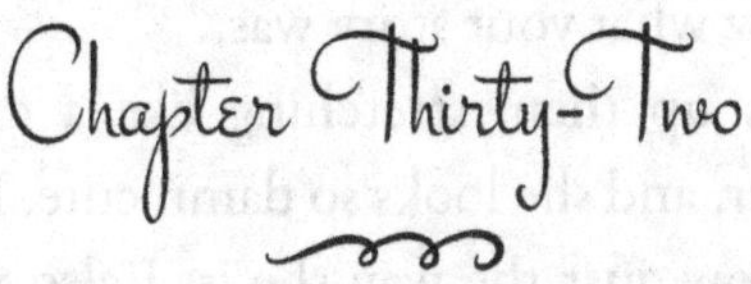

Chapter Thirty-Two

LIAM

"Are you guilty of throwing those words around?"

She nods. "What are you supposed to do when someone says they love you and you don't feel the same way?"

"I'm thinking this pertains to you and Parker?"

"Yep...So that makes two firsts that were burned on that jerk."

"You didn't mean it?"

She side eyes me while pinching her thumb and index finger together. "Not even a little bit. I always wondered what was the matter with me. Why I'd get uncomfortable when he started paying attention to me, and why I wasn't happy when he first asked me out. Everyone else thought it was great, but I wanted to hide myself away in my room or in the stables. I just wanted to be left alone."

"I'd say first impressions are on the money, but I didn't come off as a nice guy when we first met."

She pushes my chest like she's angry when she's clearly not. "I was intimidated by you, but intrigued."

"Intrigued?"

"You had the whole angry young man thing going on, and I wanted to know what your story was."

Sarah stands up then, stretching like a cat. The robe is swimming on her, and she looks so damn cute. I want to snap a picture of her now, just the way she is. I also want to tell her that love is the word that pops into my head, and my heart, when I look at her, but that is not happening. I go with a safer alternative, something that won't leave me hanging out to dry. "Just so you know, I never feel that way when you're around, the angry young man thing. These past few days, I'm just... happy."

"Same here. This has been a crazy few days, but you've made it so much better. I hope you know that."

When she reaches her hand out, I take it and coax her down to sit in my lap. "I'm glad I'm here with you."

Sarah settles in, ghosts her hands along the base of my neck until her fingers are twisted in my hair, tips her head to the side and drops a gentle kiss on my lips. Pulling back, she looks to gauge my reaction, and when she sees me smile, she goes in for more.

And this right here is everything I never knew I was missing. She feels small and soft in my arms, she smells so good I want to fill my lungs with the scent of her, and her eyes, when she breaks the kiss to look at me, are trusting. She trusts me.

I decide that I don't care if she's leaving. I'm going to soak her in, wring as much goodness from this while I can. I'm going to be with her for as long as she'll have me, and I'll be grateful when it's over, not bitter.

Easing her back onto the couch and positioning myself

over her, I kiss her lips, her neck, her collarbone, pausing to breathe her in every time I inhale. "Sarah," I whisper as I kiss a path back up to her mouth. *I want you...I need what you give me...There's no one but you.* That's what I want my kisses to tell her because I can't say the words.

"I want you," she whispers as her hand skims my chest and slides back up to cup my cheek.

"Someday," I tell her.

She says it back, her eyes soft and dreamy, "Someday."

The buzz of the dryer puts an end to our moment, but I don't ever want to forget what this feels like. A fierce sort of loyalty, an urge to shield someone from harm, a desire to be seen as good in someone's eyes—I've never felt this way about a girl before. And no one has ever looked at me the way Sarah does, like I'm her hero or something.

A few minutes later she comes out dressed in her clean clothes and hands me my clothes with an expression that tells me she's on the same sort of loopy high that I'm on.

If this ends—*when* this ends—I'll be the one left behind. I know that. For now, though, I'm going to forget about what's coming and just enjoy what I've got.

And today I've got Sarah Hamilton.

It's a good day.

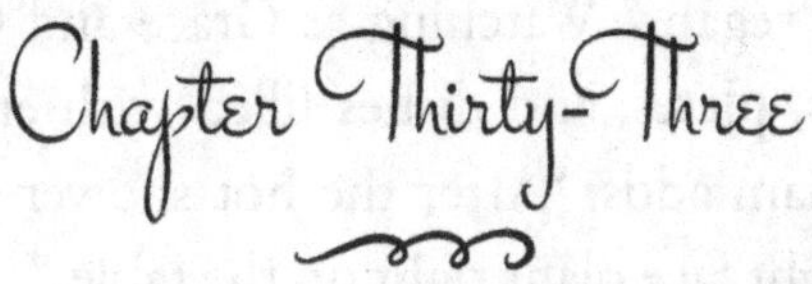

SARAH

"We got veggie wraps, chicken, roast beef—"

Owen cuts her off. "We basically got two of everything," he's teasing her and trying to ease her jittery nerves, "just in case."

She swats his shoulder. "Just in case either of you were vegan, gluten intolerant, allergic to chicken—"

"Seriously, is that even a thing?"

Grace answers him that yes, she once had a student who was allergic to turkey, but I'm only half-listening as I take in the way they move around one another, their playful back and forth. I'm only getting a glimpse, but Grace and Owen share something that brings the word *lucky* to mind, and also bears a striking resemblance to my parents' marriage. It's one thing to say you're in love, but to actually witness it like it's a living thing bouncing back and forth between two people is amazing.

My parents, that young couple from school, and now Grace and Owen—I've always had examples of true love in my life. Maybe that's why I was so uneasy most of the time while I was with Parker. I *knew* what I was missing out on, even if I didn't realize it at the time.

"I'm so hungry right now I'd scarf down a roast beef wrap even if I was a vegan." Watching as Grace and Owen put out serving platters, plates, and dishes filled with enough food to feed twenty, Liam adds, "After the hot shower and this meal, I'm afraid I might face plant right on the table."

Owen offers, "There's a guest room." Looking to Grace like the suggestion may have been a misstep, he backtracks and says, "There are *two* guest rooms. Plenty of space if you want to spend the night and then get on the road tomorrow."

I shake my head quick and say, "I really have to get back."

Grace passes me the pitcher, casually asking, "Do your parents know where you are?"

"They do now, but, um, I left yesterday without telling them where I was going." Grace takes a seat, letting my words sink in. "They know I'm at your house now. It's ok, but I told them I was heading back to New Jersey sometime later on today."

"New Jersey." It's as if she's speaking her thoughts out loud when she says, "I have so many questions."

Owen lowers his head in a way that speaks volumes. I get the impression that Grace has been in a lot of pain and Owen is the one who's been shouldering it right along with her.

"Me too," I say, reaching across to take her hand in mine. It's a small gesture, one that doesn't come close to the crushing hug I want to give and get back from her. "I have so many questions."

"Liam, do you want to bring some food down to Leo with me? We just passed by their place before and he's home alone working in his garage on something."

Without another word, Liam has his plate filled and Owen has a bag with some stuff packed. Liam leans down and lays a kiss on my hair as he grabs a bag of chips off the table. "You good?"

"Yeah."

And once the door shuts, Grace says, "He seems like a good one," referring to Liam.

"He definitely is. Hopefully my parents will come around someday."

"They don't like him?" I can tell she's now regretting the seal of approval she just bestowed on Liam.

"It's a very new thing, and let's just say there's been a lot going on these past few months." Answering her unspoken question, I say, "I didn't know I was adopted."

Grace is surprised, but to her credit, her response is measured and without a hint of judgement. "I imagine that must have been a shock. When did you find out? And how did you find out, if you don't mind me asking."

I don't mind at all. In fact, I think I could sit here for the next twenty-four hours talking to her. I can imagine Grace as the go-to person for the messed-up kids in her school.

"I kind of got blindsided in advanced biology. Which has me questioning whether or not I should major in bio, because the fact that my parents both have blue eyes and I have brown eyes never raised a red flag before that day."

"Isn't it possible?"

"Virtually *im*possible, is the way my teacher put it."

I take a bite of my sandwich even though I'm too keyed up to enjoy it. Putting it back down, I push the plate away and take another sip of my drink. She's waiting on me. "I always thought there was something odd about me. Not odd, but like...a sense that I don't belong." When Grace reaches over to stroke her thumb over my hand, I slip it back gently and put both hands in my lap. Like a seesaw in motion, I'm up and then down. I want her comfort and then I don't.

"I grew up having everything, and my parents are great, the *best*." I look to her as I emphasize that last word. Am I looking to hurt Grace? I'm not even sure. My shoulders lift in a half-hearted shrug. "I just always felt...different. It's hard to explain."

I'm surprised when I look back to her and she's fighting off tears with a smile. "But your parents were good to you. That's what I've prayed for every day."

I bite my lip to keep myself from breaking again, but I can't hold in the one word that's been eating away at me ever since I found that picture.

"Why?"

The tears are back and Grace is weeping right along with me. She stands, takes my hand and leads me to the couch. When we sit she pulls me right in, and just like before with Liam, I melt into this woman's touch, and cry what feels like a lifetime's worth of tears.

"I've spent about half of my life regretting that decision. It was the worst thing I've ever done in my life, the worst decision, and I've been paying for it ever since."

"But that day," my voice is the plaintive wail of a small child, "you could have changed your mind."

She eases back and nods. "It took me some time to even be able to go there, in my memory, back to the day you were born. Do you know I begged the social worker not to put you into my arms? I knew it would kill me. I knew it. And when she took you back, I thought I might die, right there in the bed." She looks down into her lap. "For a long time after that, I walked around in a daze. For years I really didn't care if I lived or I died." In response to my expression, she says, "There's a difference between being suicidal and having little in terms of a will to live. It's like living in black and white instead of color. You just go through the motions, wake up each day...exist."

"I'm sorry."

"You have *nothing* to be sorry about. I did that to myself." She grabs the box of tissues and offers me one before using a few to mop her own face. "Have you ever seen that show *Gilmore Girls*?"

"No."

"I feel like the universe revived that show just to mess with me." She delivers that line with a rueful laugh. "It first came out when I was in college. It's cute, borderline sappy...Hallmark movie-type stuff that I'd usually go for. But it was like a sucker punch. I'd hole up in my room, pretending I needed to study whenever my roommates watched it."

"Why?"

"Because it was what *could* have been. A young mom, the daughter she gave birth to and raised on her own, extended family, the charm of small-town life...I caught one episode and decided I could never subject myself to it again." Giving my hands a gentle squeeze, she says, "In my mind it was exactly what we could have been, me with you."

"Do Damien's parents know about me?"

"They were both deceased before I even met your father. His mother came to this country from Ireland, his father from Norway, both immigrants. When they married they settled in the Bronx, and that's where he was raised...An area called Riverdale. Damien's mother died of cancer when he was in high school, and he told me his father died of what he swore was a broken heart a few years later, when he was a freshman at Fordham University." She's wistful, back in the memory when she adds, "My parents didn't have the best marriage, but Damien described his parents as soul mates."

"What was he like?"

"He was *really* good looking...Drove a motorcycle...A decorated U.S. Marine with a crewcut. He just gave off this very capable, manly vibe." She laughs at herself. "He was a badass, but the sweetest, kindest badass. Never...I'd never met anyone like him before."

"Where did you meet?"

She rolls her eyes. "In an off-campus bar. But then he showed up out of the blue when I was on my way to class and we had lunch. He confessed to stalking me for a few days before spotting me." I nod, urging her to go on because I'm engrossed in this story of how my parents met, and so far, it's beyond romantic. "A few nights later he took me out on a proper first date, and we talked for hours." Looking to the heavens, she says, "I told him more about myself in that one night than I'd ever shared with any other person. Damien was just like that. He was a great listener."

"What Owen was about to say before...Do I look like him?"

She shakes her head and then glances up at the ceiling, or maybe towards Heaven. "You have no idea." Her brow creases before she asks, "Do you want to see a picture?"

"Of course!"

Grace gestures for me to follow to her bedroom. "I had a few pictures framed, hoping someday I could show them to you."

And the idea that she's been waiting, preparing and planning for this moment has me welling up again. But it's with gratitude and relief, not sadness.

She takes a box down from a shelf in her closet. "Here," she says, unwrapping the first frame and handing it to me. It's a picture of the two of them, a selfie where they're sitting on the bumper of a truck, facing one another.

"He loved you, and you loved him."

"With all my heart."

There's no denying it. His eyes, her smile. They are happiness personified, sharing a look that says you've found your way home and realize there's no where else you'd rather be.

She hands me another, and I notice that Grace stares at the one I just handed back to her. I wonder what it was like for her. To lose him. To find out you're having a baby and the man you loved will never be coming home to you. The life you thought you'd have...gone.

She points to the one I'm holding. "He was showing off in that one." Damien is holding a fishing pole in one hand with a pitifully small fish at the end of the line while flexing his other bicep muscle. "Damien took me camping a few times, and those trips to the river were amazing. He could set up camp, catch a fish, clean it, cook it over an open fire and serve it up." She shakes her head and then starts to laugh. "One time he even packed cilantro and limes for a marinade."

"Wow." I'm responding to the picture more than her words. Staring at this stranger's face, I see the brown hair, the dark eyes, but I don't see me. "Do you really think I look like him?"

She nods slowly. "When you smile and you're happy, your eyes sparkle the way his did. I noticed it before when Liam said something that made you laugh."

Grace stares down into her lap for a moment before handing over a smaller frame with a shrug. "This is the last one...It's just of me." She says this as if it makes the picture less valuable or important, while I'm dying to get a glimpse of the person she was back then. "He took it. I only saved it because I like how I came out in it. Back then, I always thought of myself as fat, but he made me feel gorgeous for the first time in my life." She reads my skepticism for what it is. "I trained in classical ballet from the time I was seven. 'You're getting fat,' was my teacher's way of saying, 'Good morning.'"

"That's—"

"Disturbing. I know."

"How long was this before he left?"

"Three weeks, maybe? I wanted you to see them so you'd understand...So you'd know you came from a place of so much love. I have no doubt he would have come back to me, and I know he would have been the absolute best father. He was robbed of the life he deserved.

"Back then, I'd think to myself that he was probably looking down, so disappointed in me, so angry at me for not fighting. I'd go back to the river and talk to him sometimes. When I moved back up north, I'd go to the river there, too. It was part therapy, part confessional. I think he'd forgive me, and after a lot of work, I finally came to a point where I was able to forgive myself. I hope someday you can forgive me, too."

"I don't know what I'd do if I got pregnant at nineteen, so I'd be a hypocrite to criticize you."

"If I can give you *one* piece of advice, I'd just tell you to never go it alone, no matter what problem you're facing. You think you'll be disappointing people, letting them down, but the people who love you will always be in your corner and be there to help you. I couldn't see that at the time."

Chapter Thirty-Four

SARAH

Grace looks at the clock on her stove as she sets a kettle down to make tea. "It's already six o'clock. I feel like we're on borrowed time."

I know what she means. Grace doesn't know the first thing about me, and I could ask her questions for the next who knows how long and still be left wanting.

I give her all the bullet points. She knows I ride. Knows all about Shadow. I told her about my friends, leaving out the part about my mother's hand in wrangling those relationships for me.

"So how did you meet Liam?"

"His uncle manages the stable at my club. His uncle has known me since I was eight, when I started to ride. Liam took a job at the club this past spring, so I met him there."

"And you said this is a new thing..."

She's fishing and I don't mind. I want to talk about Liam, do anything to sort through the crazy swirl of emotions I have

241

when he comes to mind. "I was dating someone else. A guy my parents," I pause to clarify, "really someone my *mother* approved of." I answer the question she's not asking, "We have money, his family has money…"

"I got that from the horse part. I didn't ride growing up, but I knew girls who did. Financially, it's no joke."

"Exactly. My mother is a good person, she's not mean or anything, but maybe she puts too much emphasis on things that aren't really important."

"And Liam being the guy who mucks the stalls at the country club rather than, say, hitting the links, isn't her top choice for you?"

"Bingo. And meanwhile, intellectually speaking, Liam is the smartest boy I've ever met. And he's a better all-around person than my boyfriend was, that's for sure."

"You drove through the town where I worked. It's basically at the bottom of the school district barrel. *So* many of those kids were smart, with so much potential, but just lacked the advantages that you and I grew up with."

"That's not your hometown?"

"No. I went to live with my aunt after I graduated. My parents had both remarried, my brother was away at school. There was nothing for me at home."

"Are you close to your family?"

"I am now. My mother and I have been repairing our relationship over the past two years. She wasn't perfect, but in all fairness, I started pushing both of them away when I was young…like twelve or thirteen. They were very busy people, and if you weren't as competitive as they were at the time, you felt like a person standing on a dock with a suitcase in your hand, watching as the boat pulled away."

"So your mother had a career?"

"They're both physicians, and so is my brother."

I can feel my eyes go wide as I acknowledge this possible link. "I'm pre-med."

"I was going to say something before when you mentioned majoring in biology, but I didn't want to push the whole, *See, we are related* thing."

"That's weird though, right?"

"Maybe, maybe not. I just know that it wasn't for me. I tried, but I just always had my head in a book, and it wasn't *Gray's Anatomy*. I've always wanted to teach."

"What about Damien?"

"He was majoring in business at Fordham. I told you his father died when he was a freshman, and then the World Trade Center was attacked at the beginning of his sophomore year. He told me a lot of Fordham alumni died, also a few people his father had worked with, and he felt like he was just sitting in class doing nothing important. So he finished out the year and then enlisted."

"Wow. Did his father work there?"

"Yes, before he died. He was a maintenance worker and a handyman on the side. His mother worked at Lincoln Center, which for me, as a fallen ballerina, was fascinating."

I sense there's a story there. "Fallen?"

She gets up from the couch, smiling. "We'll save that one for another time. Let's just say that I love to dance, not to be told *how* to dance." Looking back to the table, she asks, "Could you eat something now? I'm hungry."

"Yeah, I could eat."

We spend the next five minutes working our way through a veggie wrap we share, but it's not long before we're lobbing questions back and forth at one another again.

She tells me about visiting her brother and his wife out in

California, her friends in North Carolina, and her parents, all over the course of one summer, referring to it as the *national leg of my telling the truth tour*. This makes me laugh, even though I know there was nothing laughable about that time in her life. But the relief and closure it gave her allowed her to move on with her life. *Not to leave you behind, or Damien, but to live my life again*. She doesn't need to reassure me on this. I get it.

Then I tell her the basics around the Penny-Parker betrayal, and she's respectful enough to listen without piling judgement on either one of them. "Would you hate me if I say that I feel bad for Penny? Maybe I shouldn't but I do."

"Believe me, I've tried so hard to hate her but I can't. She was my best...No, she was my *only* friend for years. The other two friends in my group are great, but we're flighty friends. Does that make sense?"

She nods. "People you think will probably breeze in and out of your life?"

"Exactly. But Penny has been my steady since the fourth grade. I cannot wrap my head around it, why she'd do this to me."

"And Parker?"

Without taking a nanosecond to censor myself, I wave the question, his name, and every last thing about him off into thin air. "I don't give a shit about him."

This makes her clap her hands and laugh so hard she actually starts coughing. "Bravo!" she says after catching her breath.

When I get quiet, she presses me gently. "You have something on your mind. You can ask me anything, or say anything, really."

"Did you have a lot of friends growing up?"

She takes in a deep breath and lets it out. I think it soothes us both. "I had dance friends, I had friends in school, but I never really had true friends until I went away to college." She looks away for a moment, wrestling with something. "I had a hard time in high school."

"Doesn't everyone?"

"Maybe it seems that way, at least to some degree, anyway. But I've witnessed a lot in my years teaching that age group. Some people do sail through and thrive, some struggle, and most float somewhere in between. In my case, I don't think my parents splitting up helped matters. But I made it through, and then college was such a good change for me. I got matched with two roommates, and luckily, we got along great." Grace gets up and takes my plate. "Frannie and Reese, along with my two former star students, also known as the fabulous Perillo twins, are my closest girlfriends." I follow her, and looking up to me as she stacks the plates in the dishwasher, she says, "I find that I don't need a lot of friends—"

"Just true ones."

She nods in agreement. "Penny may or may not be a lost cause. What she did was really horrible, but time is a funny thing."

"Heals all wounds?"

She's talking about us when she answers, "I hope so."

Grace notices when I look down to my phone. There are two missed call notifications.

"Your mom?" Wiping her hands on a dishrag, she says, "I'd love to meet her someday. Your mother *and* your father."

It cracks me open again, hearing her refer to them as my parents, because she's that, too. Maybe it's just that I don't want to let go of this young love fairytale that's been taking root and growing in my mind. Grace and Damien and their baby. The happy family that could have been.

"Huh?"

"I said I'd like to thank them, if I ever get the chance someday."

I recover without her noticing that I spaced out there for a second. "I think you'd like them, and they'd like you."

"Adoption is complicated. I've thought about it before, but maybe never fully realized how complicated it is until you arrived on my doorstep today."

"It is, but how do you see it?"

"There's always an up and down, someone happy, and maybe someone who's not so happy." Bringing two cups of tea with her, she sits back down at the dining room table and gestures for me to follow. "What I mean is that today, this was the best possible surprise, for *me*." Those words hang in the air for a few seconds. "I've been praying for you to find me, dreaming of this day for so long. But your parents, especially because they didn't know this was coming, I'd imagine they're not feeling crazy elated the way I am today." Pushing a plate of cannolis my way, she adds, "Buckets of tears and runny noses aside, make no mistake," her eyes begin to water again, "I'm so happy you're here, Sarah."

I take one, take a bite, and swallow the emotion down. Grace hasn't given me any reason to think otherwise, but I guess I needed to hear it said out loud, plain and simple.

She's glad I came.

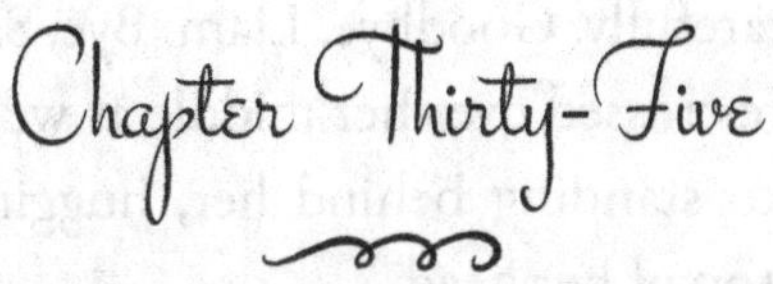

Chapter Thirty-Five

LIAM

"Thank you so much for coming." Grace is fighting off tears and Owen is standing behind her with both hands on her shoulders as the four of us stand in the driveway.

Sarah and Grace hugged before, and the moment was laced with so much pain that I had to look away.

No one is saying when exactly they'll see or speak to one another again, but all that stuff is hanging in the air. I suppose the ball is in Sarah's court. Sarah has Grace's phone number, her email and her address. Grace has Sarah's information, too, but I'm betting she'll wait for Sarah to reach out first. If I were in Grace's shoes that's what I'd do.

Once we're back in my car, they're both sporting watery smiles as they wave their goodbyes.

"Wait!" Grace calls out, and then stops short. "Do you want—"

"Oh my God, the pictures, yes!"

Owen comes over while Grace is retrieving whatever

picture it is, and leans down with one hand on the top of the car. "I can't tell you how much this means to Grace...How much it's meant to both of us." When Grace comes jogging back out with a box, he backs away. "Drive safe, you two."

"Yes, drive carefully. Goodbye, Liam. Bye, Sarah."

Her arms are crossed over her middle as we drive away, and Owen is back to standing behind her, hugging her with his chin resting on top of her head.

Sarah lets out a deep, cleansing breath once we're down the street. At the stop sign, I see a kid riding full-speed on her bike, pink tassels hanging from the handlebars and a faux purple mohawk helmet on her head.

Coming to a stop, she slaps one hand against her chest. "Oh, thank goodness I caught you!" The girl has skills, I'll give her that. Breathless and wide-eyed, she says, "I wanted to tell you I'm turning nine on September nineteenth, and you two are invited to my birthday party, ok?"

"That's really sweet, Olivia. Can we let you know? This is pretty far from where we live."

I nudge Sarah's thigh and whisper, "Just tell her yes," to which Sarah gives me a look, one that says, *I'm not lying to a little girl*. I can't help but shake my head.

"It's not too far, *please* come...Please, please, please—"

"Olivia, I told you to stay on our street."

Leo comes jogging up and tells her that he'll put her bike away for good if she disobeys him again. To which Olivia pouts and says, "You said to be," she taps her chin like she's trying to remember, "a independent thinker."

"*An* independent thinker...And don't twist my words."

Turning to us, he tells Sarah he's glad he got the chance to meet her, and then leans down to look across to me. "Remember what I said, ok?"

"The party is going to be humungous!"

"Let's go, Libs."

"Bye, Liam," she sing-songs as Leo is pulling her bike by the handlebars. "Bye, Bug!"

"She's a trip, isn't she?"

"Yeah," I agree. "A handful, but very cute."

"What was that between you and her dad?"

"Oh, Leo?"

"Yeah," she laughs, "your good buddy Leo."

"Nothing. He was just interested in knowing about how I got into fixing crap, to which I couldn't really give him an answer." I look between Sarah and the road. "You know how many times Jeff beat my ass because I was always taking shit apart?"

"He sounds like a monster."

"That's an insult to monsters." Taking the turn that has us heading back east, I tell her about being a kid, and being able to figure out how to fix stuff just by watching someone do it or just by trial and error.

"It's like people who can hear a song then sit down at the piano or some other instrument and play it. No lessons, no endless hours of honing a skill. What you have is a gift," she tells me.

I shrug, uncomfortable with being compared to the truly gifted, but lapping up her praise nonetheless. "Anyway, he said to get in touch when I'm ready to start applying for schools, said maybe he can help me with work study grants through his company. Apparently, he's some big deal."

"Great!"

"Cool your jets, Tiny. Don't go jumping on the grand plans for Liam wagon, ok?"

She's practically dancing in her seat, but then looks to me with her brow furrowed and a fake-ass frown. "Understood."

When we hit the highway, it's already after eight and the sun is going down. "The GPS says we'll be rolling in around one, one-thirty."

"I'm going to text my parents and tell them not to wait up."

"But you know they're going to."

"Maybe they won't. I'm adding, 'Can we talk first thing tomorrow?' That would be way better, don't you think?"

"For you, totally. You could do with some time to wrap your head around everything that's happened today." When I see she's chewing her nail, I reach over to lower her hand. "Why don't you close your eyes for a while and try to rest. Today was a lot."

And when I look over a few minutes later, I see her eyes are shut and I can hear the steady rhythm of her breath. Girl is done passed out. I roll down my window so the breeze can keep me alert, and I drive, alone with my thoughts.

And her phone's GPS is on the money, because it's one-twenty-eight when I turn into Sarah's long-ass driveway, making it exactly one-thirty when I cut the engine outside her house.

"Sarah, we're here."

She rouses from a deep sleep, then her eyes blink open in surprise when she sees where we are. "I'm home."

"Yep."

She stretches, making the shirt she's wearing ride up. My first thought is: *Will I ever get to see that again?* Which makes me an ass because I should be more concerned about her emotional well being at the moment. But the future has been on my mind these past few hours, and I've come to the obvious conclusion that there's not much I can do except let her know I'm in if she wants me.

"Can I call you tomorrow?"

"No," she looks at me, so serious that I can feel the bottom falling out. "I want you to come over for lunch and hang out."

"Here?"

"Yeah," she looks at me like I'm an imbecile. "You don't have to work until seven, right?"

"I should get in there by six."

"Perfect." She reaches for the door handle but turns back to me. "If we're going to do this, they're going to have to deal with it. And Liam," there's a plea in her eyes, "you have to give a little, too. There's no me without them, just like I'm going to tell my parents there's no me without you." She leans over and gives me one soft kiss. "See you tomorrow."

I nod, letting her know I'm on board because those words sound so good coming from her.

There's no me without you.

Chapter Thirty-Six

SARAH

Time to face the music.

After stretching for a solid five minutes, I hop into the shower so I can face them with a clear head. I'm going to need coffee for this also. I'm officially stalling when I start thinking about Tatiana, the person I can thank for my morning coffee addiction.

Walking into the kitchen, I'm nervous. I'm not afraid they'll be mad at me or anything, but I am afraid that by going to see Grace, I've gone ahead and fractured something between us that I won't be able to repair.

My mother is at the coffee machine with her back turned to me. "Just gimme a second. I heard you in the shower so I started the coffee."

"Mom," the word comes out choked. I walk up behind her and hug her around the waist. She's shaking with sobs the same way I am, and when she turns to embrace me, I get a glimpse of the swollen eyes that tell me she's shed at least as many tears as I have these past few days.

"I love you, Sarah, so much."

"I love you, too."

"Come," she tells me, leading me to the couch, coffee forgotten. And when we sit, I realize everything about my mother seems different. She's dressed in terrycloth sweats, her hair is piled into a messy topknot and her face is a mess from crying, but it's not that. She sounds different. There's no bright smile, no overly chipper greeting—she's not trying so hard.

"Do you want to tell me about it?"

I nod, still incapable of speech. I wipe my nose on my sleeve and take a breath that comes out in one long, shaky exhale. "I found the picture of her a couple of months ago. I tried to ask you, but—"

She lowers her head. "It was that day you were looking through your baby album. I was afraid that day. I thought maybe you knew."

"So then why?"

"Deep down, I've always been afraid that you'd find her and," she shakes her head, "this sounds so juvenile, but I've always been afraid you'd like her better, that you'd love her more than me."

"Mom."

"I realize how pathetic that sounds, believe me, but it's the truth."

"I'll never—"

She puts her hand up to stop me. "You don't have to say that. I've had a lot of time to think over the past forty-eight hours, Sarah. And it's not like I've had some epiphany or anything. You have us, and you'll *always* have me and Dad, but you also have the mother and the father who gave you life and gave you *to* us. This is the reality of adoption. It's what I knew and accepted going into this, but somewhere along the way," she sighs, "it jut became easier to...keep it simple." She shrugs and lowers her gaze. "And if you never found out, I asked myself, would that be so terrible? The fantasy I've held on to is that you'd always be ours. You'd always be mine."

I've looked at this from her side, tried my best to walk in her shoes, so what she's saying doesn't make me angry. I get it. "I understand, kind of. At least I think I do."

"I don't even know if *I* understand how I could have walked away the way I did that day, like your father and I were victorious or something. I watched," she confesses, "hidden off to the side as that girl held you in the hospital. And after it was all said and done, I pretended I left something behind, but I really just wanted one last look. Sarah," my mother croaks, "the girl was turned to the wall but I could tell she was weeping."

The admission makes me sick and desperately sad at the same time. I want to hold Grace as she was in that moment, be the friend she needed. My mother takes my hand. "A better person would have asked her if she was sure, or in the very least, if she needed help."

We're both quiet for a moment before she says, "There were times when I'd feel like a terrible person in those first few weeks, but that was offset by the crazy amount of joy I felt every time I held you in my arms.

"I hope you never know that kind of pain, Sarah. I've actually laid awake in bed at night, praying to God that you never know what it's like to ache for a baby only to be crushed by disappointment month after month." She sags back against the couch. "Do you think...you'll be able to forgive me someday?"

I nod, not looking at her, but from the corner of my eye I can see this gives her a glimmer of hope. I'm back and forth the same way I was with Grace. It's not just the adoption lie that's been between the two of us these past few years. It's way more complicated than that.

"I can't believe you saw me as a happy person." I meet the surprise in her eyes with my own disappointment. "Didn't you notice that I wasn't like everyone else?" She doesn't answer. "Maybe I didn't know for a long time, but I've always *felt* different. I don't know how to explain it, but I've just always felt like I'm on the outside looking in."

My mother looks crushed by this. "You're perfect. I hope you know that you're perfect in my eyes." A cheerless laugh escapes before she says, "And your father worships the ground you walk on. I don't have to reassure you in that department."

My smile is weak. I do know my father and my mother love me, but I don't want to fall back into what we were. I won't.

"Mom, I don't need to be reassured or anything, I know you love me...I just wish you would have been truthful with me. I think it would have spared us both a lot of grief."

"In what way?" Now it's me who doesn't answer. She looks like she's unsure of what to say or do, but makes a decision to take a breather and I'm on board for that. "Want that coffee now?" I nod, and she leaves me to go back into the kitchen.

I'm praying so hard that she uses this moment to take stock, instead of strategizing the way she normally does. I get up and join her in the kitchen, hoping for the best but expecting the usual. I don't want her to make this better, I just want her to be honest.

"Thanks." I take a sip the second she hands me the mug, noting that she went the extra mile and put cinnamon in my coffee. It conjures up a memory of her calling me her cinnamon girl while doing a god-awful rendition of that old song paired with some groovy *Look at me, I'm at Woodstock* dance. It was playful and cute in her mind, but I was cringing and on the verge of blowing a brain vessel as she performed in front of Parker.

"Why did you do that cinnamon girl thing in front of Parker? Do you remember that?"

For a nanosecond she looks lost, and I feel a seething mix of defeat and anger rising when I sense she's reverting back to clueless Audrey, fun-mom mode. But instead she locks eyes with me and nods slowly. "I remember."

"That was beyond embarrassing, it was...creepy." She visibly shrinks, but I don't care. I'm feeling mean, and she needs to hear this. "You always butt in and act like you're a part of it when my friends are over. It's like you're trying to relive your youth or something." It's hard not to scowl as I imitate her dance moves, flower-girl arms blowing in the breeze and hips swaying, when I add, "Do you realize, *Audrey*, how mortifying it is?"

She absorbs the blow and then lobs one right back at me. "Do *you* know what it's been like being *your* mother for the past couple of years? I cannot do one damn thing right in your eyes." I take a stool at the kitchen island quietly, feeling just the slightest twinge of guilt. "You shoot daggers at me every damn time I *dare* to open my mouth and speak. Do *you* remember sitting at the dinner table last week and asking Dad if he'd read the article about that rapper?"

I shake my head, to which she shoots back a look that tells me she thinks I'm full of it. "You *asked* him if he'd read that article in the business section of the Times about the company's IPO."

"So what?"

"So I was sitting right there, but you excluded me from the conversation, which, by the way, you do *all* the time." When I don't respond, she says, "I was the communications department head at the investment bank where Dad and I met." Her voice gets louder. "I know just as much, if not *more*, about the marketing of IPOs, but you treat me as if I'm incapable of adult conversation." I sit still, absorbing what is sickeningly making sense to me as I see myself through her eyes. "You sit there, *so* clever and *so* condescending. Do you think before you came into the picture that I was some pretty thing fetching coffee for the boss, or sitting home knitting booties for the children I couldn't have? I had a *life*, a big, important life."

"You never talk about your life."

She takes a seat across from me, tears pooling, looking pale and weak. "Because I gave up everything for you." All her anger is gone as her eyes search mine. "And I was glad to give it all up. When the idea of you finally seemed like it might actually become a reality, we were both over the moon. The day we got the call," she pauses, "that a college student was eight months pregnant and adamant she was going to put her child up for adoption, I handed in my resignation on the spot."

My mother lowers her head for a moment and then lifts her head from her hands, breathing out. "How did we even get here? I didn't mean for this to turn into a fight."

"We're not fighting. I mean, this is hard but maybe it's good, you know?"

"I haven't even given you a chance to tell me what happened down there."

"We've got time for that."

My father walks in the front door holding a box from my favorite bakery. He looks between us, leans down to place a kiss on my head and then asks my mother, "Should I come back?"

"Dad, just give us a few more minutes, ok?"

He nods and smiles at her, a gesture that says: *You've got this*, and his love for her has me feeling terrible for what I've put her through.

"I could just say I never realized I was hurting you when I'd cut you out of what Dad and I were doing or talking about, but honestly, there's a part of me that was doing it to punish you. I just...always got the feeling that you wanted me to be a carbon copy of you."

With genuine curiosity, she asks, "I made you feel that way?"

"By arranging my friendships, by pushing me to dress a certain way, to date certain boys...It's the same as saying, like, 'No, you're doing it wrong, I'll show you how it's done.' But I'll never look like you, I'll never be effortlessly social the way you are, I'm..."

"What?"

"I'm me. I'm plain."

She laughs out loud. "Plain? No, honey, you're stunning, with curves that girls like me would have killed for at your age." I shake my head when she sticks to defining physical traits. "But more importantly, you're smart, you're driven, and you're this petite woman who can control a mammoth horse, and that's fierce. You *do* attract people. You're just not a social butterfly...I'm starting to get that."

"I don't think I'll ever be a butterfly, but I'm good with who I am."

"I love you," she pauses to place a hand against her chest, "exactly the way you are."

My father comes back, surveys the scene and then gives us each a hug. The three of sit around the kitchen island, drinking coffee and talking about my road trip. I make sure to pepper Liam's name in liberally, to make certain there's no confusion as to where I stand with him. My mother looks to my father when I do this, but doesn't comment.

I describe Grace, give them her background story, tell them she definitely left a clear path for me to find her, and that she was happy when I did.

"Was it difficult?" my father asks.

"I felt bad for Liam, I was like a yo-yo going back and forth. *Let's go, let's go home*...I was pretty indecisive but he never pushed me one way or the other. And when I finally did meet Grace—"

My mother interrupts, "How *exactly* did it happen?"

"She knew we were on the way, so I think she was waiting for us to pull up, and then she came out and met me on their doorstep."

My father asks, "Who else was there?"

"No one at first, but then her husband Owen came home."

I tell them about Owen, that he's a History professor at Pitt, and how he was injured serving as a Marine. "They have a nice relationship." I look from him to my mother. "Their marriage seems solid. It reminded me of how you two are together."

"Owen already knew about you?"

"Yes, he was the first person she told after keeping the whole pregnancy and delivery a secret for like fifteen years. Grace told me she just worked up the courage to tell her parents, her brother and her friends a year or two ago. There were a lot of tears," I tell them, "but it felt so good to hear her talk about it. I needed so many questions answered, and she did that for me."

Remembering the pictures, I tell them to give me a second as I run upstairs to retrieve the box. Carefully, I take out the one I love the most and unwrap it. "This is Grace, and my father, Damien Erikson."

Peeking up, I see that my father doesn't seem the least bit slighted, and I'm grateful. I don't want to have to tightrope my way around titles for the rest of my life just to spare everyone's feelings.

It's like my mother said, this is the reality of adoption. There will always be my birth parents, Grace Dawson and Damien Erikson, and my mother and father, Audrey and Daniel Hamilton, the two people who have loved me and cared for me my entire life. Each and every one of those four people are a part of me.

The doorbell rings. I hop off my stool and announce with a smile, "Liam's here."

Chapter Thirty-Seven

LIAM

"What's so funny?"

I look around at what I'm assuming is called the foyer, with it's thirty-foot ceiling, massive chandelier, and an artwork collection that is certainly full of originals. A specific song has been running through my head for the twenty-five minutes it takes to ride over here, because while I'll admit to being a little nervous, there is something undeniably ridiculous about this peace summit.

"Have you ever heard the song *Punk Rock Girl*?"

"Nope. Who sings it?"

"Dead Milkmen. It's old. Just...sort of fits this particular *meet the parents* situation."

Sarah eyes me suspiciously. "Is this like a Neidermeyer thing?"

"Huh?"

"*Animal House*? I watched it after you caught me feeding Shadow that carrot. Ring a bell?"

He starts cracking up. "Yeah, sorry 'bout that."

"I watched it as soon as I came home that day. First off, you could never make a movie like that today."

He nods. "It's beyond politically incorrect."

"But the Neidermeyer thing was funny."

"And spot on."

"Whatever you say." As she turns and gestures for me to follow her inside, I take her wrist. "How did it go?"

"It was a lot, but it's good. We're good now."

I don't know if the *we're* she's referring to means Sarah and her parents, or that her parents are on board with me and Sarah. Door number two isn't likely so I won't be holding my breath.

In the kitchen, it's dead quiet except for the hissing sound of the coffee machine. Her mom is smoothing her messy hair back from off her face and her father is standing there just waiting to greet me. They're both dressed casually, possibly even in the clothes they slept in. That alone has me feeling like I've walked into an alternate universe.

Mr. Hamilton steps forward, smiling with eyes that tell me he hasn't gotten much sleep. "Good Morning, Liam. Thank you for driving Sarah, and for making sure she was all right. We appreciate it." He shakes my hand, a firm grip with eye contact.

"Don't thank me. I was happy to do it."

"Liam," her mother approaches me with an outstretched hand. "I'm Audrey Hamilton. We haven't properly met, and I'm truly sorry about the way our last conversation went."

I don't say anything, because *the way our last conversation went* implies that I spoke, when in fact, I just stood there while she lobbed accusations and called me names. I hesitate, but for Sarah's sake I take her outstretched hand as I study her. Her skin is washed out, her face is swollen and her eyes are bloodshot. The angry, ramrod-straight posture she had the other day when she was screaming bloody murder is gone. Now she has her free hand resting on the kitchen island to support herself.

Her breath stutters as she closes her eyes. Does she find the idea of me in their life so awful she can't bring herself to really look at me? It's either that or she's ashamed to face me after calling me trash. I drop my hand when the moment drags on too long, and she turns to go back and fuss at the coffee machine. "Liam, how do you take your coffee?"

"I don't drink coffee, but thanks."

"Oh," she turns back to look at me, and then she doesn't know what to do with her hands. I'm not enjoying her discomfort, but I'm not unhappy about it either.

Mr. Hamilton says, "Would you like a soda, a water?"

And while I want to say no just to punish them by keeping this uncomfortable silence going, I can see Sarah from the corner of my eye looking nervously between me and her father. "Water would be great, thank you."

He hands me a cut crystal water glass. "Sarah said you're starting school in September?"

I shoot Sarah a look, hoping she hasn't gone and tried to sell the idea of me to her parents. If so, I could have told her not to waste her energy. What *I'm* selling? Mr. and Mrs. Hamilton *definitely* aren't buying.

I give the briefest of nods. "Community college."

Mrs. Hamilton says my name, and I'm thinking she's about to launch into some *that's great* bullshit, to tell me how community college is a great start or something, and just the sound of her voice has me on the verge of boiling over. So I'm surprised when her next words aren't directed at me, but at them. "Can you two give us a minute?"

"Can we sit?" she asks me.

I take a seat across from her and see that she's looking at my shirt. I spent a few minutes changing the oil in my car before coming over, so there's a little grease on my Dunes t-shirt. I'd like to say it was an accident, but honestly, Maeve pointed it out to me before I left. I guess I subconsciously wanted both of them, but especially this snob sitting across from me, to notice the dirt, the grime, the *trash*.

"What I said the other day..." She's twisting the rock on her left ring finger nervously and her eyes are looking here, there and everywhere. I'm not doing shit to make this any easier for her, and if she thinks she can apologize without even making eye contact, she can shove it. But it's as if she can hear me, or she's telling herself the exact same thing. She stops her fidgeting, breath shuddering as she draws in air to steady herself, and then looks me in the eye. "What I said was horrible, and thoughtless, and it wasn't true."

I look down at the counter, surprised but not satisfied or happy in the least. Shame is my kryptonite. Maybe it's everyone's. Once an insult, hatred, or judgement is dished out, a simple sorry doesn't just wipe the slate clean. Maybe she is genuinely sorry, but I'm still sitting in this grand kitchen wearing my stained shirt, with my stained past, coming from my dilapidated house and my low class family.

But is that her judging me right now, or am I judging myself? For years I've worn this uniform of hardship with pride, with a giant *fuck you* to anyone who finds me lacking, but who am I kidding in this grease-stained shirt? I left the house knowing I had a clean spare in the backseat of my car because I'd *never* show up to work in a dirty shirt, even for a job that requires cleaning tap lines, carrying kegs, and assorted other filthy tasks. So who is this little performance for? What do I gain from making her despise me?

Deep breath, Liam. "I accept your apology."

Her head is tilted to the side, searching to make contact with my downcast eyes. When she does, she gives me a reassuring nod with her watery smile. "I'll do better."

Chapter Thirty-Eight

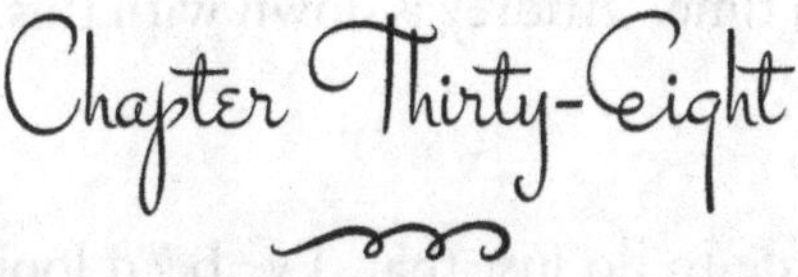

LIAM

My damn heart skips a beat when she comes out of the house with an overnight bag slung over her shoulder.

I bounce out to get her door before she reaches the car. "Hey, you."

"Thank you kindly," she says, curtsying like a wiseass before getting in.

I'm about to ask her if she packed the bikini she wore the other day— my personal favorite—when I see that her mother is standing in the doorway watching us. She smiles when our eyes meet. She's trying, I guess, but I'm still not convinced she's on board with the idea of me. Whatever, I'm not letting her ruin this just when it's getting good.

"Hi, Mrs. Hamilton."

"Hi, Liam. Have fun, you two," she says, waving once before going back inside.

Turning to Sarah as I start down the driveway, I ask, "She's all right with this?"

"She'd be all right if I was driving off with Parker, so why not with you?"

"Um, because it's me?"

She rolls her eyes as if she's tired of revisiting this topic for the umpteenth time. "Audrey is down with this."

"Right."

"Let it go."

And I decide to do just that. I've been looking forward to this weekend, and I'm not going to let Audrey Hamilton ruin it. If I'm being honest, she *has* gone out of her way to make me feel welcome in their home these past few weeks, but I'd still bet my last dime she's praying that I'll be dust in her daughter's rear-view mirror come September.

"I'm glad we decided on staying local. I don't think she's got another epic quest in her." I lovingly caress the dashboard of the car I used to disdain. "And I need her to last through this year before selling her off to the highest bidder."

"Maybe Leo will buy it."

I shoot her a side eye. "I don't know if I'm so high on Leo after what he said about my ink."

"You know he was just trying to be helpful. And, um, you have to admit, letting Mike *practice* on you might not have been a wise decision."

I look down at the mermaid on my left forearm, the one who's more ripped than Conor McGregor. "You've got a point."

"Have you ever gone camping before?"

"With Mike's family. You?"

"Nope. I'm relying on you for *everything*."

I reach over to stroke my hand up her smooth thigh. "You're in luck...I'm *very* reliable."

She leans her head back and sighs. Sarah looks content, and

if I've had anything to do with the blissed-out mood she's been in lately, I'm grateful.

She's been in contact with Grace, talking on the phone once a week, and she usually calls me after to relay their conversations and to process it all.

It's a lot. She's balancing her mother's feelings on one side and her desire to connect with Grace on the other. Mr. Hamilton has been a steady presence through it all. He's good and he's patient with both Sarah and with his wife. I decided within a week of coming back from our grand adventure that he is, in fact, a good dude.

He went to bat for me at their club, and after securing my settlement and getting my uncle a raise, the club turned around and rescinded their membership.

I don't know about Sarah's mother, but I'm pretty sure her father was relieved, if not thrilled. The only problem was Shadow. Kicking the Hamiltons out meant the horse couldn't stay, but like my Aunt Maeve is always saying, *When God closes a door he opens a window.*

And Mr. Hamilton? His kind of money can open doors, windows, the Hoover Dam...

He's decided to fund a program that helps disabled children and adults by exposing them to riding, or just interacting with gentle horses. I'd never heard of equine therapy before, but it sounds really interesting. It's just in the planning phase now, but he's been talking to my uncle about taking over the stable operations once the charity is up and running.

Shadow, in the meantime, will board near campus, so Sarah can ride him, feed him carrots, and talk to her horse on the regular.

Campus.

She's leaving. The clock is ticking. I know this but I put it out of my mind. Worry is wasted time in my book, and I'm not looking to waste one minute of the time we've got left together.

Sarah has mentioned that she'll be close by a few times—actually showed me her GPS so I could see for myself that she'll only be a *quick one hour and forty-seven minute drive away*, but aside from that, we've both done a good job of avoiding the topic.

I tell myself that I'll be busy, too. I'll be working at a car dealership in town, doing oil changes and changing brakes, I suppose, so that will keep me occupied after classes. Sock away money, get a perfect GPA while I'm in community college, research the universities I plan on applying to—I don't talk much about my goals, but I've got a long list of them.

I've been channeling Sarah's mantra: *Know it and you'll own it.* It's something she learned from one of those high-paid consultants her father's company hired to lead a seminar. She has me visualizing the actual moment when I open the acceptance letter to the university of my choosing, complete with my scholarship offer. She instructs me to not only see myself walking to class on this beautiful campus, but to feel it. *You have to feel it with every cell in your being,* she coaches as I sit across from her, meditating with my eyes closed. Does this voodoo manifesting stuff even work? I don't know but I'm willing to try.

I do *not* tell Sarah that I also visualize her coming to visit me on this picturesque, leafy-green campus. That I see her, clear as day, walking towards me with a big smile on her face and her arms open wide to receive the crushing hug I'm about to give her.

Know it and you'll own it.

Driving with her hand resting in mine, I send up a silent

prayer, asking for the one thing I truly want. I want to own Sarah, heart and soul, the same way she owns me.

"We're here!"

Sarah booked a campsite down by Cape May, right on the beach. She told me it's costing us a hundred dollars each, which sounds crazy—camping should be free, am I right?—but when I see our set up, I get the feeling that she shaved more than a few dollars off my share.

"What kind of campsite is this? Are the Kardashians in the neighboring tent?"

"It's called a yurt." She can't even say the word with a straight face. "And this, my friend, is called *glamping*."

"I'm familiar with that asinine term." And while I have to admit that our private little site, complete with a fire pit, is pretty great, I'm slightly conflicted.

She reads my expression and says, "Liam, there were no spots at Lake Absegami, or basically anywhere else. I never knew people reserve spots so far in advance. And this," she holds her hands out to her sides as she does a full three-sixty, "is great. They've got bikes we can use to ride into town, paddle boards, a—"

"A coffee machine. Who has a damn coffee machine set-up on a campsite complete with organic coffee pods and almond milk?"

"They also have half and half if you're a purist."

Biting into a giant chocolate-chip cookie from our welcome basket, I moan because it's maybe the best I've ever tasted. "I guess I'll survive."

"Come on," she says as she's stripping down, "the forecast

is calling for clouds and drizzle tomorrow, so let's swim before the sun goes down."

I don't answer, dumbstruck from the sight of her in her suit. I come to as she takes off running down the beach and then diving in without checking to see if the water is cold, if it's rough, or if it's filled with the red jellyfish we dread every August. She just goes, and I follow.

Coming up for air, she looks so damn happy it's infectious. "Come here," I tell her as I drag her in close. "You wore my favorite." I slide my hand up her leg and under the fabric to cup her ass. "That was nice of you."

"This old thing?" Her voice is breathy before I even make contact, and when we're pressed together close, she shivers, then whispers, "Wait until you see my sleepwear."

"In my experience, campers sleep fully clothed to protect themselves from bugs and wild animals."

"Not this camper," she murmurs against my neck as her hand slides down the front of my board shorts. "And *glamp*-sites don't have bugs or wild animals."

"Is that so?" I don't even know what we're talking about anymore. I just know that her hand feels so, so good, and I cannot wait until the sun sets and I've got this girl all to myself.

Experienced. Some people would call me that. And I'm not Sarah's first, so she's quote-unquote experienced, too. But we're not. I was a scared kid my first time. Something was taken from me. And the few experiences I've had since that awful time in my life weren't paired with anything real. But this? I still can't believe this girl desires me. She looks at me as if I've hung the moon sometimes, and she lets me know that she sees me as someone who's worthwhile and deserving.

Sarah told me last week that I was her person. *You're my person*, she said as she rested her tired head on my chest. She'd just told me about her latest phone call with Grace, and how nervous she was to tell Sarah that her and Owen are expecting. *Did she really think I'd be upset, or...jealous? That I'd be anything but happy for them?* I listen mostly, as she can and does work it out on her own every time.

I want to be a steady presence for her, the same way she's been there for me. I don't initiate or offer much up spontaneously, but I find myself talking about my complicated past because she knows how to ask the right questions. She knows more about my life than anyone else—about my complicated relationship with my mother, with Jeff, about my father and my future. Talking about the tough stuff, who knew it could feel so good?

Sarah Hamilton is my person, too.

She's mine until the summer ends.

Chapter Thirty-Nine

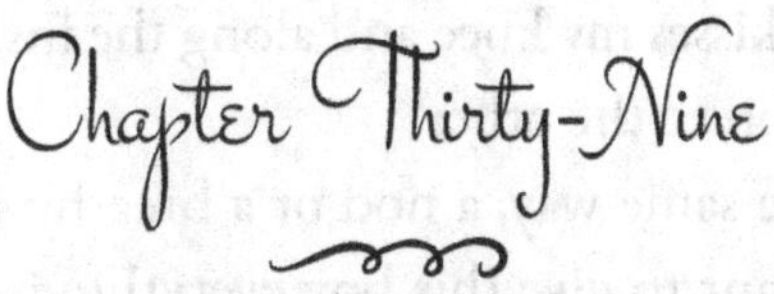

SARAH

There's an outdoor shower set-up, but we run right past it and head straight from the ocean to our yurt, which I will heretofore refer to as our nest. Yurt is just...a weird word.

I don't care about the sand in my hair or the salty spray on our skin, and neither does Liam.

As he busies himself zipping us in and tying the strings that add a second layer of nonexistent security, I undo the strings on my bikini and take a deep calming breath. This isn't our first time—we jumped that hurdle two weeks ago when my parents spent the night in Manhattan—but this feels extra special. We're away together, on our own, no work or obligations, no distractions to come between us.

When he turns and takes in the sight of me, I feel relieved when I see the look on his face change from surprised to something I can only describe as wonder. He likes what he sees.

"You're amazing, you know that?" Liam inches closer, eases

my knees apart and fixes his eyes *there*. My instinct is to lock my knees together, but I trust him. I trust him completely.

"So beautiful," he murmurs, his hands feather-light as they skim along my bare skin. "Can I?" he asks, and when I nod he dips down and kisses my knee and along the inside of one thigh before moving on to the other.

I answer the same way, a nod or a breathy *yes*, whatever he asks of me. I want to give this boy everything. And when he's finally inside of me, it's how I want it to be and how I want us to stay: connected, joined as one. Liam Murphy, forever mine.

He's become the center of my life since that day we took off in his car together. We don't talk about the summer coming to an end. I truly don't know how I'll leave him next week, yet I know that I will. But leaving and moving on are two different things. I don't see myself moving on from him.

I'll never see an ending to our story.

He holds me after, lays me across his strong body and covers me with his arms. "I could die a happy man right now." When I look at his face, I see that his eyes are closed and the smile that lingers tells me he's content.

I rest my head down again before asking, "Do you *not* want me to tell you that I love you? Because I do, Liam. I love you."

He shifts us so that we're side by side and he's propped on one elbow looking down at me. "You think I wouldn't want to know that you love me?"

"Just because," I pause as I consider whether or not to say it out loud, "it's only a week away."

"I love *you*, Sarah. I don't care that you're leaving next week. Right now is all that matters. Right now, you love me and I love you."

"The way you say that…You see everything changing between us, don't you?"

"Everything does change. You leave next week, I stay here. Next September I don't know where I'll be. No one knows what's around the corner. I'm not looking to end this," he tips my chin up, "because I've never been happier than I've been this summer with you. But whatever happens, I have you *now*. I love you, *now*."

"I want it to be forever."

"So do I. And maybe it will be. Or maybe you'll meet—"

"Stop!" I push his hand away. "I don't want to think about meeting anyone else."

"I don't either." He takes my hand back, kisses the inside of my wrist. "And I'm full of crap, by the way." He sprawls out on his back again, looking up and smiling. "I have this recurring fantasy where I get a full ride to Pitt, I work with Leo while I'm in school, I get to see you every time you come to visit Grace, and then after we graduate I get a kick-ass job and we live on their street." He starts to laugh. "I also picture a yard full of kids like Garth and Sienna's."

I laugh then, too. "Hold on there, mister. I'd be satisfied with two or three." Snuggling in close again, I tell him, "It's not so far-fetched, your fantasy. That could all happen."

But even as I say it, I know Liam is right. No one knows what lies around the corner, and there's no sense making plans when you could be using that time, our *now*, to live in the moment.

Sleepy and content, he murmurs, "I love you, Sarah Hamilton."

Wide awake and already grieving the loss of him, I whisper back, "I love you, too, Liam Murphy, and I always will."

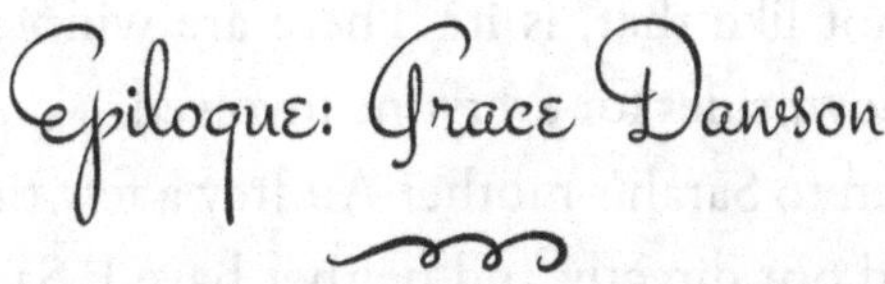

Epilogue: Grace Dawson

I still have to remind myself that I am now, legally and officially, Grace Dawson-Hanson. I took Owen's name this past May. I wanted to take it on our wedding day, but I wouldn't risk doing anything that might put a roadblock in the way of my daughter finding me.

And she did, Sarah found me.

Sarah. It fits her, I suppose. Back when I was pregnant with her, I wouldn't let myself even think about names. But I know she would have been Bernadette if I'd kept her, named after Damien's mother. He would have loved that.

Sarah Hamilton. You make up this persona for the people you don't know, but it's nothing like the real thing, live and in person. I always imagined her in all superlatives, and she is— she's amazing, talented, good-hearted and so bright. I want my parents to meet her, my brother and his family, Frannie and Reese someday, too.

I want too much.

I want what I can't have.

No one *really* talks about adoption. We only acknowledge

the couple longing for the child they can't conceive, and then there's the baby. Far off in the background is the mother of this motherless child. Problem, meet the perfect solution.

It's all good.

But it's not like that, is it? There are winners and losers, upsides and downsides for everyone involved.

I've spoken to Sarah's mother Audrey a few times now. She hasn't reached out directly and neither have I. Sarah passes the phone to her mother on occasion during one of our weekly calls, and now that she's in school, the opportunity to do this doesn't come up often. The first time we spoke she was friendly, but I think it was uncomfortable for both of us.

She got what she wanted eighteen years ago, but I imagine she's lived in fear of the moment when her daughter wanted to find me, and also this time we find ourselves in now, with her daughter wanting to forge some sort of relationship with me.

It's assumed that I got to live my life, free and unburdened. I was able to finish college and start over with a clean slate. And maybe it feels that way for some women, but I'll never see myself as anything but the loser in all this. I lost my firstborn child, lost the only piece of Damien left in this world, lost hope for a long time, and I lost years mourning and beating myself up for a decision I made when I was little more than a child myself.

And then there's Sarah. Being adopted seems to have landed her in a state of limbo and confusion. She's adjusting to college well, I think. From what I can read in her voice over the telephone, and what I saw the one time she's visited since last summer, she appears to be happy. But it's taking time to absorb it all. I'm not surprised by this, but I never imagined how hard it would be to stand on the sidelines and watch like a lowly bystander. The instinct to step in and make it all better is so strong, but I can't dole out advice or step in to counsel her. She is their daughter, but she's a part of me, too. Sarah is my flesh and blood.

I've told myself time and time again not to look back and waste time on regrets, but it's so much easier said than done. For years I've reimagined it. I held her that morning in the hospital, but in the revised version, I shook my head and told the social worked I'd changed my mind when she gestured for me to hand her back over. I nuzzled my nose into her baby-soft skin, ran my fingers over that tuft of black hair as I whispered, *It'll be all right, Birdie. You and me... We'll be just fine.*

But that's not how it went down, so I tell myself to be grateful for every single thing she gives me—every phone call, every email, every secret.

When she came here last month with her Liam, she was shocked when she walked in the door, same way I'm shocked and thrilled every time I turn profile in the mirror. I wasn't really sure I wanted to know the sex of the baby, but my intuition told me to find out so that I could prepare Sarah. I used to ignore that inner voice of mine, but I don't anymore.

We asked her to be the godmother for our baby girl—something I'd agonized over for months—and she said yes. She didn't give off the vibe that she was anything but happy for us, and I hope that's truly the case. I suspect there have to be some mixed emotions—it would only be natural—but she's either not there yet or she's looking to spare my feelings.

In the kitchen together after lunch, she walked up to me and tentatively traced that spot at the nape of my neck. I'd pulled my hair up for a reason. I desperately wanted her to know, but I thought it would seem too staged or forced to point it out myself.

"My birthday," she whispered.

"I had it done on the first anniversary of Damien's passing."

"Why the bird?"

I turn to face her, trying but failing to keep my emotions in check. "It was your hair. You had this thick mass of black hair on your head, and for those few minutes when I held you, I kept running my fingers through it. It was soft and so glossy, like Damien's, like a blackbird's." I hold in the tears when I smile at her. "In my heart, that's what I've always called you... Birdie."

She comes closer, and I wrap my arms around her, holding her close. Sarah will never know how I thought of her every day, or how her birthdays were laced with sorrow, hope and prayers every year. To try and convince her, or to make her believe—the words sound cheap to my own ears so I don't say them.

All I can do is let her know that I'll always be here for her, that she will always be welcome in our home and in my life. I'll give her a helping hand or a shoulder to cry on whenever she needs one. I'll show her through actions, not words, that in my heart, she will *always* be my daughter.

I'll keep doing the best that I can.

Every day of her life.

* * *

A Note from Lily

Writing the end of a book is an emotional experience, as you're saying goodbye to characters that have been in your head and in your heart for some time. The end of a series is even more intense, as you're closing the door on a fictional world you created.

The Blackbird series has been a six-year-long journey with starts and stops along the way. Yes, four books in six years. To some people that's a snail's pace, but it's my pace. It took me over two years to complete the first book in the series, *When the Night is Over*. Similarly, *All Your Life* has been a long labor of love.

The complexity of mother-daughter relationships is something I revisit regularly in my work, as being a woman is an endlessly complex and fascinating journey. The feedback I get from readers, in personal emails and in posted reviews, tells me we all have joys, sorrows, times when we succeed and others when we struggle. We all have stories to tell.

I am grateful you chose my book out of the many, *many* novels out there. Thank you for reading, and if my words touched you in some way, please consider leaving a review. Your opinion matters, and reviews are the perfect way to point your fellow readers towards books you have enjoyed and to authors they might not otherwise come across. Best of all, unlike books, reviews only take a few moments to write.

With Gratitude,
Lily

Also by Lily Foster

THE LET ME SERIES

Let Me Be the One

Let Me Love You

Let Me Go

Let Me Heal Your Heart

Let Me Fall

When I Let You Go

THE BLACKBIRD SERIES

When the Night is Over

Your Hand in Mine

Ghost on the Shore

All Your Life

9 798988 606208